Over
5,000,000
Copies of
A. Merritt's
Books Sold
In Avon Editions

OUT OF THE FANTASTIC WORLDS OF A.
MERRITT comes another bizarre and
compelling journey into a life you have
never known before. Here is the beautiful Priestess of Love, the sinister God of
Evil, his black-bearded Babylonian
priest, and the American adventurer.
All the forces of black magic are used
to hold the American as he sails toward
disaster on THE SHIP OF ISHTAR.

A. MERRITT

THE SHIP OF ISHTAR

AN AVON BOOK

AVON BOOKS
A division of
The Hearst Corporation
959 Eighth Avenue
New York, New York 10019

First Avon Printing, November, 1944
Fourth Avon Printing, August, 1966

Cover illustration by Doug Rosa

Printed in the U.S.A.

PART I

The Coming of the Ship

1

A TENDRIL of the strange fragrance spiralled up from the great stone block. Kenton felt it caress his face like a coaxing hand.

He had been aware of that fragrance—an alien perfume, subtly troubling, evocative of fleeting unfamiliar images, of thought-wisps that were gone before the mind could grasp them—ever since he had unsheathed from its coverings the thing Forsyth, the old archæologist, had sent him from the sand shrouds of ages-dead Babylon.

Once again his eyes measured the block—four feet long, a little more than that in height, a trifle less in width. A faded yellow, its centuries hung about it like a half visible garment. On one face only was there inscription, a dozen parallel lines of archaic cuneiform; carved there, if Forsyth were right in his deductions, in the reign of Sargon of Akkad, sixty centuries ago. The surface of the stone was scarred and pitted and the wedge shaped symbols mutilated, half obliterated.

Kenton leaned closer over it, and closer around him wound the scented spirals clinging like scores of tendrils, clinging like little fingers, wistful, supplicating, pleading——

Pleading for release!

What nonsense was this he was dreaming? Kenton drew

himself up. A hammer lay close at hand; he lifted it and struck the block, impatiently.

The block answered the blow!

It murmured; the murmuring grew louder; louder still, with faint bell tones like distant *carillons* of jade. The murmurings ceased, now they were only high, sweet chimings; clearer, ever more clear they rang, drawing closer, winging up through endless corridors of time.

There was a sharp crackling. The block split. From the break pulsed a radiance as of rosy pearls and with it wave after wave of the fragrance—no longer questing, no longer wistful nor supplicating.

Jubilant now! Triumphant!

Something was inside the block! Something that had lain hidden there since Sargon of Akkad, six thousand years go!

The *carillons* of jade rang out again. Sharply they pealed, then turned and fled back the endless corridors up which they had come. They died away; and as they died the block collapsed; it disintegrated; it became a swirling, slowly settling cloud of sparkling dust.

The cloud whirled, a vortex of glittering mist. It vanished like a curtain plucked away.

Where the block had been stood—a ship!

It floated high on a base of curving waves cut from lapis lazuli and foam-crested with milky rock crystals. Its hull was of crystal, creamy and faintly luminous. Its prow was shaped like a slender scimitar, bent backward. Under the incurved tip was a cabin whose seaward sides were formed, galleon fashion, by the upward thrust of the bows. Where the hull drew up to form this cabin, a faint flush warmed and cloudy crystal; it deepened as the sides lifted; it gleamed at last with a radiance that turned the cabin into a rosy jewel.

In the center of the ship, taking up a third of its length, was a pit; down from the bow to its railed edge sloped a deck of ivory. The deck that sloped similarly from the stern was jet black. Another cabin rested there, larger than that at the bow, but squat and ebon. Both decks continued in wide platforms on each side of the pit. At the middle of the ship the ivory and black decks met with an odd suggestion of contending forces. They did not fade into each other. They ended there abruptly, edge to edge; hostile.

6

Out of the pit arose a tall mast; tapering and green as the core of an immense emerald. From its cross-sticks a wide sail stretched, shimmering like silk spun from fire opals; from mast and yards fell stays of twisted dull gold.

Out from each side of the ship swept a single bank of seven great oars, their scarlet blades dipped deep within the pearl crested lapis of the waves.

And the jewelled craft was manned! Why, Kenton wondered, had he not noticed the tiny figures before?

It was as though they had just arisen from the deck . . . a woman had slipped out of the rosy cabin's door, an arm was still outstretched in its closing . . . and there were other women shapes upon the ivory deck, three of them, crouching . . . their heads were bent low; two clasped harps and the third held a double flute. . . .

Little figures, not more than two inches high. . . . Toys!

Odd that he could not distinguish their faces, nor the details of their dress. The boys were indistinct, blurred, as though a veil covered them. Kenton told himself that the blurring was the fault of his eyes; he closed them for a moment.

Opening them he looked down upon the black cabin and stared with deepening perplexity. The black deck had been empty when first the ship had appeared—that he could have sworn.

Now four manikins were clustered there—close to the edge of the pit!

And the baffling haze around the toys was denser. Of course it must be his eyes—what else? He would lie down for a while and rest them. He turned, reluctantly; he walked slowly to the door; he paused there, uncertainly, to look back at the shining mystery——

All the room beyond the ship was hidden by the haze!

Kenton heard a shrilling as of armies of storm; a roaring as of myriads of tempests; a shrieking chaos as though down upon him swept cataracts of mighty winds.

The room split into thousands of fragments; dissolved. Clear through the clamor came the sound of a bell—one —two—thr——

He knew that bell. It was his clock ringing out the hour of six. The third note was cut in twain.

The solid floor on which he stood melted away. He felt

7

himself suspended in space, a space filled with mists of silver.

The mists melted.

Kenton caught a glimpse of a vast blue wave-crested ocean—another of the deck of a ship flashing by a dozen feet below him.

He felt a sudden numbing shock, a blow upon his right temple. Splintered lightnings veined a blackness that wiped out sight of sea and ship.

2

The First Adventure

KENTON lay listening to a soft whispering, persistent and continuous. It was like the breaking crests of sleepy waves. The sound was all about him; a rippling susurration becoming steadily more insistent. A light beat through his closed lids. He felt motion under him, a gentle, cradling lift and fall. He opened his eyes.

He was on a ship; lying on a narrow deck, his head against the bulwarks. In front of him was a mast rising out of a pit. Inside the pit were chained men straining at great oars. The mast seemed to be of wood covered with translucent, emerald lacquer. It stirred reluctant memories.

Where had he seen such a mast before?

His gaze crept up the mast. There was a wide sail; a sail made of opaled silk. Low overhead hung a sky that was all a soft mist of silver.

He heard a woman's voice, deep toned, liquidly golden. Kenton sat up, dizzily. At his right was a cabin nestling under the curved tip of a scimitared prow; it gleamed rosily. A balcony ran round its top; little trees blossomed on that balcony; doves with feet and bills crimson as though dipped in wine of rubies fluttered snowy wings among the branches.

At the cabin's door stood a woman, tall, willow-lithe, staring beyond him. At her feet crouched three girls. Two

Within the blackness of the ship's stern roared the thunder of the serpent drum.

The blackness thinned. A face stared out, half veiled, bodiless, floating in the shadow. It was the face of the man Klaneth—and yet no more his than that which challenged it was the woman Sharane's. The pale eyes had become twin pools of hell flames; pupilless. For a heart beat the face hovered, framed by the darkness. The shadow dropped over it and hid it.

Now Kenton saw that this shadow hung like a curtain over the exact center of the ship, and that he crouched hardly ten feet distant from where that curtain cut the craft in twain. The deck on which he lay was pale ivory and again memory stirred but did not awaken. The radiance from the roseate orb struck against the curtain of shadow and made upon it a disk, wider than the ship, that was like a web of beams spun from the rays of a rosy moon. Against this shining web the shadow pressed, straining to break through.

From the black deck the thunder of the serpent drum redoubled; the brazen conches shrieked. Drum-thunder and shrieking horn mingled; they became the pulse of Abaddon, lair of the damned.

From Sharane's three women, shot storm of harpings, arpeggios like gusts of tiny arrows and with them shrill javelin pipings from the double flute. Arrows and javelins of sound cut through the thunder hammering of the drum and the bellow of the horns, sapping them, beating them back.

A movement began within the shadow. It seethed. It spawned.

Over the face of the disk of radiance black shapes swarmed. Their bodies were like monstrous larvæ, slugs; faceless. They tore at the web; stove to thrust through it; flailed it.

The web gave!

Its edge held firm, but slowly the center was pushed back until the disk was like the half of a huge hollow sphere. Within that hollow crawled and writhed and struck the monstrous shapes. From the black deck serpent drum and brazen horns bellowed triumph.

Again rang the golden trumpet cry from the deck of ivory. Out of the orb streamed an incandescence intolerable. The edges of the web shot forward and curved.

11

They closed upon the black spawn; within it the black spawn milled and struggled like fish in a net. Like a net lifted by some mighty hand the web swung high up above the ship. Its brightness grew to match that of the orb. From netted shapes of blackness came a faint, high pitched, obscene wailing. They shrank, dissolved, were gone.

The net opened. Out of it drifted a little cloud of ebon dust.

The web streamed back into the orb that had sent it forth.

Then, swiftly, the orb was gone!

Gone too was the shadow that had shrouded the black deck. High above the ship the snowy doves circled, screaming victory.

A hand touched Kenton's shoulder. He looked up into the shadowy eyes of the woman called Sharane; no goddess now, only woman. In her eyes he read amazement, startled disbelief.

Kenton sprang to his feet. A thrust of blinding pain shot through his head. The deck whirled round him. He tried to master the dizziness; he could not. Dizzily the ship spun beneath his feet; and beyond in wider arcs dizzily spun turquoise sea and silver horizon.

Now all formed a vortex, a maelstrom, down whose pit he was dropping—faster, ever faster. Around him was a formless blur. Again he heard the tumult of the tempests; the shrillings of the winds of space. The winds died away. There were three clear bell notes——

Kenton stood within his own room!

The bell had been his clock, striking the hour of six. Six o'clock? Why the last sound of his own world before the mystic sea had swept it from under him had been the third stroke of that hour clipped off in mid-note.

God—what a dream! And all in half a bell stroke!

He lifted his hand and touched a throbbing bruise over his right temple. He winced—well, that blow at least had been no dream. He stumbled over to the jewelled ship. He stared at it, incredulous.

The toys upon the ship had moved—new toys had appeared!

No longer were there four manikins on the black deck. There were only two. One stood pointing toward the starboard platform near the mast, his hand resting on the

12

shoulder of a red bearded, agate eyed soldier toy clad all in glittering chain mail.

Nor was there any woman at the rosy cabin's door as there had been when Kenton had loosed the ship from the block. At its threshold were five slim girls with javelins in hands.

The woman was on the starboard platform, bent low beside the rail!

And the ship's oars were no longer buried in the waves of lapis lazuli. They were lifted, poised for the downward stroke!

3

The Ship Returns

ONE BY ONE Kenton pulled at the manikins, each toy. Immovable, gem hard, each was, seemingly part of the deck itself; no force he could exert would move them.

Yet something had shifted them—and where were the vanished ones? From where had the new ones come?

Nor was there any haze around the little figures, nor blurring; each lineament stood out clean cut. The pointing toy on the black deck had dwarfed, bowed legs; his torso was that of a giant; his bald pate glinted and in his ears were wide discs of gold. Kenton recognized him —the beater of the serpent drum.

There was a tiny silver crescent upon the head of the bending woman toy, and over its tips poured flood of red-gold hair——

Sharane!

And that place at which she peered—was it not where he had lain on that other ship of his dream?

That—other ship? He saw again its decks ebon and ivory, its rosy cabin and its emerald mast. It had been this ship before him—no other! Dream? Then what had moved the toys?

Kenton's wonder grew. Within it moved a sharp unease, a sharper curiosity. He found he could not think

13

clearly with the ship filling his eyes; it seemed to focus all his attention upon it, to draw it taut, to fill him with a tense expectancy. He unhooked a hanging from the wall and threw it over the gleaming mystery. He walked from the room, fighting with each step an imperative desire to turn his head. He dragged himself through the doorway as though hands were gripping his ankles, drawing him back. Head still turned away Kenton lurched shoulders against the door; closed it; locked it.

In his bathroom he examined the bruise on his head. It was painful enough, but nothing serious. Half an hour of cold compresses fairly well removed all outward marks of it. He told himself that he might have fallen upon the floor, overcome by the strange perfumes—he knew that he had not.

Kenton dined alone, scarce heeding what was set before him, his mind groping through perplexities. What was the history of the block from Babylon? Who had set the ship within it—and why? Forsyth's letter had said that he had found it in the mound called 'Amran, just south of the Qser or crumbled "palace" of Nabopolasser. There was evidence, Kenton knew, that the 'Amran mound was the site of E-Sagilla, the ziggurat or terraced temple that had been the Great House of the Gods in ancient Babylon. The block must have been held in peculiar reverence, so Forsyth had conjectured, since only so would it have been saved from the destruction of the city by Sennacherib and afterwards have been put back in the re-built temple.

But why had it been held in such reverence? Why had such a miracle as the ship been imprisoned in the stone?

The inscription might have given some clue had it not been so mutilated. In his letter Forsyth had pointed out that the name of Ishtar, Mother Goddess of the Babylonians—Goddess of Vengeance and Destruction as well —appeared over and over again; that plain too were the arrowed symbols of Nergal, God of the Babylonian Hades and Lord of the Dead; that the symbols of Nabu, the God of Wisdom, appeared many times. These three names had been almost the only legible words on the block. It was as though the acid of time which had etched out the other characters had been held back from them.

Kenton could read the cuneatic well nigh as readily as

14

his native English. He recalled now that in the inscription Ishtar's name had been coupled with her wrathful aspect rather than her softer ones, and that associated always with the symbols of Nabu had been the signs of warning, of danger.

Forsyth had not noticed that, evidently—or if he had he had not thought it worth mentioning. Nor, apparently, had he been aware of the hidden perfumes of the block.

Well—there was no use thinking of the inscription. It was gone forever with the dust into which it had turned.

Kenton impatiently thrust back his chair. He knew that for the past hour he had been out temporizing, divided between the burning desire to get back to the room where the ship lay and the dread that when he did he would find all that adventure had been illusion, a dream; that the little figures had not really moved; that they were as they had been when he had first loosed the ship; that it was only a toy manned by toys—nothing more. He would temporize no longer.

"Don't bother about me any more to-night, Jevins," he told his butler. "I've some important work to do. If there are any calls say that I am away. I'm going to lock myself in and I don't want to be disturbed for anything less than Gabriel's trumpet."

The old servant, a heritage from Kenton's father, smiled.

"Very well, Mr. John," he said. "I'll let no one bother you."

To reach the room wherein was the ship, Kenton's way led through another in which he kept the rarest of his spoils from many a far away corner of the world. Passing, a vivid gleam of blue caught his eye and stayed him, like a hand. The gleam came from the hilt of a sword in one of the cabinets, a curious weapon he had bought from a desert nomad in Arabia. The sword hung above an ancient cloak in which it had been wrapped when the furtive Arab had slipped into his tent. Unknown centuries had softened the azure of that cloak, through whose web and woof great silver serpents writhed, cabalistically entwined.

Kenton unhooked the sword. Silver serpents, counterparts of those on the garments, twined about its hilt. From the hilt sprang a rod of bronze, eight inches long and three thick, round as a staff. This rod flared and flattened

15

out into a leaf shaped blade two feet long and full six inches wide across its center. Set in the hilt had been one large stone of cloudy blue.

The stone was no longer clouded. It was translucent, shining like an immense sapphire!

Obeying some half-formed thought that linked this new enigma with the ship's shifting toys, he drew down the cloak and threw it over his shoulders. The sword in hand, he unlocked the further door, closed and fastened it behind him; walked over to the shrouded ship; swept off its covers.

Pulses leaping, Kenton drew back.

On it now were two figures only—the drummer, crouched with head in arms upon the black deck, and on deck of ivory a girl, leaning over the rail and looking down upon the oarsmen!

Kenton snapped out the electrics and stood waiting.

Minute after minute crept by. Fugitive gleams from the lights on the Avenue penetrated the curtains of the windows, glimmered on the ship. Muted but steady came the roar of the traffic, punctuated by horn blasts, explosions through mufflers—New York's familiar voice.

Was that a halo growing round the ship . . . And what had become of the traffic's roar.

The room was filling with silence as a vessel is filled with water. . . .

Now a sound broke that silence; a sound like the lapping of little waves, languorous, caressing. The sounds stroked his lids, slumbrously; pressed them down. By enormous effort he half raised them.

A wide mist was opposite him, a globular silvery mist floating down upon him. Within that mist drifted a ship, its oars motionless, its sail half-filled. Wavelets crisped at its sickled bow, wavelets of pale turquoise with laced edges of foam.

Half the room was lost in the ripples of that approaching sea . . . the part on which he stood was many feet above the waves . . . so far below were they that the deck of the ship was level with his feet.

Closer drew the ship. He wondered why he heard no rushing winds, no clamoring tempests; no sound save the faint whispering of the foam-tipped waves.

Retreating, he felt his back press against the farther

wall. Before him drifted that misty world, the ship upon its breast.

Kenton leaped, straight for the deck.

The winds roared about him now; vast winds howled and shrieked—again he heard but felt them not at all. And suddenly the clamor died.

Kenton's feet struck solid surface.

He stood upon an ivory deck, facing a rosy cabin whose little blossoming trees were filled with cooing crimson billed, vermilion footed, doves. Between him and the cabin's door was a girl, her soft brown eyes filled with wonder and that same startled disbelief he had seen in those of Sharane when first her gaze had fallen upon him at the foot of the emerald mast.

"Are you Lord Nabu that you came thus out of the air and in his cloak of wisdom, his serpents twining within it?" she whispered. "Nay that cannot be—for Nabu is very old—and you are young. Are you his messenger?"

She dropped to her knees; crossed her hands, palms outward, over her forehead. She leaped to her feet; ran to the closed door of the cabin.

"*Kadishtu!*" she struck it with clenched hands. "Holy One—a messenger from Nabu!"

The door of the cabin was flung open. Upon its threshold stood the woman called Sharane. Her glance swept him; then darted to the black deck. He followed it. The beater of the serpent drum squatted there; he seemed to sleep.

"Watch, Satalu!" breathed Sharane to the girl.

She caught Kenton's hand; she drew him through the door. Two girls were there who stared at him. She thrust them forward.

"Out!" she whispered. "Out and watch with Satalu."

They slipped from the cabin. She ran to an inner door; dropped a bar across it.

She turned, back against it; then stepped slowly to Kenton. She stretched out slim fingers; with them touched his eyes, his mouth, his heart—as though to assure herself that he was real.

She cupped his hands in hers, and bowed, and set her brows against his wrists; the waves of her hair bathed them. At her touch desire ran through him, swift and flaming. Her hair was a silken net to which his heart flew, eager to be trapped.

17

He steadied himself; he drew his hands from hers; he braced himself against her lure.

She lifted her head; regarded him.

"What has the Lord Nabu to say to me?" her voice rocked Kenton with perilous sweetnesses, subtle provocations. "What is his word to me, messenger? Surely will I listen—for in his wisdom has not the Lord of Wisdom sent one to whom to listen ought not be—difficult?"

There was a flash of coquetry like the flirt of a roguish fan in the misty eyes turned for an instant to his.

Thrilling to her closeness, groping for some firm ground, Kenton sought for words to answer her. Playing for time, he looked about the cabined space. There was an altar at the far end. It was sown with luminous gems, with pearls and pale moonstones and curdled, milky crystals. From seven crystal basins set before it arose still silvery flames. There was an alcove behind the altar, but the glow of the seven lights hid whatever was within. He had a swift sense of tenancy of that flame veiled alcove—something dwelt there.

At the far side was a low, wide divan of ivory inlaid with the milky crystals and patterned with golden arabesques. Silken tapestries fell from the walls, multi-colored, flower woven. Soft deep silken rugs covered the cabin's floor, and piles of cushions. At back, at left, two wide low windows opened; through them streamed silver light.

A bird flew upon the sill of one; a snowy bird with scarlet beak and feet; it scanned him, it preened itself, it cooed and flew away——

Soft hands touched him; Sharane's face was close, eyes now with doubt more deeply shadowed.

"You—do come from Nabu?" she asked, and waited for reply; and still he found no words to answer her. "Messenger you must be," she faltered, "else—how could you board the Ship of Ishtar? . . . And you are clad in Nabu's cloak . . . and wear his sword . . . many times have I seen them in his shrine at Uruk . . . and I am weary of the Ship," she whispered. "I would see Babylon again! Ah dearly, do I long for Babylon."

Now words came to Kenton.

"Sharane," he said boldly. "I do bear a message for you. It is the truth, and our Lord Nabu is Lord of Truth

18

—therefore it must be from him. But before I give it to you, tell me—what is this ship?"

"What is the Ship!" she drew back from him, doubt enough now in her face— "But if you come indeed from Nabu—you must know that!"

"I do not know," he told her, "I do not even know the meaning of the message I carry—it is for you to interpret. Yet here am I, upon the ship, before you. And in my ears I hear command—whispered it may be by Nabu himself—that I must not speak until you have told me—what is this ship."

For a long moment she stood, scanning him, studying him.

"The ways of the gods are strange," she sighed at last. "They are hard to understand. Yet—I obey."

PART II
The Sin of Zarpanit

4

SHE slipped down upon the divan and beckoned him beside her. She laid a hand lightly upon his heart. His heart leaped beneath the touch; she felt it, too, and moved a little from him, smiling, watching him through downcast, curving lashes. She drew her slender, sandaled feet beneath her; mused with white hands clasped between rounded knees. When she spoke her voice was low, words half intoned.

"The sin of Zarpanit; the tale of her sin against Ishtar; Ishtar the Mighty Goddess; Mother of the Gods and of men; Lady of the Heavens and of Earth—who loved her!"

"High Priestess of Ishtar at her Great House in Uruk was Zarpanit. *Kadishtu*, Holy One, was she. And I, Sharane, who come from Babylon, was closest to her; her priestess; loved by her even as she was loved by Ishtar. Through Zarpanit the Goddess counseled and warned, rewarded and punished, Kings and men. Into the body of Zarpanit the Goddess came as to a shrine, seeing through her eyes, speaking with her lips.

"Now the temple in which we dwelt was named the House of the Seven Zones. In it was the sanctuary of Sin, God of Gods, who lives in the Moon; of Shamash his son; whose home is the Sun, of Nabu, the Lord of Wisdom; of Ninib, the Lord of War; of Nergal, the Dark

Hornless one, Ruler of the Dead; and of Bel-Merodach, the Mighty Lord. Yet most of all was it the House of Ishtar, who dwelt there of his own right—temple themselves within her holy home.

"From Cuthaw in the north, from the temple there which Dark Nergal ruled as Ishtar ruled at Uruk, came a priest to sit over the Zone of Nergal in the House of the Seven Zones. His name was Alusar—and close as was Zarpanit to Ishtar as close was he to the Lord of the Dead. Nergal made himself manifest through Alusar, spoke through him and dwelt at times within him even as did Ishtar within her Priestess Zarpanit. With Alusar came retinue of priests, and among them that spawn of Nergal's slime—Klaneth. And Klaneth was close to Alusar as I to Zarpanit."

She raised her head and looked at Kenton through narrowed lids.

"I know you now," she cried. "A while ago you lay upon the ship and watched my strife with Klaneth! Now I know you—although then you had no cloak nor sword; and vanished as I looked upon you!"

Kenton smiled at her.

"You lay with frightened face," she said. "And stared at me with fearful eyes—and fled!"

She half arose; he saw suspicion sweep her anew; the scorn in her voice lashed him into quick, hot rage. He drew her down beside him.

"I was that man," he said. "Nor was it fault of mine that then I went away—I who have returned as quickly as I could? And your own eyes lied to you. Nor ever think again that mine hold fear of you! Look into them!" he bade her, fiercely.

She looked—long; sighed and bent away, sighed again and swayed toward him, languorously. His arms gripped her.

"Enough," she thrust him away. "I read no hasty script in new eyes. Yet I retract—you were not fearful. You did not flee! And when you speak I shall no doubt understand. Let be!"

"Between Ishtar and Nergal," she took up the interrupted tale, "is and ever must be unending hatred and strife. For Ishtar is Bestower of Life and Nergal is Taker of Life; she is the Lover of Good and he is the Lover of Evil. And how shall ever Heaven and Hell be linked; or life and death; or good and evil?

21

"Yet she, Zarpanit, *Kadishtu,* the Holy One of Ishtar, her best beloved, did link all these. For where she should have turned away—she looked with desire; and where she should have hated—she loved!

"Yea—the Priestess of the Lady of Life loved Alusar the Priest of the Lord of Death! Her love was a strong flame by whose light she could see only him—and him only. Had Zarpanit been Ishtar she would have gone to the Dwelling Place of the Lost for Alusar, even as did the Goddess for her lover Tammuz—to draw him forth or to dwell there with him.

"Yea—even to dwell with him there in the cold darkness where the dead creep feebly, calling with the weak voices of birds. In the cold of Nergal's domain, in the famine of Nergal's abode, in the blackness of his city where the deepest shade of earth would be a ray of sunlight, Zarpanit would have been happy—knowing that she was with Alusar.

"So greatly did she love!

"I helped her in her love—for love of her," she whispered. "But Klaneth crept ever behind Alusar waiting for chance to betray him and to take his place. Yet Alusar trusted him. There came a night——"

She paused, her face drawn with memoried terror.

"There came . . . a night when Alusar lay with Zarpanit . . . within her chamber. His arms were about her . . . hers around his neck . . . their lips together. . . .

"And that night down came Ishtar from her Heavens and entered and possessed her! . . .

"While at the same instant from his dark city came Nergal . . . and passed into Alusar. . . .

"And in each other's arms, looking into each other's eyes, caught in the fire of mortal love . . . were . . . Ishtar and Nergal . . . Heaven and Hell . . . the Soul of Life mated to the Soul of Death!"

She quivered and wept and long minutes went slowly by before again she spoke.

"Straightway those two who clasped were torn from each other. We were buffeted as by hurricanes, blinded by lightnings; scourged and thrown broken to the walls. And when we knew consciousness the priests and priestesses of all the Seven Zones had us. All the sin was known!

"Yea, even though Ishtar and Nergal had not . . . met . . . that night still would be sinning of Zarpanit and

22

Alusar have been known. For Klaneth, whom we had thought on guard, had betrayed them and brought down upon them the pack!

"Let Klaneth be cursed!" Sharane raised arms high, and the pulse of her hate beat upon Kenton like a hammer of flame. "Let Klaneth crawl blind and undying in the cold blackness of Nergal's abode! But Goddess Ishtar! Wrathful Ishtar! Give him to me first that I may send him there as I would have him go!"

5

How The Gods Judged

"FOR A TIME," she said, "we lay in darkness, Zarpanit and I together—and Alusar we knew not where. Great had been the sin of those two, and in it I had shared. Not quickly was our punishment to be decided. I comforted her as best I might, loving her, caring naught for myself—for her heart was close to breaking, knowing not what they did with him she loved.

"There fell another night when the priests came to us. They drew us from our cell and bore us in silence to the portal of the *Du-azzaga*, the Brilliant Chamber, the Council Room of the Gods. There stood other priests with Alusar. They opened the portal, fearfully, and thrust us three within.

"Now in truth my spirit shrank and was afraid, and beside mine I felt the shuddering soul of Zarpanit.

"For the *Du-azzaga* was filled with light, and in the places of the Gods sat not their images but the Gods themselves! Hidden each behind a sparkling cloud the Gods looked at us. In the place of Nergal was a fiery darkness.

"Out of the shining azure mist before the Shrine of Nabu came the voice of the Lord of Wisdom.

" 'So great is your sin, woman,' it said, 'and yours, priest, that it has troubled even us the Gods! Now what have you to say before we punish?"

"The voice of Nabu was cold and passionless as the light of far flung stars—yet in it was understanding.

"And suddenly my love for Zarpanit swelled, and I held fast to it and it gave me strength; while beside me I felt her soul stand erect, defiant, her love flinging itself before her as a shield. She did not answer—only held out her arms to Alusar. His love stood forth unafraid even as hers. He clasped her.

"Their lips met—and the judging Gods were forgotten!

"Then Nabu spoke again:

" 'These two bear a flame that none but Ishtar can quench—and it may be not even she!'

"At this Zarpanit drew from her lover's arms; came close to the glory in which hid Ishtar; did homage and addressed her:

" 'Yea, O Mother, are you not the mother of that fire we call love? Did you not create it and set it as a torch above Chaos? And having made it, did you not know how mighty was the thing you made? It was that love of which you are the mother, O Holy Ishtar, that came uncalled into this temple of my body which was yours, and still is yours though you have abandoned it. Is it my fault that so strong was love that it broke the doors of your temple, or my fault that its light blinded me to all save him on whom it shone? You are the creator of love, O Ishtar; and if you did not mean it to conquer then why made you it so mighty? Or if Love be grown stronger than you who made it can we—a man and woman—be blamed that we could not overcome it? And if love be not stronger than you, still did you make it stronger than man. Therefore punish love, your child, O Ishtar—not us!'

"It was the Lord Nabu who broke the silence of the Gods:

" 'Truth is in what she says. The flame they bear is one whose ways you know, O Ishtar, far better than do we. Therefore it is for you to answer her.'

"From the glory veiling the Goddess a voice came, sweet but small with bitter anger:

" 'There *is* truth in what you say, Zarpanit, whom once I called daughter. Now because of that truth I will temper my anger. You have asked me whether love is stronger than I who created it. We shall learn! You and your lover shall dwell in a certain place that shall be opened to you. Ever together shall you be. You may look upon each other, your eyes may meet—but never lips nor hands! You may speak to each other—but never of this flame called love! For when it leaps and draws you together then I, Ishtar, will enter you, Zarpanit, and give it battle! Nor shall it be the Ishtar you have known. Nay, that Sister-Self of mine whom men name the Wrathful, the Destroyer—*she* shall possess you. And so it shall be until the flame within you conquers her, or that flame perishes!'

"The voice of Ishtar was still. The gods sat, silent. Then out of the fiery blackness of Nergal's shrine bellowed the voice of the Lord of Death!

" 'So say you, Ishtar! Then I, Nergal, tell you this—I stand with this man who is my priest! Nor am I much displeased with him, since it was by him that I looked so closely into your eyes, O Mother of Life!'—the Blackness shook with laughter—'I shall be with him, and I will meet you, Ishtar the Destroyer! Yea, with craft to match yours and strength to grapple with you—until I, not you, have blown out that flame. For in my abode is no such fire—and I would quench it in them that my darkness be not affrighted when at last these two come to me!'

"And again the laughter shook the ebon cloud, while the glory that covered the Goddess quivered with her wrath.

"But the three of us listened with despair—for ill as it had gone with us, far worse was it to hear this jesting of the Dark Hornless One with the Mother of the Heavens.

"Came Ishtar's voice, smaller still:

" 'Be it so, O Nergal!'

"There was silence for a little time among the other gods; and I thought that behind their veils they looked at each other askance. Came at last the passionless voice of Nabu:

" 'What of this other woman——?'

"The voice of Ishtar, impatient:

" 'Let her fate be bound with Zarpanit's. Let Zarpanit have her retinue in that place to which she goes.'

"Then Nabu again:

" 'The priest Klaneth—is he to go free?'

" 'What! Shall not my Alusar have his retinue as well?' mocked Nergal. 'Nay, set Klaneth and others beside him to minister to him.'

25

"Again I thought that the Gods looked at each other askance; then Nabu asked:

" 'Shall it be so, O Ishtar?'

"And Ishtar answered:

" 'Let it be so!'

"The *Du-azzaga* faded; I was one with the nothingness.

"When we awoke we were on this haunted ship, on this strange sea, in this strange world and all the gods had decreed in the *Du-azzaga* had come to pass. With Zarpanit was I and half a score of the temple girls she had loved. And with Alusar was Klaneth and a pack of his black acolytes. They had given us oarsmen, sturdy temple slaves —a twain for each oar. They had made the ship beautiful, and they had seen to it that we lacked nothing."

A flame of anger pulsed for an instant through her eyes.

"Yea," she said, "the kindly gods did all for our comfort—and then they launched the ship on this strange sea in this strange world as battleground for Love and Hate, arena for Wrathful Ishtar and Dark Nergal, torture chamber for their priestess and priest.

"It was in this cabin that Zarpanit awakened—with the name of Alusar upon her lips. Then straightway she ran out the door, and from the black cabin came Alusar calling her name. I saw her reach that line where black deck meets this—and, lo, she was hurled back as though by thrust of arms. For there is a barrier there, messenger—a barrier built by the gods over which none of us upon the ship may pass—but then we knew nothing of that. And Alusar, too, was hurled back.

"Then as they arose, calling, stretching hands, striving to touch finger to finger, straightway into Zarpanit poured that Sister-Self of Ishtar, the Angry One, the Destroyer, while around Alusar black shadows deepened and hid him. At last—the shadows parted—and what had been the face of Alusar peered from them and it was the face of Nergal, Lord of the Dead!

"So it was—even as the gods had decreed. And that immortal twain within the bodies of those mortal two who loved each other so—battled and flung their hates like brands against each other, while the slaves chained to their oars in the pit cowered and raved or fell senseless under the terrors loosed above them. And the temple girls cast themselves upon the deck or ran screaming into the cabin that they might not see. Only I did not cry out or flee—who, since I had faced the gods in the *Du-azzaga,* could never again feel fear.

"And so it fared; how long, how long I do not know, in this place where time seems not to be, since there is neither night nor day as we knew them in Babylon.

"Yet ever Zarpanit and Alusar strove to meet, and ever Wrathful Ishtar and Dark Nergal thrust them apart. Many are the wiles of the Lord of the Shades and countless are his weapons. Many are the arts of Ishtar, and is not her quiver always full? Messenger, how long the pair endured I know not. Yet always they strove to break that barrier through, driven by their love. And always——

"The flames within them burned on," she whispered. "Nergal nor Ishtar could dim them. Their love did but grow stronger. There came a day——

"It was in mid-battle. Ishtar had taken possession of Zarpanit and stood where this deck touches the pit of the oarsmen. Nergal had poured himself into Alusar and hurled his evil spawn across the pit against the goddess's lightnings.

"And as I crouched, watching, at this cabin's door, I saw the radiance that covered Ishtar tremble and dull. I saw the face of Ishtar waver and fade—the face of Zarpanit look out from where the face of Ishtar had been.

"The darkness that shrouded the Lord of the Dead lightened as though a strong flame had shot up within it!

"Then Ishtar took one step—and another and another—toward the barrier between black deck and this. But it came to me that not by her will did she so move. No! She went haltingly, reluctantly, as though something stronger than herself pushed her on. And as she moved, so moved Nergal within his shadows to meet her!

"Closer they came and closer. And ever the radiance of Ishtar would wax and wane. Ever the shadows clothing Nergal would lighten, darken, lighten again. Yet ever—slowly, unwillingly, but inexorably they drew closer and closer to each other. I could see the face of Alusar, the priest, thrusting itself into sight, stripping itself of Nergal's mask.

"Slowly, slowly the white feet of Zarpanit carried Ishtar to the barrier; and slowly, slowly, ever matching her tread, came Alusar to meet her. And they met!

"They touched hands, touched lips, clasped—ere conquered god and goddess could withdraw from them.

"They kissed and clasped. They fell upon the deck—dead. Dead—in each other's arms.

"Nor Ishtar nor Nergal had conquered! Nay! Love of man and love of woman—these had conquered. Victors over god and goddess—the flames were free!

"The priest had fallen on the hither side of the barrier. We did not unclasp their arms. We set them adrift, alock, face to face—their bodies.

"Then I ran forth to slay Klaneth. But I had forgotten that neither Ishtar nor Nergal had conquered one the other. Lo, into me poured the goddess, and into Klaneth returned Nergal! As of old these two powers battled. And again as of old the unseen barrier was strong, holding back from each other those on ivory deck and black.

"Yet I was happy—for by this I knew that Zarpanit and Alusar had been forgotten by them. It came to me that the strife had gone beyond those two who had escaped. That now it mattered not either to Wrathful Ishtar or to Nergal that priestess and priest had gone—since in my body and in Klaneth's they could still strive against each other for possession of the ship. . . .

"And so we sail—and fight, and sail—and fight. . . . How long, I do not know. Many, many years must have passed since we faced the gods in Uruk—but see, I am still as young as then and as fair! Or so my mirror tells me," she sighed.

6

"Am I Not—Woman!"

KENTON sat silent, unanswering. Young and fair she was indeed—and Uruk and Babylon mounds of time-worn sands these thousands of years!

"Tell me, Lord"—her voice roused him; "tell me, has the Temple at Uruk great honor among the nations still? And is Babylon proud in her supremacy?"

He did not speak, belief that he had been thrust into some alien, reality wrestling with outraged revolt of reason.

And Sharane, raising her eyes to his troubled face, stared at him with ever growing doubt. She leaped from beside him, stood quivering like a blade of wrath in a sweetly flowered sheath.

"Have you word for me?" she cried. "Speak—and quickly!"

Dream woman or woman meshed in ancient sorceries, there was but one answer for Sharane—the truth.

And tell her truth Kenton did, beginning from the arrival of the block from Babylon into his house; glossing no detail that might make all plain to her. She listened, her gaze steadfast upon him, drinking in his words— amazement alternating with stark disbelief; and these in turn replaced by horror, by despair.

"For even the site of ancient Uruk is well-nigh lost," he ended. "The House of the Seven Zones is a windswept heap of desert sand. And Babylon, mighty Babylon, has been level with the wastes for thousands of years!"

She leaped to her feet—leaped and rushed upon him, eyes blazing, red-gold hair streaming.

"Liar!" she shrieked. "Liar! Now I know you—you phantom of Nergal!"

A dagger flashed in her hand; he caught the wrist just in time; struggled with her; bore her down upon the couch.

She relaxed, hung half fainting in his arms.

"Uruk dust!" she whimpered. "The House of Ishtar dust! Babylon a desert! And Sargon of Akkad dead six thousand years ago, you said—six thousand years ago!" She shuddered, sprang from his embrace. "But if that is so, then what am I?" she whispered, white lipped. "What—am I? Six thousand years and more gone since I was born—and I alive! Then what am I?"

Panic overpowered her; her eyes dulled; she clutched at the cushions. He bent over her; she threw white arms around him.

"I am alive?" she cried. "I am—human? I am—woman?"

Her soft lips clung to his, supplicating; the perfumed tent of her hair covered him. She held him, her lithe body pressed tight, imperatively desperate. Against his racing heart he felt the frightened pulse of hers. And ever between her kisses she whispered: "Am I not a woman—and alive? Tell me—am I not alive?"

Desire filled him; he gave her kiss for kiss; tempering the flame of his desire was clear recognition that neither swift love for him nor passion had swept her into his arms.

It was terror that lay behind her caresses. She was afraid—appalled by that six-thousand year wide abyss between the life she had known and his. Clinging to him she fought for assurance. She had been driven back to woman's last intrenchment—the primal assertion of the woman-self—the certainty of her womanhood and its unconquerable lure.

No, it was not to convince him that her kisses burned his lips—it was to convince herself.

He did not care. She was in his arms. He gave her kiss for kiss.

She thrust him from her; sprang to her feet.

"I am a woman, then?" she cried triumphantly. "A woman—and alive?"

"A woman!" he answered thickly, his whole body quivering toward her. "Alive! God—yes!"

She closed her eyes; a great sigh shook her.

"And that is truth," she cried, "and it is the one truth you have spoken. Nay—be silent!" she checked him. "If I am a woman and alive, it follows that all else you have told me are lies—since I could be neither were Babylon dust and it six thousand years since first I saw the ship. You lying dog!" she shrilled, and with one ringed hand struck Kenton across the lips.

The rings cut deep. As he fell back, dazed both by blow and sudden shift of fortune, she threw open the inner door.

"Luarda! Athnal! All!" wrathfully she summoned. "Quick! Bind me this dog! Bind him—but slay him not!"

Streamed from the cabin seven warrior maids, short kirtled, bare to their waists, in their hands light javelins. They flung themselves upon him. And as they wound about him Sharane darted in and tore the sword of Nabu from his hand.

And now young, fragrant bodies crushed him in rings of woman flesh, soft, yet inexorable as steel. The blue cloak was thrown over his head, twisted around his neck. Kenton awoke from his stupor—awoke roaring with rage. He tore himself loose, hurled the cloak from him, leaped toward Sharane. Quicker than he, the lithe bodies of the maids screened her from his rush. They thrust him with their javelins, pricking him as do the matadors to turn a charging bull. Back and back they drove him, ripping his clothing, bringing blood now here, now there.

Through his torment he heard her laughter.

"Liar!" she mocked. "Liar, coward and fool! Tool of Nergal, sent to me with a lying tale to sap my courage! Back to Nergal you go with another tale!"

The warrior maids dropped their javelins, surged forward as one. They clung to him; twined legs and arms around him, dragged him down. Cursing, flailing with his fists, kicking—caring no longer that they were women—Kenton fought them. Berserk, he staggered to his feet. His foot struck the lintel of the rosy cabin's door. Down he plunged, dragging his wildcat burden with him. Falling they drove against the door. Open it flew, and out through it they rolled, battling down the ivoried deck.

There was a shouting close behind him, a shrill cry of warning from Sharane—some urgent command, for grip of arms and legs relaxed; clutching hands were withdrawn.

Sobbing with rage, Kenton swung to his feet. He saw that he was almost astride the line between ivoried deck and black. It came to him that this was why Sharane had whistled her furies from him; that he had dragged them too close to its mysterious menace.

Again her laughter lashed him. She stood upon the gallery of little blossoming trees, her doves winging about her. The sword of Nabu was in her hand; derisively she lifted it.

"Ho, lying messenger!" mocked Sharane. "Ho, dog beaten by women! Come, get your sword!"

"I'll come, damn you!" he shouted, and leaped forward.

The ship pitched. Thrown off his balance, Kenton staggered back, reeled to the line where black and ivory decks met.

Reeled over it—unhurt!

Something deeper than his consciousness registered that fact; registered it as of paramount importance. Whatever the power of the barrier, to it Kenton was immune. He poised himself to leap back to the ivory deck.

"Stop him!" came the voice of Klaneth.

In mid-spring long, sinewy fingers gripped his shoulder, swung him round. He looked into the face of the beater of the serpent drum. The drummer's talons lifted him and cast Kenton like a puppy behind him.

And panting like some outraged puppy, Kenton swayed

up on his feet. A ring of black-robed men was closing in upon him, black-robed men whose faces were dead white, impassive; black-robed men closing in upon him with clutching hands. Beyond the ring stood the mailed warrior with the red beard and the pale agate eyes; and beside him the Black Priest.

Naught cared Kenton for any or all of them. He rushed. The black robes curled over him, overwhelming him, pinned him down.

Again the ship lurched, this time more violently. Kenton, swept off his feet, slid sidewise. A wave swished over him. The hands that clutched him were washed away. Another wave lifted him, flung him up and out. Deep he sank; fought his way upward; dashed the water from his eyes and looked for the ship.

A roaring wind had risen. Under it the ship was scudding—a hundred yards away. He shouted; swam toward her. Down went the sail, down dipped the oars, straining to keep her before the wind. Faster, faster flew the ship before the blast.

She was lost in the silvery mists.

Kenton ceased his efforts; floated, abandoned in an unknown world.

A wave smote him; he came up behind it, choking. The spindrift whipped him. He heard the booming surf, the hiss of combers thrown back by ramparts of rock. Another wave caught him. Struggling on its crest he saw just ahead of him a pinnacle of yellow stone rising from a nest of immense boulders upon which the billows broke in fountains of spume.

He was lifted by a gigantic comber; dashed straight against the yellow pillar.

The shock of his impact was no greater than that of breaking through thick cobweb. For infinite distances it seemed to him he rushed on and on through a soft thick darkness. With him went the shrieking clamor of vast tempests. Abruptly his motion ended, the noise of the tempests ceased.

He lay prone; his fingers clenched some coarse fabric that crumpled stubbornly in his grip. He rolled over, hands thrust out; one of them gripped cool, polished wood. He sat up——

He was back in his own room!

Kenton dragged himself to his feet, stood swaying, dazed.

What was that darkening the rug at his feet? It was water —water that was dripping from him, strangely colored water—crimsoned water.

He realized that he was wet to the skin, drenched. He licked his lips—there was salt upon them. His clothing was ripped and torn, the salt water dripped from it.

And from a score of wounds his blood mingled with the water!

He stumbled over to the jewelled ship. On the black deck was a little group of manikins, leaning and looking over the rail.

Upon the gallery of the rosy cabin one tiny figure stood——

Sharane!

He touched her—jewel hard, jewel cold, a toy!

And yet—Sharane!

Like returning wave his berserk rage swept him. Echoes of her laughter in his ears, Kenton, cursing, sought for something to shatter the shining ship. Never again should Sharane mock him!

He caught a heavy chair by the legs, swung it high overhead, poised for an instant to send it crashing down——

And suddenly beneath the salt upon his lips Kenton tasted the honey musk of her kisses—the kisses of Sharane!

The chair fell from his hands.

"Ishtar! Nabu!" he whispered, and dropped upon his knees. "Set me again upon the ship! Ishtar! Do with me as you will—only set me again upon your ship!"

7

Slave Of The Ship

SWIFT was his answer. He heard far away a bellowing roar as of countless combers battering against a rock ribbed coast. Louder it grew.

With a thunder of vast waters the outward wall of his room disappeared. Where wall had been was the crest

33

of an enormous leaping wave. The wave curled down over Kenton, lifted him up, rolled him far under it; shot him at last, gasping for breath up and up through it.

He was afloat again upon the turquoise sea!

The ship was close. Close! Its scimitared bow was striking down by his head; was flying past him. A golden chain hung from it, skittering over the crests. Kenton clutched at it—missed it.

Back he fell. Swift raced the shining side of the ship past him. Again he threw himself high. There was another chain; a black one spattering over the wave tips and hanging from the stern.

He gripped it. The sea tore at his thighs, his legs, his feet. Grimly he held fast. Hand over hand, cautiously, he drew himself up. Now he was just below the rail. Slowly he raised his head to peer over.

Long arms swept down upon him; long hands gripped his shoulders, lifted him, hurled him down upon the deck, pinned him there. A thong was drawn round his ankles, his arms were pinioned to his sides.

He looked into the face of the frog-mouthed beater of the serpent drum. And over one of the drummer's enormous shoulders stared the white face of Klaneth. He heard his voice:

"Carry him in, Gigi."

He felt himself lifted by the drummer as easily as though he had been a babe; and cradled in the huge hands he was carried through the black cabin's door.

The drummer set Kenton on his feet, regarding him with curious, half-amused eyes. Agate eyes of the red bearded warrior and pale eyes of Klaneth dwelt upon him as curiously.

Kenton took stock of the three. First the black priest—massive, elephant thewed; flesh pallid and dead as though the blood flowed through veins too deeply imbedded to reveal the creep of its slow tide; the face of Nero remodelled from cold clay by numbed hands.

Then Gigi—the drummer. His froglike face with the pointed ears; his stunted and bowed legs; his giant's body above the hips; the gigantic shoulders whence swung the long and sinewy and apish arms whose strength Kenton had felt; the slit of a mouth in whose corners a malicious humor dwelt. Something of old earth gods about him; a touch of Pan.

34

Red beard—a Persian out of that time when Persia's hordes were to the world what later the Roman legions were to be. Or so Kenton judged him by his tunic of linked light mail, the silken sheathed legs, the high buskins and the curved daggers and the scimitar in his jewelled belt. And human as Kenton himself. About him was none of the charnel flavor of Klaneth nor the grotesqueness of Gigi. The full red lips beneath the carefully trimmed beard were sensual, life loving; the body was burly and muscular; the face whiter than Kenton's own. But it was sullen and stamped deep with a half-resigned, half desperate boredom that even his lively and frank curiosity about Kenton lightened little.

In front of him was a wide slab of bloodstone. Six priests knelt upon it, worshipping something that stood within a niche just above the slab. What it was he could not tell—except that it breathed out evil. A little larger than a man, the thing within the niche was black and formless as though made of curdling shadows. It quivered, pulsated—as though the shadows that were its substance thickened constantly about it, passed within it and were replaced swiftly by others.

Dark was that cabin, the walls somber as dull black marble. Other shadows clung to the dark walls and clustered in the corners; shadows that seemed only to await command to deepen into substance.

Unholy shadows—like those that clothed the thing within the niche.

Beyond, as in the cabin of Sharane, was another chamber, and crowding at the door between were a dozen or more of the black robed, white faced priests.

"Go to your places," Klaneth turned to them, breaking the silence. They slipped away. The black priest closed the door upon them. He touched the nearest of the kneeling priests with his foot.

"Our Lord Nergal has had enough of worship," he said. "See—he has swallowed your prayers!"

Kenton looked at the thing within the niche. It was no longer misty, shadowed. It stood out, clear cut. Its body was that of a man and its face was that same awesome visage of evil into which he had seen the black priest's turn on that first adventure of his upon the ship.

The face of Nergal—Lord of the Dead!

What had been the curdled, quivering shades enveloping the statue?

He felt the eyes of Klaneth searching him, covertly. A trick! A trick to frighten him. He met the black priest's gaze squarely; smiled.

The Persian laughed.

"Hai, Klaneth," he said. "There was a bolt that fell short. Mayhap this stranger has seen such things before. Mayhap he is a sorcerer himself and can do better things. Change your play, Klaneth."

He yawned and seated himself upon a low settle. The black priest's face grew grimmer.

"Best be silent, Zubran," he said. "Else it may be that Nergal will change his play for you in a way to banish forever your disbelief."

"Disbelief?" echoed the Persian. "Oh, Nergal is real enough. It is not disbelief that irks me. It is the eternal monotony. Can you do nothing new, Klaneth? Can Nergal do nothing new? Change his play for me, eh? By Ahriman —that is just what I wish he would do, if he can!"

He yawned again, ostentatiously. The black priest growled; turned to the six worshippers.

"Go," he ordered, "and send Zachel to me."

They filed through the outer door. The black priest dropped upon another settle, studying Kenton; the drummer squatted, also watching him; the Persian muttered to himself, playing with his dagger hilts. The door opened and into the cabin stepped a priest who held in one hand a long whip whose snaky lash, metal topped, was curled many times around his forearm. He bowed before Klaneth.

Kenton recognized him. When he had lain on the deck close to the mast he had seen this man sitting on a high platform at the foot of that mast. Overseer of the galley slaves, the oarsmen, was Zachel, and that long lash was measured to flick the furtherest of them if they lagged.

"Is this he whom you saw upon the deck some sleeps ago?" asked Klaneth. "He who lay there and, you say, vanished when the drab of Ishtar yonder bent over to touch him?"

"He is the same, master," answered the overseer, coming close to Kenton and scanning him.

"Where went he then?" asked Klaneth, more to himself than to the other. "To Sharane's cabin? But if so—

why did she drive him out, her cats clawing him? And whence came that sword she waved and bade him come retake? I know that sword——"

"He did not go into her cabin at that time, master," interrupted Zachel. "I saw her seek for him. She went back to her place alone. He had vanished."

"And his driving forth," mused Klaneth, "that was two sleeps ago. And the ship has sailed far since then. We saw him struggling in the waves far behind us. Yet here he is upon the ship again—and with his wounds still fresh, still bleeding as though it had been but a moment gone. And how passed he the barrier? Yea—how passed he the barrier?"

"Ah, at last you have stumbled on a real question," cried the Persian. "Let him but tell me that—and, by the Nine Hells, not long will you have me for companion, Klaneth."

Kenton saw the drummer make a covert warning gesture to Zubran; saw the black priest's eyes narrow.

"Ho! Ho!" laughed Gigi. "Zubran jests. Would he not find life there as tiresome as he pretends to find it with us? Is it not so, Zubran?"

Again he made the fleet, warning sigh. And the Persian heeded it.

"Yes, I suppose that is so," he answered grudgingly. "At any rate—am I not sworn to Nergal? Nevertheless," he muttered, "the gods gave women one art that has not grown tiresome since first they made the world."

"They lose that art in Nergal's abode," said the black priest, grimly. "Best remember that and curb that tongue of yours lest you find yourself in a worse place than here —where at least you have your body."

"May I speak, master?" asked Zachel; and Kenton felt threat in the glance the overseer shot at him.

The black priest nodded.

"I think he passed the barrier because he knows naught of our Lord," said Zachel. "Indeed—may be an enemy of our Lord. If not—why was he able to shake off the hands of your priests, vanish in the sea—and return?"

"Enemy of Nergal!" Klaneth muttered.

"But it does not follow that he is friend of Ishtar," put in the drummer, smoothly. "True if he were sworn to the Dark One he could not pass the barrier. But true is it also that were he sworn to Ishtar equally would that have been impossible."

"True!" Klaneth's face cleared. "And I know that sword —Nabu's own blade."

He was silent for a moment; thoughtful. When he spoke there was courtesy in the thick voice.

"Stranger," he said, "if we have used you roughly, forgive us. Visitors are rare upon this craft. You—let me say —startled us out of our manners. Zachel, loose his bonds."

The overseer bent and sullenly set Kenton free of his thongs.

"If, as I think, you come from Nabu," went on the black priest, "I tell you that I have no quarrel with the Wise One òr his people. Nor is my Master, the Lord of Death, ever at odds with the Lord of Wisdom. How could he be when one carries the keys of knowledge of this life, and the other the key that unlocks the door of the ultimate knowledge? Nay, there is no quarrel there. Are you a favored one of Nabu? Did he set you on the ship? And —why?"

Silent was Kenton, searching desperately for some way to answer the black priest. Temporize with him as he had with Sharane, he knew he could not. Nor, he knew, was it of any use to tell him the truth as he had told her— and been driven out like a hunted rat for it. Here was danger; peril, greater than he had faced in the rosy cabin. Klaneth's voice cut in:

"But favored of Nabu as you may be, it seems that could not save you from losing his sword, nor from the javelins of Ishtar's women. And if that is so—can it save you from my whip, my chains?"

And as Kenton stood, still silent, wolf light flared in the dead pupils and the black priest leaped to his feet crying:

"Answer me!"

"Answer Klaneth!" roared Gigi. "Has fear of him killed your tongue?"

Under the apparent anger of the drummer's voice Kenton sensed a warning; friendliness.

"If that favor could have saved me, at least it did not," he said sullenly.

The black priest dropped back upon the settle, chuckling.

"Nor could it save you if I decreed your death," he said.

38

"Death—if he decrees it," croaked Gigi.

"Whoever you are," went on the black priest, "whence you come, or how—one thing seems true. You have power to break a chain that irks me. Nay, Zachel, stay," he spoke to the overseer who had made a move to go. "Your counsel is also good. Stay!"

"There is a slave dead at the oars," said the overseer. "I would loose his chains and cast him over."

"Dead," there was new interest in Klaneth's voice. "Which was he? How did he die?"

"Who knows?" Zachel shrugged his shoulders. "Of weariness, maybe. He was one of those who first set sail with us. He who sat beside the yellow haired slave from the North whom we bought at Emakhtila."

"Well—he had served long," said the black priest. "Nergal has him. Let his body bear his chains a little longer. Stay with me."

He spoke again to Kenton, deliberately, finally:

"I offer you freedom. I will give you honors and wealth in Emakhtila, where we shall sail as soon as you have done my bidding. There you shall have priesthood and a temple if you want them. Gold and women and rank—if you will do what I desire."

"What must I do to win me all this?" asked Kenton.

The black priest arose and bent his head so that his eyes looked straight into Kenton's own.

"Slay Sharane!" he said.

"Little meat in that, Klaneth," the Persian spoke, mockingly. "Did you not see her girls beat him? As well send to conquer a lioness a man who has already been whipped by her cubs."

"Nay," said Klaneth, "I did not mean for him to pass over the open deck where surely her watchers would see him. He can clamber round the ship's hull—from chain, ledge to ledge. There is a window behind the cabin wherein she sleeps. He can creep up and through it."

"Best swear him to Nergal before he takes that road, master," Zachel interrupted. "Else we may never have him back again."

"Fool!" Gigi spoke. "If he makes his vows to Nergal perhaps he cannot go at all. How do we know that then the barrier will not be closed to him as it is to us who are sworn to the Dark One, even as it is to those who are sworn to Ishtar?"

"True," nodded the black priest. "We dare not risk that. Well spoken, Gigi."

"Why should Sharane be slain?" asked Kenton. "Let me take her for slave that I may repay her for her mockery and her blows. Give her to me—and you may keep all the riches and honors you have offered."

"No!" The black priest leaned closer, searching more intently his eyes. "She must be slain. While she lives the Goddess has a vial into which to pour herself. Sharane dead—Ishtar has none on this ship through whom she may make herself manifest. This, I, Klaneth, know. Sharane dead, Nergal rules—through me! Nergal wins—through me!"

In Kenton's mind a plan had formed. He would promise to do this—to slay Sharane. He would creep into her cabin, tell her of the black priest's plot. Some way, somehow, make her believe him.

Too late he saw by the black priest's face that Klaneth had caught his thought! Too late remembered that the sharp eyes of the overseer had been watching him, losing no fleeting change of expression; interpreting.

"Look, master!" Zachel snarled. "Look! Can you not read his thought, even as I? He cannot be trusted. You have held me here for counsel and have called my counsel good—then let me speak what is in my mind. I thought that this man had vanished from beside the mast, even as I told you. But did he? The gods come and go upon the ship as they will. But no man does. We thought we saw him struggling in the waves far behind the ship. But did we? By sorcery he may have lain all this while, hid in Sharane's cabin. Out of her cabin we saw him come——"

"But driven forth by her women, Zachel," broke in the drummer. "Cast out. Beaten. Remember that. There was no friendship there, Klaneth. They were at his throat like hounds tearing down a deer."

"A play!" cried Zachel. "A play to trick you, master. They could have killed him. Why did they not? His wounds are but pin pricks. They drove him, yes, but where? Over to us! Sharane knew he could cross the barrier. Would she have made gift to us of new strength unless—she had a purpose? And what could that purpose have been, master? Only one. To place him here to slay you—even as you now plan to send him to slay her!

"He is a strong man—and lets himself be beaten by

40

girls! He had a sword, a sharp blade and a holy one—
and he lets a woman take it. Ho! Ho!" laughed Zachel.
"Do you believe all this, master? Well—I do not!"

"By Nergal!" Klaneth swore, livid. "Now by Nergal——!"

He gripped Kenton by the shoulders, hurled him through
the cabin door and out upon the deck. Swiftly he followed him.

"Sharane!" he howled. "Sharane!"

Kenton raised his head, dizzily; saw her standing beside the cabin door, arms around the slim waists of two
of her damsels.

"Nergal and Ishtar are busy elsewhere," mocked the
black priest. "Life on the ship grows dull. There is a slave
under my feet. A lying slave. Do you know him,
Sharane?"

He bent and lifted Kenton high, as a man a child. Her
face, cold, contemptuous, did not change.

"He is nothing to me—Worm," she answered.

"Nothing to you, eh?" roared Klaneth. "Yet it was by
your will that he came to me. Well—he has a lying
tongue, Sharane. By the old law of the slaves shall he be
punished for it. I will pit four of my men against him. If
he master them I shall keep him for awhile—to amuse us
further. But if they master him—then shall his lying
tongue be torn from him. And I will give it to you as a
token of my love—O, Sacred Vessel of Ishtar!"

"Ho! Ho!" laughed the black priest as Sharane shrank,
paling. "A test for your sorceries, Sharane. To make that
tongue speak! Make it—" the thick voice purred—"make
it whisper of love to you. Tell you how beautiful you are,
Sharane. How wonderful—ah, sweet Sharane! Reproach
you a little, too, perhaps for sending it to me to be torn
out!"

"Ho! Ho!" laughed Klaneth; then as though he spat the
words, "You temple slut!"

He thrust a light whip in Kenton's hands.

"Now fight, slave!" he snarled, "fight for your lying
tongue!"

Four of the priests leaped forward, drawing from beneath their robes thongs tipped with metal. They circled,
and before Kenton could gather his strength they were
upon him. They darted about him like four lank wolves;
slashing at him with their whips. Blows flailed upon his

41

head, his naked shoulders. Awkwardly he tried to parry, to return them. The metal tips bit deep. From shoulders, chest, back, a slow rain of blood began to drip.

A thong caught him across the face, half blinding him. Far away, he heard the golden voice of Sharane, shrill with scorn.

"Slave—can you not even fight?"

Cursing, he dropped his useless whip. Close before him was the grinning face of the priest who had struck him. Ere his lash could be raised again the fist of Kenton had smashed squarely on the leering mouth. He felt beneath his knuckles the bones of the nose crumble, the teeth shatter. The priest crashed back; went rolling to the rail.

Instantly the other three were upon him; tearing at his throat, clawing him, striving to drag him down. He broke loose. The three held back for an instant; then rushed. One there was a little in front of the others. Kenton caught him by an arm, twisted that arm over his shoulder, set hip to prisoned flank, heaved and hurled the priest through air against the pair poised to strike. Out flung the body; fell short. The head crashed against the deck. There was a sharp snap, like a breaking faggot. For a moment the body stood, shoulders touching deck, legs writhing as though in grotesque midsomersault. Then crumpled and lay still.

"Well thrown!" he heard the Persian shout.

Long fingers clutched his ankles; his feet flew from beneath him. As he fell he caught glimpse of a face staring up at him, a face that was but one red smear; the face of the first priest he had battered down. Falling, Kenton swept out his arms. Claws clutched his throat. There flashed into Kenton's mind a dreadful thing he had seen done in another unequal combat upon a battlefield in France. Up swept his right hand, the first two fingers extended. They found place in the eye sockets of the throttler; pressed there cruelly; pressed there relentlessly. He heard a howl of agony; tears of blood spurted over his hands; the choking fingers dropped from his throat. Where eyes had been were now two raw red sockets with dreadful pendants.

Kenton leaped to his feet. He stamped upon the crimson smeared face looking up at him stamped once, twice, thrice—and the grip about his ankles was gone.

42

He caught a glimpse of Sharane, white faced, wide-eyed; realized that the laughter of the black priest was stilled.

At him rushed the fourth acolyte, a broad-leafed knife gleaming in his grip. Kenton bent his head, rushed to meet him. He caught the hand that held the blade; bent the arm back; heard the bone snap. The fourth priest shrieked and fell.

He saw Klaneth, mouth loose, staring at him.

Straight for the black priest's throat he leaped, right fist swinging upward to the jaw as he sprang. But the black priest thrust out his arms, caught him in mid-leap; lifted him high, over his head; balanced him to dash him down upon the deck.

Kenton closed his eyes—this, then, was the end.

He heard the voice of the Persian, urgent:

"Hai, Klaneth! Hai! Kill him not! By Ishak of the Hollow Hell—kill him not. Klaneth! Save him to fight again!"

Then the drummer——

"Nay, Klaneth! Nay!" He felt the talons of Gigi catch him; hold him tight in double grasp. "Nay, Klaneth! He fought fairly and well. He would be a rare one to have with us. Mayhap he will change his mind—with discipline. Remember, Klaneth—he can pass the barrier."

The great bulk of the black priest trembled. Slowly his hands began to lower Kenton.

"Discipline? Ha!" it was the snarling voice of the overseer. "Give him to me, master, in the place of the slave who died at the oar. I will teach him—discipline."

The black priest dropped Kenton on the deck; stood over him for a moment. Then he nodded, turned and stalked into his cabin. Kenton, reaction seizing him, huddled; hands clasping knees.

"Unchain the dead slave and cast him over, Zachel," he heard Gigi say. "I will watch this man till you return."

Kenton heard the overseer patter away. The drummer bent over him.

"Well fought, wolf cub," he whispered. "Well fought! Now to your chains. Obey. Your chance shall come. Do as I say, wolf cub—and I will do what I may."

He walked away. Kenton, wondering, raised his head. He saw the drummer stoop, lift the body of the priest with the broken neck and with one sweep of his long arm send it whirling over the ship's rail. Bending again he sent after it the body of him upon whose face Kenton had stamped.

He paused speculatively before the wailing, empty-socketed horror stumbling and falling about the deck. Then, grinning cheerfully, he lifted it by the knees and tossed it overboard.

"Three less to worry about hereafter," muttered Gigi.

A tremor shook Kenton; his teeth chattered; he sobbed. The drummer looked down on him with amused wonder.

"You fought well, wolf cub," he said. "Then why do you quiver like a whipped hound whose half chewed bone has been cast away?"

He laid both hands on Kenton's bleeding shoulders. Under their touch he steadied. It was as though through Gigi's hands flowed some current of strength of which his soul drank. As though he had tapped some ancient spring, some still pool of archaic indifference both to life and death, the current ran through him.

"Good!" said Gigi, and stood up. "Now Zachel comes for you."

The overseer was beside Kenton; he touched his shoulder; pointed down a short flight of steps that led from the black deck to the galley-pit. Zachel behind him, Kenton groped down those steps into the half darkness of the pit. He stumbled along a narrow passage-way; was brought to halt at a great oar over whose shank a head, golden haired, long haired as any woman's, bent from muscle-gnarled shoulders. This golden haired oarsman slept. Around his waist was a thick bronze ring. From this ring a strong chain swung, its end fastened to a staple sunk deep in the back of the bench on which he sat. His wrists were manacled. The oar on which his head rested was manacled, too. Between manacled wrists and manacled oar two other strong chains stretched.

There was an empty chained circlet at the sleeper's left side; on the oar at his left two empty manacles hung from chains.

Zachel pushed Kenton down on the bench beside the sleeping oarsman; girdled his waist with the empty bronze circlet; snapped it close; locked it.

He thrust Kenton's unresisting hands through the manacles dangling from the oar; closed them on him; locked them.

And suddenly Kenton felt warmth of eyes upon him; looked behind him; saw leaning over the rail the face of

Sharane. There was pity in her face; and dawning of something that set his heart to beating wildly.

"I'll discipline you—never fear!" said Zachel.

Kenton looked behind him again.

Sharane was gone.

He bent over his oar beside the sleeping giant.

Bent over his oar——

Chained to it.

Slave of the ship!

8

The Tale Of Sigurd

KENTON awakened to the shrilling of a whistle. Something flicked his shoulder like the touch of a hot iron. He jerked his head up from the bed of his arms; looked stupidly at the chained wrists. Again the flick upon the shoulder, biting into the flesh.

"Up, slave!" he heard a snarling voice say—a voice he knew and struggled with deep drugged mind to place. "Up! Stand to your oar!"

Then another voice, close beside him, whispering, hoarse, but with warmth of comradeship in it:

"On your feet before his whip covers your back with the blood runes."

He struggled upright; hands falling mechanically into two smooth, worn hollows in the wooden shaft to which he was chained. Standing thus upon the bench, his eyes looked out upon a tranquil, turquoise ocean, waveless, within a huge inverted bowl of silver mists. In front of him were four men, two standing, two sitting, at shanks of great oars which, like that he clutched, thrust through the side of a ship. Beyond them sloped a black deck——

Memory rushed upon him, banishing the last of sleep. The first voice had been that of Zachel, and the hot touches on his skin the bite of his whip. He turned his head. A score of other men, black and brown, sat and stood at other great sweeps, bending and rising, sending the Ship

45

of Ishtar cutting through the still blue sea. And there on a platform at the mast step was Zachel, grinning derisively. Out at Kenton flicked the long lash once more.

"Look not back! Row!" snarled Zachel.

"I will row," whispered the second voice. "Stand and sway with the oar till strength comes to you."

He looked down on a head fair haired, long haired as any woman's. But there was nothing womanish in the face that was lifted for an instant to his. Ice cold and ice blue were the eyes in it, though thawed now by a rough kindliness. The skin was storm beaten, tempest tanned. Nor was there aught womanish in the muscles that swelled on shoulders, back, and arms as he swung the great sweep, handling it as easily as a woman a broom.

Norseman from tip to toe; a Viking straight out of some ancient Saga—and, like Kenton, a slave to the ship; the giant who had been asleep over the oar when Kenton's own chains had been locked upon him.

"Sigurd, Trygg's son, I," muttered the Norseman. "What Norn of ill-luck set you on this ship of warlocks? Speak low—bend to your oar. The devil with the lash has sharp ears."

To the motion of the oar Kenton bent and rose, standing there on the bench. The benumbment that had held his mind was passing; passed ever more swiftly as his tightened grip on the oar began to send the blood more swiftly through his veins. The man beside him grunted approval.

"No weakling, you," he whispered. "The oar wearies—yet up it flows strength from the sea. But sip that strength slowly. Grow strong—slowly. Then it may be that you and I together——"

He paused; shot a wary side glance at Kenton.

"By your looks, you are a man of Eirnn, of the Southern Isles," he whispered. "No grudge bear I against them. They met us always sword to sword and breast to breast. Many the blows we have struck between us, and the hovering Valkyries went never empty-handed back to Valhalla when we met the men of Eirnn. Brave men, strong men, men who died shouting, kissing sword blade and spear point as gayly as a bride. Are you one of these?"

Kenton thought swiftly. He must shape his answer cunningly to bind this comradeship so plainly offered him; neither bewilder by whole truth nor be so vague as to rouse suspicion.

46

"Kenton, my name," he answered softly. "My fathers were of the Eirnn. They knew well the Vikings and their ships—nor have they handed down to me any grudge against them. I would be friend of yours, Sigurd, Trygg's son, since for how long neither of us knows I must labor here beside you. And since you and I—together——"

He paused meaningly, as had the Viking. The Norseman nodded, then again shot that keen side glance at him.

"How fell this bane upon you?" he muttered. "Since they drove me aboard this ship at Isle of Sorcerers we have entered no harbor. You were not here when they chained me to the oar."

"Sigurd—by Odin All-Father—I do not know!" The Norseman's hand quivered at the name of his god. "A hand that I could not see plucked me out of my own land and set me here. That son of Hela who rules the black deck offered me freedom—if I would do a thing of shame. I would not. I battled with his men. Three I slew. And then they chained me to this oar."

"You slew three!" The Viking looked up at Kenton, eyes blazing, teeth bared. "You slew three! Skoal! Comrade! Skoal!" he shouted.

Something like a flying serpent hissed by Kenton; hissed and struck the Norseman's back. It withdrew, blood spurting from where it had bitten. It struck and struck again.

Zachel's voice snarled through the hissing of the lash:

"Dog! Sow spittle! Have you gone mad? Shall I flay you then!"

Under the lash the body of Sigurd, Trygg's son, shuddered. He looked up at Kenton, bloody froth on his lips. Suddenly, Kenton knew that it was not from the pain of the blows—that it was from the shame of them and from rage; that the whiplash was drawing redder drops from his heart, threatening to break it.

And Kenton, leaning over, thrust his own bare back between that lash and the bloody shoulders; took the blows itself.

"Ha!" shouted Zachel. "You want them, do you? Jealous of my whip's kisses, are you? Well, then—take your fill of them!"

Mercilessly the lash hissed and struck, hissed and struck. Kenton endured its bite stoically, never shifting the shield of his body from the Norseman; meeting each sharp agony

47

by thought of what he would do to repay when his time had come——

When he had mastered the ship!

"Stop!" Through pain-misted eyes he saw the drummer leaning over the pit. "Would you kill the slave, Zachel? By Nergal, if you do I'll ask Klaneth as gift to me to chain you to his oar for a while!"

Then Zachel, sullenly:

"Row, slave!"

Silently, half fainting, Kenton bent over the oar. The Norseman caught a hand, held it in iron grip.

"Sigurd, Trygg's son, am I! Jarl's grandson! Master of Dragons!" His voice was low, yet in it was a clanging echo of smiting swords; and he spoke with eyes closed as though he stood before some altar. "Blood brotherhood is there now between us, Kenton of the Eirnn. Blood brothers—you and I. By the red runes upon your back written there when you thrust it between me and the whip. I shall be your shield as you have been mine. Our swords shall be as one sword. Your friend shall be my friend, and your enemy my enemy. And my life for yours when need be! This by Odin All-Father and by all the Aesir I swear—I, Sigurd, Trygg's son! And if ever I break faith with you, then may I lie under the poison of Hela's snakes until Yggdrasill, the Tree of Life, withers, and Ragnarak, the Night of the Gods, has come!"

The heart of Kenton swelled and grew warm.

The grip of the Norseman tightened. He withdrew his hand and bent once more to the oar. Nothing more said he—but Kenton knew the vow was sealed.

The whip of the overseer cracked, a shrill whistle sounded. The four rowers in front lifted high their oars, shunted them into a niche. The Viking raised his sweep, set it in a similar rest.

"Sit," he said. "They wash us now and feed."

A cascade of water fell over Kenton, and another. The salt of it stung his wounds, brought tears to his eyes.

"Quiet!" warned Sigurd. "Soon the pain passes, and the salt will heal."

Then down over him swished the water. Two brown men, naked to the waists, backs scarred, went by. In each hand they held buckets, raised them, and poured the water over two of the men at the stroke oars. They turned and went back along the narrow way between the benches.

48

Powerful were their bodies. Their faces were those of men come to life out of some ancient Assyrian frieze, narrow, hook-nosed, full-lipped. No mind dwelt behind those faces. Their eyes were staring, empty.

The pair came back with other buckets which they dashed over the floor of the rowers' pit, washing it clean. And when this was done two other slaves set upon the bench between Kenton and the Norseman a rough platter and a bowl. On the platter were a dozen long pods and a heap of round cakes resembling the cassava bread the tropical folk press out and bake in the sun. The bowl was filled with a dark, thick liquid, purplish red.

He munched the pods; they were fleshy, with a curious meaty flavor. The round cakes tasted exactly like what they resembled—cassava bread. The liquid was strong, pungent, a trace of fermentation in it. There was strength in that food and drink. The Norseman smiled at him.

"No lash now, so we speak not too loudly," he said. "It is the rule. So while we eat and drink ask what you will of me without fear, blood brother."

"Two things I would first know of many," said Kenton. "How came you on the ship, Sigurd? And how comes this food here?"

"From here and there comes the food," answered the Viking. "It is a ship of warlocks and a cursed one. Not long may it stop at any place, nor at any place is it welcome. Nay, not even at Emakhtila, which is full of warlocks. Where it harbors they bring food and gear quickly and with fear. Quickly do they give to speed it quickly away, lest the demons who possess it grow angry and destroy. They have strong magic—that pale son of Helan and the woman on the white deck. Sometimes I think her a daughter of Loki, whom Odin chained for his wickedness. And sometimes I think her a daughter of Freya, the Mother of Gods. But whatever she be, she is very fair and has a great soul. I have no hatred toward her."

He lifted the bowl to his lips.

"And as for how I came here," he went on, "that is a short tale enough. Southward I had sailed with the fleet of Ragnor Red Spear. Twelve great dragons had we when we set forth. Southward sailed we through many seas, raiding as we went. Then after long, with six of our ten dragons left us, we came to a city in the land of the Egyptians.

49

It was a very great city and full of temples to all the gods in the world—except our gods.

"It irked us that among all these temples Odin All-Father had none. It irked us, and we grew wroth. So one night when we had drunk overdeep of the Egyptian wine six of us set forth to take a temple, cast out its god, and give it to Odin for a home.

"We came to a temple and entered. It was a dark temple and full of black robes like these on board the ship. When we told them what we meant to do, they buzzed like bees and rushed us like a wolfpack. Many then we slew, shouting. And we would have won that temple for Odin, the six of us fighting in a ring, but—a horn blew!"

"Summoning too many for you?" asked Kenton.

"Not at all, blood brother," said Sigurd. "It was a warlock horn. A horn of sleep. It blew sleep through us as the storm wind blows the spray through a sail. It turned our bones to water, and our red swords dropped from hands that could not longer feel their hilts. And down we all dropped, sodden with sleep, among the slain.

"When we awoke we were in a temple. We thought it the same temple, for it was as dark and the same black-robed priests filled it. We were in chains, and they whipped us and made us slaves. Then we found we were no longer in the land of the Egyptians, but in a city named Emakhtila, on an isle of warlocks set in a sea of what I think a warlock world. Long I slaved for the black robes, I and my comrades, till they dragged me to this ship that had dropped anchor in Emakhtila harbor. And here ever since I have bent over my oar, watching their wizard-ries and fighting to keep my soul from being sucked from me."

"A horn that poured out sleep!" said Kenton, puzzled. "But that I do not understand, Sigurd."

"You will, comrade," Sigurd said grimly. "Soon enough you will. Zachel plays it well—listen—it begins."

From behind them a deep, droning, mellow horn note sounded. Low pitched, vibrant, continuous, it crept into the ears, and seemed to pour through them along every nerve, touching them, caressing them with the soft fingers of the very soul of poppied sleep.

The note droned on, dripping sleep.

The Viking's eyes were fierce and strained with struggle against slumber. Slowly, slowly the lids closed over them.

His hands relaxed, the fingers opened, his body swayed, his head dropped upon his chest. He slumped down upon the bench.

The note droned on.

Fight as hard as Kenton might, he could not thrust away the soft, clinging slumber that pressed inexorably in on him from every side. A numbness crept through his body. Sleep, sleep—swarms of infinite particles of sleep were drifting through him, drifting with his blood through every vein, along every nerve, clogging his brain.

Lower and lower dropped his own lids.

And suddenly he could no longer fight. Chains rattling, down against Sigurd he fell. . . .

Something deep within Kenton whispered to him to awaken; something reached down into the abysses of his charmed slumber and drew to its surface his consciousness. Slowly his heavy lids began to rise—then stopped, obeying some subtle warning. He looked out through narrowest slits. The chains that bound his wrists to the riveted manacles of the oar were long. He had moved in his sleep and now lay with head on arm stretched along the back of the low bench. He faced the ivory deck.

There, at its edge, looking down upon him, was Sharane. Veils of palest blue, through which the hands of long dead Assyrian maids had woven golden lotuses, draped her breast, coiled round her slender waist, and fell to the delicate, sandaled feet. Her black haired maiden Satalu beside her, she leaned over, scanning him.

"Mistress," he heard Satalu say, "he cannot be man of Nergal, since Nergal's men have chained him there."

"No," mused Sharane. "No—in that I was wrong. And had he been of Nergal, never could he have crossed the barrier. Nor would Klaneth have taunted me—as he did—"

"He is very handsome and young," sighed Satalu—"and strong. He fought the priests like a lion lord."

"Even a cornered rat will fight," answered Sharane, scornful. "He let himself be led to his chains like a whipped dog. And he lied to me! He came to me in borrowed plumes bearing a sword he could not use!

"Oh," cried Sharane—and half of that cry was a sob—"oh, Satalu, I am ashamed! Liar and coward and slave—

still he stirs something in my heart that never yet has stirred for man. Oh, I am ashamed—I am ashamed, Satalu!"

"Lady Sharane, do not weep!" Satalu caught the fluttering hands. "He may be none of these. How do you know? Perhaps he did speak the truth. How know we what has happened in that world of ours so long lost to us? And he is very handsome—and young!"

"At least," said Sharane and bitterly, "he is a slave."

"Sh-h!" warned Satalu. "Zachel comes."

They turned; walked toward Sharane's cabin out of Kenton's vision.

The wakening whistle shrilled. There was a stir among the slaves, and Kenton groaned, raised himself, rubbed eyes, and gripped the oar.

Exultation was in his heart. There could be no mistaking Sharane's words. He held her. By a slender thread, it might be; but still—he held her. And if he were not a slave—when slave he ceased to be—what then? By no slender thread then would he hold her. He laughed—but softly, lest Zachel hear. Sigurd looked at him curiously.

"The sleep horn must have brought you gay dream," he murmured.

"Gay, indeed, Sigurd," he answered. "The kind of dream that will thin our chains until we can snap them."

"Odin send more dreams like it," grunted the Norseman.

9

The Bargaining Of Sharane

WHEN Zachel blew the horn again Kenton had no need of it to send him to sleep. The sharp eyes of the overseer had seen through Sigurd's self-sacrificing stratagem, and he had watched Kenton continually, lashing him if he faltered or let the whole burden of the oar fall upon the Norseman. His hands were blistered, every bone and muscle ached, and his mind lay dulled in his weary body. And thus it was between the next five sleeps.

Once he roused himself enough to ask Sigurd a question that had been going round and round in his brain. Half the rowers in the pit were behind the line that separated black deck from ivory—that line which neither Klaneth and his crew nor Sharane and her women could cross. Yet Zachel roamed at will from one end of that pit to the other; other priests, too, for he had seen them. And although he had not seen Klaneth or Gigi or the Persian there, he did not doubt that they could come and go if they so wished. Why, then, did not the black robes swarm up the farther side and overwhelm the rosy cabin? Why did not Sharane and her women drop into the pit and lay siege to the ebon cabin? Why did they not launch their javelins, their arrows, over the pit of the rowers into the wolfpack of the black priest?

It was a warlock ship, the Viking had repeated, and the spell upon it no simple one. The slave who had died had told him that he had been on the ship since the gods had launched her, and that the same unseen, mysterious barrier shut off the side of the rowers that rimmed Sharane's deck. Nor could javelin or arrow or other missile other than those hurled by god and goddess penetrate it.

Humanly, each opposing camp was helpless against the other. There were other laws, too, the slave had told Sigurd. Neither Sharane nor Klaneth could leave the ship when it hove to in harbor. Sharane's women could. The black priest's men, yes—but not for long. Soon they must return. The ship drew them back. What would happen to them if they did not return? The slave had not known, had said that such thing was impossible, the ship would draw them back.

Kenton pondered over all this as with aching back he pushed and pulled at the oar. Decidedly these were practical, efficient deities who had doomed the ship, overlooking no detail, he thought, half amused.

Well, they had created the game, and certainly they had the right to make that game's rules. He wondered whether Sharane could roam at will from stem to stern when he had conquered the ship. Wondering still, he heard the drone of Zachel's horn begin, and pitched, content, into the bottomless oubliette of sleep it opened.

He awoke from that sixth sleep with mind crystal clear, an astonishing sense of well being, and a body once more free from pain and flexible and vigorous. He pulled at his oar strongly and easily.

"Strength flows up to you from the sea even as I foretold," grunted Sigurd.

Kenton nodded absently, his sharpened mind grappling with the problem of escape from his chains.

What went on in the pit and on the ship while the rowers were asleep? What chance would offer then to free himself and the Viking if he could stay awake?

If he could stay awake!

But how could he close his ears to that horn which poured sleep into them as the sirens of old poured with their songs fatal fascination into the ears of sailors strayed within their ken?

The sirens! The story of crafty Ulysses' adventure with those sea women flashed into his memory. How desire had come upon that wanderer to hear the siren song—yet no desire to let it draw him to them. How he had sailed into their domain; had filled his oarsmen's ears with melted wax; had made them bind him to the mast with open ears, and then, cursing, straining at his bonds, mad with desire to leap into their white arms, had heard their enchanted measures—and sailed safe away.

A wind arose—a steady wind that filled the sail and drove the ship through gently cresting waves. Came command to rest oars. Kenton slouched down upon the bench. Sigurd was in one of his silent moods, face brooding, gaze far away, filled with dreams of other days when his dragons cleft the Northern Ocean.

Kenton dropped his hands upon the silken rags upon his legs; his fingers began, seemingly idly, to unravel their threads, twist and knot them into little silken cylinders. He worked on, the Viking unheeding. Now two were finished. He palmed one, rubbed as idly the side of his face, and so rubbing slipped the little silken cylinder into an ear. He waited for a time; slipped in the other ear the second plug. The roaring of the wind sank to a loud whispering.

Carefully, unhurrying, he drew them out; twisted more threads around them. Again he set them in place. Now the wind's roar was only a murmuring, faint and far away. Satisfied, he slipped the silken cylinders under his torn girdle.

On sped the ship. And after a while the slaves came and

dashed their buckets over him and the Viking; brought them food and drink.

On the very edge of the sleep-horn drone Kenton slumped down upon the bench, face on forearms, the silken cylinders hidden under thumbs. Swiftly he slipped them in his ears. Then he let every muscle go limp. The droning diminished to a faint, hardly heard humming. Even so, a languor crept through him. He fought it. He beat the languor back. The humming ceased. He heard the overseer go by him; looked after him through half-raised lids; saw him ascend that pit's steps and pass over the deck to Klaneth's cabin.

The black deck was empty. As though shifting in slumber, Kenton rolled over, threw an arm across the back of the bench, rested his head upon it, and through lowered lashes took stock of what lay behind him.

He heard laughter, golden, chiming. To the edge of her deck, black haired Satalu beside her, walked Sharane. She seated herself there, unbound her hair, shook the flaming red gold cloud of it over face and shoulders; sat within it as though within a perfumed, silken red gold tent. Satalu raised a shining tress; began to comb it.

Through that web of loveliness he felt Sharane's eyes upon him. Involuntarily his own opened wide; clung to her hidden ones. She gasped, half rose, parted the curtains of her hair, stared at him in wonder.

"He is awake!" she whispered.

"Sharane!" he breathed.

He watched shame creep again into her eyes—her face grow cold. She raised her head, sniffed daintily.

"Satalu," she said, "is there not a stronger taint from the pit?" Again she tilted her nose. "Yes—I am sure there is. Like the old slave market at Uruk when they brought the new slaves in."

"I—I notice it not, mistress," faltered Satalu.

"Why, yes—of course." Sharane's voice was merciless. "See there he sits. A new slave; a strange slave who sleeps with open eyes."

"Yet he—he looks not like a slave," again faltered her handmaiden.

"No?" questioned Sharane sweetly. "What has happened to your memory, girl? What is the badge of a slave?"

The black haired girl did not answer; bent low over the locks of her mistress.

"A chain and the brand of whips," mocked Sharane. "These are the slave's badge. And this new slave has both —in plenty."

Still Kenton was silent beneath her mockery; made no movement; indeed scarce heard her, his burning eyes drinking in her beauty.

"Ah, but I dreamed one came to me with great words, a bearer of promises, fanning hope in my heart," sighed Sharane. "I opened my heart to him—in that dream, Satalu. All my heart! And he repaid me with lies—and his promises were empty—and he was a weakling—and my girls beat him. And now it seems to me that there sits that liar and weakling of my dreams with brand of whip upon his back and weak hands chained. A slave!"

"Mistress! Oh, Mistress!" whispered Satalu.

But Kenton kept silence, although now her mockery began to sting.

And suddenly she rose, thrust hands through shining locks.

"Satalu," she murmured, "would you not think that sight of me would awaken even a slave? That any slave, so he were young and strong, would break his chains— for me?"

She swayed, turned; through her thin robes gleamed exquisite, rosy curves of breast and thigh; lithe loveliness. She spread wide the nets of her hair, peered through them at him with wanton eyes; preened herself, thrust out a tiny, rosy foot, a dimpled knee.

He raised his head recklessly, the hot blood rushing through.

"The chains will break, Sharane!" he called. "I will break them—never fear! And then——"

"And then—" she echoed, "and then my girls shall beat you as before!" she mocked, and sped away.

He watched her go, pulse beating like drums. He saw her halt and whisper to Satalu. The black haired girl turned, made him a warning gesture. He closed his eyes, dropped head on arm. And soon he heard the feet of Zachel striding down the steps, go by him. The waking whistle shrilled.

Why, if her mockery had been real, had she warned him?

Sharane looked down upon him again from her deck.

Time had gone by since she had stood there mocking him. Time had gone, but how measured in his own lost world Kenton had no means of telling, meshed as he was in the ship's timeless web.

Sleep after sleep he had lain on his bench, watching for her. She had kept to her cabin—or if she had not, she had kept herself from his sight.

Nor had he told the Viking that he had broken the spell of the sleep horn. Sigurd he trusted, heart and soul. Yet he was not sure of the Norseman's subtlety; not certain that he could feign the charmed slumber as Kenton did. He could not take the risk.

And now again Sharane stood and looked down upon him from the platform close to the emerald mast. The slaves slept. There was none at watch on the black deck. There was no mockery now in Sharane's face. And when she spoke she struck straight home to the heart of her purpose.

"Whoever you are, whatever you may be," she whispered, "two things can you do. Cross the barrier. Remain awake when the other slaves must sleep. You have told me that you can break your chains. Since those two things you can do—I find belief within me that of the third you also speak the truth. Unless——"

She paused; he read her thought.

"Unless I lied to you about that as I lied to you before," he said levelly. "Well, those were no lies I told you."

"If you break your chains," she said, "will you slay Klaneth?"

He feigned to consider.

"Why should I kill Klaneth?" he asked at last.

"Why? Why?" Scorn tinged her voice. "Has he not set his chains upon you? Had you whipped? Made you slave?"

"Did not Sharane drive me forth with javelins?" he asked. "Did not Sharane pour salt in my wounds with her mockery—her laughter?"

"But—you lied to me!" she cried.

Again he feigned consideration.

"What will this liar, weakling, and slave gain if he kills the black priest for you?" he asked bluntly.

"Gain?" she repeated blankly.

"What will you pay me for it?" he said.

"Pay you? Pay you! Oh!" The scorn in her eyes scorched him. "You shall be paid. You shall have freedom—the pick of my jewels—all of them——"

57

"Freedom I shall have when I have slain Klaneth," he answered. "And of what use to me are your jewels on this cursed ship?"

"You do not understand," she said. "The black priest slain, I can set you on any land you wish in this world. In all of them jewels have value."

She paused, then: "And have they no worth in that land from whence you come, and to which, unchained, it seems you can return whenever danger threatens?"

Her voice was honeyed poison. But Kenton only laughed.

"What more do you want?" she asked. "If they be not enough—what more?"

"You!" he said.

"Me!" she gasped incredulously. "I give myself to any man—for a price! I—give myself to you! You whipped dog!" She stormed. "Never!"

Up to this Kenton's play with her had been calculated; but now he spoke with wrath as real and hot as hers.

"No!" cried Kenton. "No! You'll not give yourself to me! For, by God, Sharane, I'll take you!"

He thrust a clenched, chained hand out to her.

"Master of this ship I'll be, and with no help from you—you who have called me a liar and slave and now would throw me butcher's pay. No! When I master the ship it will be by my own hand. And that same hand shall master—you!"

"You threaten me!" Her face flamed wrath. "You!"

She thrust a hand into her breast, drew out a slender knife—hurled it at him. As though it had struck some adamantine wall, invisible, it clanged, fell to her feet, blade snapped from hilt.

She paled, shrank.

"Hate me!" jeered Kenton. "Hate me, Sharane; For what is hate but the flame that cleans the cup for wine of love!"

With no soft closing of her cabin door did she go within it. And Kenton, laughing grimly, bent his head over his oar; was soon as sound asleep as the Norseman snoring beside him.

10

On The Ship A-Sailing

HE AWAKENED to a stirring and humming through all
the ship. On ivory deck and black the ship's folk stood,
pointing, talking, gesticulating. A flock of birds, the first
he had seen in this strange world, hovered above him.
Their wings were shaped like those of great butterflies. Their plumage shone as though lacquered in glowing vermilions and pale golds. From their opened beaks
came a chiming tumult as of little tinkling bells.

"Land!" the Viking exclaimed. "We run into harbor.
Food and water must be low."

There was a brisk wind blowing and the oars at rest.
Careless of Zachel's lash, Kenton leaped upon the bench,
looking over the bow. The overseer gave no heed, his
own eyes intent upon what lay before.

It was a sun yellow isle, high and rounded, and
splashed with craters of color like nests of rainbows.
Save for these pansied dapplings, the island curved all
glowing topaz, from its base in the opalescent shallows of
the azure sea to its crest, where feathered trees drooped
branches like immense panaches of ostrich plumes dyed
golden amber. Over and about that golden isle shot flashes
of iridescences from what seemed luminous flying flowers.

Closer drew the ship. At the bow the damsels of
Sharane clustered, laughing and chattering. And upon her
balcony was Sharane, watching the isle with wistful eyes.

Now it was close indeed. Down ran the peacock sail.
The ship rowed slowly and more slowly to the shore; not
until the curved prow had almost touched that shore did
the steersman shift the rudder and bring the ship sharply
about. As they drifted, the plumes of the strange trees
swept the deck with long leaves, delicately feathered as
those the frost etches on the winter pane. Topaz yellow
and sun amber were those leaves; the branches from which

they hung glistened as though cut from yellow chrysolite. Immense clusters of flowers dropped from them, lily shaped, flame scarlet.

Slowly, ever more slowly, drifted the ship. It crept by a wide cleft that cut into the heart of the isle. The sides of this vale were harlequined with the cratered colors, and Kenton saw that these were fields of flowers, clustered as though they filled deep circled amphitheaters. The flashing iridescences were birds—birds of every size from smallest dragon flies to those whose wingspread was that of condors in the high Andes. Large and small, on each glittered the lacquered butterfly wings.

The isle breathed fragrance. Of green upon it there was none, save for the emerald glintings of the birds.

The valley slid behind them. Ever more slowly the feathered trees brushed the deck. The ship slipped into the mouth of a glen at whose end a cataract dropped rain of pearl into a golden ferned pool. There was the rattling of a chain; an anchor splashed. The bow of the ship swung in; nosed through the foliage; touched the bank.

Over the rail climbed the women of Sharane, upon their heads great baskets. From her balcony Sharane looked after them with deeper wistfulness. The women melted within the flower spangled boskage; fainter and fainter came their voices; died away. Sharane, chin cupped in white hands, drank in the land and with wide and longing eyes. Above her red gold hair streaming through the silver crescent a bird hovered—a bird all gleaming emeralds and flashing blues, chiming peals of fairy bells. Kenton saw tears upon her cheeks. She caught his gaze, dashed them away angrily. She half turned as though to go; then slipped down woefully behind one of her balcony's tiny blossoming trees where he could no longer see her weeping.

Now her women filed back along the bank, their baskets filled with plunder; fruits, gourds purple and white, and great clusters of those pods he had eaten when first he had broken fast upon the ship. Into the cabin they trooped, and out again with baskets empty. Time upon time they came and went. At last they bore away skins instead of the woven hampers; water bags which they filled from the pool of the cataract. Time upon time they brought them back, swollen full, upon their shoulders.

60

They trooped out once more, burdenless; darted joyously over the rail; doffed their scanty enough robes and plunged into the pool. Like water nymphs they swam and played, the pearly flow caressing, streaming from delicately delicious curves—pale ivory, warm rose, soft olive. They sprang from the pool, wove flower crowns and with sprays of the fragrant lily blooms in arms clambered, reluctant, over the side and into the rosy cabin.

Now crawled over the rail the men of Klaneth. They slipped on and off the ship with their burdens, poured their last water skins into the casks.

Again there was stir upon the ship. The chains rattled, the anchor lifted. Up and down flashed the oars, drawing the ship from the bank. Up rose the peacock sail. The ship veered, caught the wind, swam slowly through the amethystine shallows. Faster swung the sweeps. The golden isle diminished, was saffron shadow in the mists; vanished.

On sailed the ship.

And on and on—by what signs or reckonings or to what port Kenton could not know. Sleep after sleep it sailed. The huge bowl of silver mists whose edge was the horizon, contracted or expanded as those mists thickened or thinned. Storms they met and weathered; roaring storms that changed the silver of the mists to lurid copper, ambered jet, darkness deeper than night. Sudden storms threaded with lightnings weird and beautiful. Lightnings that were like the shatterings of immense prisms, the breakings of rainbows of jewels. Storms that trod on feet of thunder. Thunder that was metallic, tintinnabulary; hurricanes of clashing cymbals following showers of multicolored, flaming gems.

Steadily strength of the sea poured into Kenton up his oar blade, even as Sigurd had promised; remaking him, hardening him, turning all his body into a machine as finely tempered as a rapier and as flexible.

Between sleeps Sigurd chanted to him Viking tales, Sagas unsung, lost epics of the Norse.

Twice the black priest sent for him; questioned him, threatened him, cajoled him—vainly. And each time with blacker face sent him back to his chains.

Strife of god and goddess there was none. And Sharane during the sleep time of the slaves kept to her cabin. Awake, he could not turn his head to seek her without inviting the bite of Zachel's lash. So often he let the horn of sleep have its way—what use to keep awake while Sharane hid?

There came a time when, lying awake, he heard steps coming down the pit's stair. He turned, face against the back of his bench, as though in troubled slumber. The steps paused beside him.

"Zubran," it was the voice of Gigi, "this man has become a young lion."

"Strong enough," grunted the Persian. "It is a pity that his strength is wasted here—driving this ship from one place of weariness to another as bad."

"I think as you," said Gigi. "Strength he now has. Also he has courage. You remember how he slew the priests."

"Remember!" There was no boredom in Zubran's voice now. "Can I forget! By the heart of Rustam—could I forget! It was the first draft of life given me, it seemed, for centuries. I owe him something for that."

"Also," went on Gigi, "he has loyalty where his heart turns. I told you how he shielded with his own back the man who sleeps beside him. I liked him well for that, Zubran."

"As a gesture," said the Persian, "it was excellent. A trifle florid, perhaps, for perfect taste. But still—excellent."

"Courage, loyalty, strength," mused the drummer; then slowly, a hint of mirth in his voice, "And cunning. Unusual cunning, Zubran, since he has found a way to shut his ears to the sleep horn—and lies here now wide awake."

Kenton's heart stopped; began to beat furiously. How did the drummer know? Did he know? Was it only a guess? Desperately he strove against quivering nerves; forced his body to remain inert.

"What!" exclaimed the Persian, incredulously. "Awake! Gigi—you dream!"

"Nay," said Gigi quietly. "I have watched him when he saw me not. He is awake, Zubran."

Suddenly Kenton felt his paw upon his breast, pressing upon his pounding heart. The drummer chuckled; withdrew the hand.

"Also," he said, approvingly, "he has caution. A little he trusts me—but not too much. Nor does he know you well enough as yet, Zubran, to give you any trust at all.

Therefore he lies quiet, saying to himself: 'Gigi cannot really know. He cannot be sure as long as I do not open my eyes.' Yes, he has caution. But see, Zubran, he cannot keep the blood from stealing up into his face, nor slow his heart to the calm rhythm of sleep."

Again he chuckled, half-maliciously.

"And there is other proof of his caution, in that he has not told his comrade that the horn has no power over him. Hear the long haired one snore? No mistaking that for wakefulness. I like that too—he knows that a secret shared by two runs risk of being none."

"He seems sound asleep to me." Kenton felt the Persian bend down over him doubtfully.

His eyelids fought to rise; by sheer will he kept them down, breathing regularly, motionless. How long would they stand there looking at him?

At last Gigi broke the silence.

"Zubran," he said, quietly, "like you, I tire of the black priest and this fruitless strife between Ishtar and Nergal. Yet bound by our vows neither you nor I may come to grips with Klaneth, nor may we harm his men. It matters not that by trickery those vows were gotten from us. We made them—and they bind. As long as Nergal's priest rules Nergal's deck we may not give him battle. But suppose Klaneth no longer ruled—that another hand thrust him to his dark master?"

"A mighty hand that! Where on these seas could we find such a hand? And if found, how persuade it to close on Klaneth?" jeered the Persian.

"I think—it is here." Kenton felt again the drummer's touch. "Courage and loyalty and strength, quick wit and caution. He has all these. Beside—he can pass the barrier!"

"By Ahriman! That is so!" whispered the Persian.

"Now I would make another vow," said Gigi. "A vow in which you would join. If this man's chains were—broken, easily then could he pass to Sharane's cabin; easily now, I think, regain his sword."

"Well, what then?" asked Zubran. "He would still have Klaneth to meet and all his pack. And we could not help him."

"No," answered the drummer. "But neither would we hinder him. Our vows do not bind us to fight for the black priest, Zubran. Were I this man—with my chains

63

broke—and sword regained—I would find way to release this comrade sleeping beside him. He, I think, could keep off the pack while this wolf cub, who is now no longer cub but grown, could match himself against Klaneth."

"Well—" the Persian began doubtfully; then changed to cheerfulness—"I would see him loosed, Gigi. At the least, it would give break to this cursed monotony. But you spoke of a vow."

"A vow for a vow," answered Gigi. "If broken were his chains, if he regained sword, if he met Klaneth and we fought not against him at Klaneth's side, and if he slew Klaneth, would he vow comradeship with you and me, Zubran? I wonder?"

"Why should he make that vow to us," asked Zubran, "unless—we loosed his chains?"

"Exactly," whispered Gigi. "For if he made that vow—I would loose them!"

Hope sprang flaming up in Kenton. Cold doubt followed. Was this all a trap? A trick to torment him? He would take no chance—and yet—freedom!

Gigi again bent over him.

"Trust me, Wolf," he said, low. "Vow for vow. If you accept—look at me."

The dice were offered him. Were they straight or weighted, he would cast them. Kenton opened his eyes, stared straight for an instant into the twinkling beads of jet so close. Then he closed them tight; resumed his slow breathing; his semblance of deepest slumber.

And Gigi rose from him, laughing. He heard the two move away, up the pit's steps.

Freedom again! Could it be true? And when would Gigi—were it true and no trap—when would Gigi loose his chains? Long he lay between fiery hope and chilling doubt. Could it be true?

Freedom! And——

Sharane!

11

Gigi Snaps The Chains

NOT LONG did Kenton have to wait. Hardly had the next faint hum of the sleep horn died than he felt a touch on his shoulder. Longer fingers twitched his ears, raised his eyelids. He looked into the face of Gigi. Kenton pulled out the little silken cylinders that shut off the compelling slumber of the horn.

"So that is how you do it." Gigi examined them with interest. He squatted down beside him.

"Wolf," he said, "I have come to have a talk with you, so that you may know me a little better. I would continue to sit here beside you, but some of those cursed priests may come prowling around. Therefore, in a moment I shall seat myself on Zachel's stool. When I have done so, turn you around facing me, taking that highly deceptive attitude I have so often watched you assume."

He stepped up on the bench. "Zubran is with Klaneth, arguing about the gods. Zubran, although sworn to Nergal, thinks him a rather inferior copy of Ahriman, the Persian god of darkness. He is also convinced that this whole matter of warfare between Nergal and Ishtar for the ship lacks not only originality and ingenuity, but taste— something, indeed, that his own gods and goddesses would not do; or if they did, would do much better. This angers Klaneth, which greatly rejoices Zubran."

Once more he arose and looked about him.

"However," he went on, "this time he is arguing to keep Klaneth and especially Zachel away while we talk, since Klaneth leans a great deal upon Zachel in these arguments. I have told them that I cannot bear their talk, and that I will watch on Zachel's seat until it is finished. And it will not be finished until I return, for Zubran is clever, oh, very clever and he expects our talk to lead, ultimately, to permanent relief of his boredom."

He glanced slyly at the ivory deck.

"So do not fear, Wolf." He swayed upon his dwarfed legs. "Only as I go, slip sideways and keep your eyes on me. I will give you warning if warning is needed."

He waddled away, climbed into the overseer's seat. Kenton, obeying him, turned sleepily; rested arm on bench and head on arm.

"Wolf," said Gigi suddenly, "is there a shrub called the chilquor in the place from whence you came?"

Kenton stared at him, struck dumb by such a question. Yet Gigi must have some reason for asking it. Had he ever heard of such a shrub? He searched his memory.

"Its leaves are about so large." Gigi parted finger-tips for inches three. "It grows only upon the edge of the desert and it is rare—sorrowfully rare. Look you—perhaps you know it by another name. Perhaps this will enlighten you. You bruise the buds just before they open. Then you mix them with sesamum oil and honey and a little burned ivory and spread it like a paste over your head. Then you rub and rub and rub—so and so and so—" he illustrated vigorously upon his bald and shining pate.

"And after a little," he said, "the hair begins to sprout; like grain under the rains of spring it grows, until soon —lo—naked dome is covered. Instead of the light flying off affrighted from shining dome it plays within new hair. And once more the man who was bald is beautiful in the eyes of woman!

"By Nadak of the Goats; By Tanith, the dispenser of delights!" cried Gigi with enthusiasm. "That paste grows hair! How it does grow hair! Upon a melon would it grow it. Yes, even those planks rightly rubbed by it would sprout hair like grass. You are sure you do not know it?"

Struggling with his amazement Kenton shook his head.

"Well," said Gigi, sorrowfully. "All this the chilquor buds can do. And so I search for them—" here he sighed mightily—"who would once more be beautiful in woman's eyes."

He sighed again. Then one by one he flecked the backs of the sleeping slaves with Zachel's whip—even the back of Sigurd.

"Yes," he murmured, "yes, they sleep."

His black eyes twinkled on Kenton, the slit mouth grinned.

"You wonder," he said, "why I talk of such trivial matters as shrubs and hair and bald pates, while you lie chained. Well, Wolf, these matters are far from trivial. They brought me here. And were I not here—would you have hope of freedom, think you? Ah, no," said Gigi. "Life is a serious matter. Therefore all parts of it must be serious. And therefore no part of it can be trivial. Let us rest for a moment, Wolf, while you absorb that great truth."

Again, one by one, he flecked the backs of the sleeping slaves.

"Well, Wolf," he went on, "now I shall tell you how I came aboard this ship because of the chilquor, its effect on hair and because of my bald pate. And you shall see how your fortune rests upon them. Wolf, when I was but a child in Nineveh, girls found me singularly attractive.

" 'Gigi!' they would cry as I passed by them. 'Gigi, little love, little darling! Kiss me, Gigi!' "

Gigi's voice was ludicrously languishing; Kenton laughed.

"You laugh, Wolf!" observed the drummer. "Well—that makes us understand each other better."

His eyes twinkled impishly.

"Yes," he said, " 'Kiss me,' they cried. And I would kiss them, because I found them all as singularly attractive as each found me. And as I grew, this mutual attraction increased. You have no doubt noticed," said Gigi complacently, "that I am an unusual figure of a man. But as I passed from adolescence my greatest beauty was, perhaps, my hair. It was long and black and ringleted, and it fell far over my shoulders. I perfumed it and cared for it, and the tender little vessels of joy who loved me would twine their fingers in it when I lifted them upon my head or when my head was on their knees. They joyed in it even as I.

"And then I had a fever. When I recovered, all my beautiful hair was gone!"

He paused to sigh again.

"There was a woman of Nineveh who pitied me. She it was who anointed my head with the chilquor paste; told me how to make it; showed me the growing shrub. After years of—ah, mutual attraction—I had fever again. And again my hair vanished. I was in Tyre then, Wolf, and made what haste I could to return to Nineveh. When I did return, the kindly woman was dead and a sand storm had covered the spot where she had pointed out to me the chilquor shrubs!"

He sighed, prodigiously. Kenton, amused and fascinated by his tale as he was, could not forbear a suspicious glance after that melancholy exhalation. It seemed overdone.

"Then before I could search further," went on Gigi, hurriedly, "word came to me that one who loved me—a princess,—was on her way to Nineveh to see me. Shame was mine and anguish! I could not meet her with a bald pate. For no one loves a bald man!"

"Nobody loves a fat man," grinned Kenton. He had spoken, it seemed, in his own tongue for the drummer apparently had not understood.

"What did you say?" he asked.

"I said," answered Kenton, gravely, "that for one whose excellencies are as great as yours, the loss of your hair should have been of no more consequence to a woman than the falling of one feather from a pet bird."

"That is a fine tongue of yours," remarked Gigi, stolidly. "That it can say so much in so few sounds."

"Well," he continued. "I was distressed indeed. I could have hidden—but I feared my will would not be strong enough to keep me hid. She was a very lovely princess, Wolf. Besides, I knew that if she found that I was in Nineveh, as find out she surely would, she would rout me out. She was a fair woman. And this is the one difference between the fair women and the dark—that the latter wait for you to come for them, but the former search for you. And I could go to no other city to hide —for in each of them were other women who admired me. What was I to do?"

"Why didn't you get a wig?" asked Kenton, so interested now in Gigi's tale that his chains were forgotten.

"I told you, Wolf, that they loved to thread their fingers through my locks," answered Gigi, severely. "Could any wig stay in place under such treatment? Not when the women were such as loved me—No! No! I will tell you what I did. And here is where you will see how my lost hair and you are entangled. The High Priest of

68

Nergal in Nineveh was a friend of mine. I went to him and asked him first to work a magic that would plant my head afresh with hair. He was indignant—said that his art was not to be debased for such a common purpose.

"It was then, Wolf, that I began to have my suspicions of the real power of these sorcerers. I had seen this priest perform great magic. He had raised phantoms that had raised my hair—when I had it. How much easier then ought it to have been for him to have raised my hair without the trouble of raising the phantoms too? I suggested this. He grew more indignant—said that he dealt with gods, not barbers!

"But now I know better. He could not do it! I made the best of the matter, however, and asked him to put me for a while where my princess could not find me and where, weak willed as I am, I could not go to her. He smiled, and said he knew just the place. He inducted me as an acolyte to Nergal and gave me a token that he said would insure me recognition and good will from one he named Klaneth. Also he sealed me with certain vows, not to be broken. I took them cheerfully, thinking them but temporary, and his friend Klaneth the high priest of some hidden temple where I would be safe. I went to sleep that night trustfully, happy as a child. I awakened, Wolf—here!

"It was a sorry jest," muttered Gigi, angrily. "And a sorry jest would it be for that Ninevite priest if I knew the way back to him!

"But here I have been ever since," he added, briskly. "Barred by my acolytage to Nergal from crossing to that other deck where there is a little vessel of joy named Satalu whom I would fain take within my hands. Barred by other vows from leaving the ship wherever it may touch for food and gear—since it was sanctuary I asked from which I could not go nor my princess come to me."

"By Tiamat of the Abyss—I got the sanctuary I asked!" he exclaimed, ruefully enough. "And by Bel who conquered Tiamat—I am as weary of the ship as Zubran himself!

"Yet were I not here," he added, as by afterthought, "who would loose you of your chains? A shrub and lack of hair, an amorous princess and my vanity—these brought me on the ship to set you free when you came. Of such threads do the gods weave our destinies."

He leaned forward, all malice gone from twinkling eyes, a grotesque tenderness on the froglike mouth.

"I like you, Wolf," he said, simply.

"I like you, Gigi," all Kenton's defenses were down. "Greatly, indeed, do I like you. And trust fully. But— Zubran——"

"Have no doubts about Zubran," snapped Gigi. "He, too, was tricked upon this ship and is even more eager than I to be free. Some day he shall tell you his story, as I have mine. Ho! Ho!" laughed the drummer. "Ever seeking the new, ever tiring of the known is Zubran. And this is his fate—to be shot into a whole new world and find it worse than his old. Nay, Wolf, fear not Zubran. With shield and sword will he stand beside you—until he tires even of you. But even then will he be loyal."

He grew solemn, kept unwinking gaze on Kenton, searching, it seemed, his soul.

"Consider well, Wolf," he whispered. "The odds are all against you. We two may not help you as long as Klaneth is lord of his deck. It may be that you cannot free the long-haired one beside you, You have Klaneth to face and twenty of his men—and, it may be, Nergal! And if you lose—death for you—and after long, long torture. Here, chained to your oar, you are at least alive. Consider well!"

Kenton held out to him his prisoned wrists.

"When will you loose my chains, Gigi?" was all he said.

Gigi's face lighted, his black eyes blazed, he sprang upright, the golden loops in his pointed ears dancing.

"Now!" he said. "By Sin, the Father of Gods! By Shamash his Son and by Bel the Smiter—now!"

He thrust his hands between Kenton's waist and the great circlet of bronze that bound it; pulled it apart as though it had been made of putty; he broke the locks of the manacles on Kenton's wrists.

"Run free, Wolf!" he whispered. "Run free!"

With never a look behind him, he waddled to the pit's steps and up them. Slowly Kenton stood upon his feet. His chains dropped from him. He looked down at the sleeping Viking. How could he unfasten his links? How, if he could unfasten, awaken him before Zachel came hurrying down among the slaves?

Again he looked about him. At the foot of the overseer's high stool lay a shining knife, long-bladed, thin-bladed, dropped there by Gigi—for him? He did not know. But he did know that with it he might pick the Viking's locks. He took a step toward it——

How long he was in taking the second step.

And there was a mist before his eyes.

Through that mist the sleeping forms of the oarsmen wavered—were like phantoms. And now he could no longer see the knife.

He rubbed his eyes, looked down on Sigurd. He was a wraith!

He looked at the sides of the ship. They melted away even as he sought them. He had a glimpse of sparkling turquoise sea. And then—it became vaporous. Was not! Cease to be!

And now Kenton floated for an instant in thick mist shot through with silvery light. The light snapped out. He hurtled through a black void filled with tumult of vast winds.

The blackness snapped out! Through his closed lids he saw light. And he was no longer falling. He stood, rocking, upon his feet. He opened his eyes——

Once more he was within his own room!

Outside hummed the traffic of the Avenue, punctuated by blasts of auto horns.

Kenton rushed over to the jeweled ship. Except for the slaves, on it was but one little figure—one toy. A manikin who stood half way down the pit steps, mouth open, whip at feet, stark astonishment in every rigid line.

Zachel, the overseer!

He looked down into the galley pit. The slaves lay asleep, oars at rest——

And suddenly he caught sight of himself in the long mirror! Stood, wondering, before it!

For what he saw was never the Kenton who had been borne out of that room upon the breast of the inrushing mystic sea. His mouth had hardened, eyes grown fearless, falcon bright. Over all his broadened chest the muscles ran, not bulging, bound—but graceful, flexible, and steel hard. He flexed his arms, and the muscles ran rippling along them. He turned, scanned his back in the mirror.

Scars covered it, healed teeth marks of the lash. The lash of Zachel——

Zachel—the toy?

71

No toy had made those scars!

No oars of toy had brought into being those muscles!

And suddenly all Kenton's mind awoke. Awoke and was filled with shame, with burning longing, despair.

What would Sigurd think of him when he awakened and found him gone—Sigurd with whom he had sworn blood brotherhip? What would Gigi think—Gigi, who had made vow for vow with him; and trusting him, had broken his chains?

A frenzy shook him. He must get back! Get back before Sigurd or Gigi knew that he was no longer on the ship.

How long had he been away? As though in answer a clock began chiming. He counted. Eight strokes!

Two hours of his own time had passed while he had been on the ship. Two hours only? And in those two hours all these things had happened? His body changed to—this?

But in those two minutes he had been back in his room what had happened on the ship?

He must get back! He must. . . .

He thought of the fight before him. Could he take his automatics with him when he went back—if he could go back? With them he could match any sorceries of the black priest. But they were in another room, in another part of his house. Again he looked at himself in the glass. If his servants saw him—thus! They would not know him. How could he explain? Who would believe him?

And they might tear him away—away from this room where the ship lay. This room that held his only doorway back into Sharane's world!

He dared not risk going from that room.

Kenton threw himself upon the floor; grasped the golden chains that hung from the ship's bow—so thin they were, so small on this the ship of jeweled toys!

He threw his will upon the ship! Summoning it! Commanding it!

The golden chains stirred within his grasp. They swelled. He felt a tearing wrench. Thicker grew the chains. They were lifting him. Again the dreadful wrenching, tearing at every muscle, nerve and bone.

His feet swung free.

The vast winds howled around him—for a heartbeat

only. They were gone. In their place was the rushing of wind driven waves. He felt the kisses of their spray.

Beneath him was a racing azure sea. High above him curved the prow of the Ship of Ishtar. But not the ship of jeweled toys. No! The ensorcelled ship of which the toy ship was the symbol; the real ship on which blows were actual and death lurked—death that even now might be watching him, poised to strike!

The chain he clutched passed up the side of the bow and into the hawser port painted like a great eye between the bowward wall of the cabin and the curved prow. Behind him the great oars rose and fell. He could not be seen from them; the oarsmen's backs were toward him and the oar ports were covered with strong leather, through which the shanks slipped; shields to protect the rowers from waves dashing past those ports. Nor, under the hang of the hull as he was, could he be seen from the black deck.

Slowly, silently, hand over hand, pressing his body as close to the hull as he could, he began to creep up the chain. Up to Sharane's cabin. Up to that little window that opened into her cabin from the closed bit of deck beneath the great scimitar.

Slowly, more slowly, he crept; pausing every few links to listen; he reached at last the hawser port; he threw a leg over the bulwark, and dropped upon the little deck. He rolled beneath the window; flattened himself against the cabin wall; hidden now from every eye upon the ship; hidden even from Sharane, should she peer through that window.

Crouched there—waiting.

12

Master Of The Ship:

KENTON raised his head, cautiously. The chains passed through a hawser port, wound around a crude windlass and were fastened to a thin, double hook that was more like a grappling iron than anchor. Evidently, although control of steering gear, mast and rowers' pit was in the hands of the black priest, the women of Sharane looked after anchorage. He noted, with some anxiety, a door leading out of the cabin's farther side—the portion that housed her warrior maids. But it was not likely, he thought, that any would come out as long as the ship was under sail and oar. At any rate he would have to take that risk.

Through the opened window above him he could hear the hum of voices. Then that of Sharane came to him scornful.

"He broke his chains, even as he had promised—and then fled!"

"But mistress," it was Satalu. "Where could he go? He did not come here. How do we know that Klaneth did not take him?"

"No mistaking Klaneth's wrath," answered Sharane. "No mistaking the scourging he gave Zachel. Both were real. Satalu."

So the black priest had scourged Zachel had he, well, that, at any rate, was good news.

"Nay, Satalu," said Sharane, "why argue? He had grown strong. He broke his chains. He fled. And so proved himself the coward I called him—and never believed he was—till now!"

There was silence in the cabin. Then Sharane spoke again.

"I am weary, Luarda—watch outside the door. You others to your cabin to sleep—or what you will. Satalu, brush my hair a little and then leave me."

Another silence; a longer one. Then Satalu's voice:

"Mistress, you are half asleep. I go."

Kenton waited—but not long. The sill of the window was about as high above the anchor deck as his chin. He raised himself gently; peered within. His gaze rested first on the shrine of the luminous gems, the pearls and pale moonstones, the milky curdled crystals. He had the feeling that it was empty, tenantless. There were no flames in the seven little crystal basins.

He looked down. The head of the wide divan of ivory with its golden arabesques was almost beneath him. Upon it lay Sharane, face down upon its cushions, clothed only in one thin silken veil and the floods of her red gold hair, and weeping; weeping like any woman with bruised heart.

Weeping for—him?

A gleam of sapphire, a glint of steel caught his eyes. It was his sword—the sword of Nabu. The sword he had vowed he would not take from her hands—would take, unaided, with his own. It hung upon a low rack on the wall just above her head; so close that she need but reach up a hand to grasp it.

He drew back, waited impatiently for her weeping to cease. Love for her—or lust—he had in full. But search his heart now as he might—no pity.

And soon her sobbing lessened; died away. And after another while of waiting he slowly thrust his head again through the window. She lay asleep, face turned toward the cabin door, tears still on the long lashes—breast rising and falling softly in the measured respiration of slumber.

Kenton gripped the sill, drew himself softly up until shoulders and breast were within. Then he bent over until his waist rested on the ledge. Now his hands touched the softnesses of one of the rugs upon the floor. He slid down, gripping the sill with his insteps. Slowly, like a tumbler, he brought his legs down; lay prone, full length, at the head of Sharane's bed.

Again he waited. Her measured breathing did not change. He drew himself up on his feet. He slipped to the door that lay between this cabin and that of the warrior maids. There was a low murmuring of voices there. He saw a bar that, lowered, slipped into a metal clutch on the other side, securing it. Noiselessly he dropped it, fastened it. Those cats were caged, he thought, grinning.

He glanced over the cabin. Upon a low stool lay a small piece of silk; over a settle a long one, scarf-like. He picked up the small piece and rolled it deftly into a serviceable gag. He took the long piece and tested it. It was heavy and strong, just what he needed, he reflected —but not enough. He slipped to a wall, unhooked a similar hanging.

He tiptoed over to Sharane's bed. She stirred, uneasily, as though she felt his eyes on her; as though she were awakening.

Before she could raise her lids Kenton had opened her mouth and thrust the silken gag within. Then throwing himself over her, holding her down by sheer weight, he jerked up her head, wound the scarf tightly around her mouth, tied it. As swiftly he raised her from the hips and wound the balance of the scarf around her arms, pinioning them to her sides.

Eyes blazing with wrathful recognition, she tried to roll from beneath him, struck up at him with her knees. He shifted his weight, lay across her thighs, bound knees and ankles with the second scarf that he had torn from the wall.

Now she lay motionless, glaring at him. He sent her a kiss, mockingly. She tried to throw herself upon the floor. Noiselessly still, he took other hangings, wrapped her round and round with them. And finally he passed a pair of heavy cords under and over the bed; bound her fast with them to the divan.

Heedless of her now, he walked to the outer door. In some way he must get the handmaiden she called Luarda within the cabin, make her as helpless as her mistress—and as silent. He opened the door the merest slit, peered through it. Luarda sat close beside it, back turned to him, gaze upon the black deck.

He stole away, found another small piece of silk; snatched from the wall another hanging. The small piece he fashioned into another gag. Then he opened the door as before, placed his lips to the crack, pitched his voice high and softly; as femininely as he could, called to her:

"Luarda! The mistress wants you! Quick!"

She leaped to her feet. He shrank back, pressing himself against the wall close beside the door frame. Unsuspiciously, she opened the door; stepped within it, and paused for an instant, open-mouthed, at the sight of Sharane, bound and helpless.

That instant was all Kenton needed. One arm was around her neck, throttling her. With his free hand he thrust the gag into her mouth; in the same moment closed the door with his foot. The girl in his arms wriggled like a snake. He managed to keep her mouth closed until he had wound the hanging around jaws and throat. Her hands swept up, clawing him; she strove to wind her legs around his. He drew the silk tighter around her neck, strangling her. When her struggles grew feeble, he bound her arms to her side. He laid her on the floor, and pinioned, as he had Sharane's, her ankles and knees.

Helpless as her mistress now she lay. He picked her up; carried her over to the divan; rolled her under it.

Not till then did he reach up and take down his sword. He stood before Sharane.

There was no fear in the burning eyes that stared up at him. Rage enough and to spare was there—but no fear.

And Kenton laughed low, bent over her, and pressed his lips to her own gagged and bound ones. He kissed each wrathful eye.

"And now, Sharane," he laughed. "I go to take the ship—without your help! And when I have taken it, I'll come back and take—you!"

He walked to the door, opened it softly, swept gaze over the ship.

Upon the black deck squatted Gigi, forehead resting on the edge of the serpent drum, long arms trailing disconsolately down its sides. There was a forlornness about the drummer that made Kenton want to cry out to him. It was an impulse to which the sight of Zachel's head put speedy check. He could see just the top of it over the low rail between Sharane's deck and the rowers' pit.

He crouched low, until the head was out of sight—knowing that in that position Zachel could not see him. He knotted the sword in his girdle. On hands and knees he crept out of the cabin door. He saw that there was a window in the place where Sharane's women slept. But there was no outward door. They must pass through her cabin to gain the deck. If they suspected something amiss with their mistress, found the door barred, undoubtedly they would come through that window. Well—he would have to take his chances on that; only hope that he could get most of the work ahead of him done before they were aroused.

And if he could surprise Klaneth in his den, strike swiftly and silently—then he and the Viking could make short work of the rest, and the women could do what they pleased. They could neither help nor hinder. It would be too late.

He flattened himself to the deck; wriggled beneath the window; listened. There was no sound of voices now. Slowly raising himself he saw that from this point the overseer was hidden from him by the mast. Keeping a cautious eye on the disconsolate Gigi, he stood up and peered within the second cabin. There were eight girls there asleep; some pillowed on each other's breasts, some curled up on the silken cushions. He reached in, closed the window noiselessly.

Again he lay flat and squirmed along the side of the cabin to the starboard rail. He slipped over it. He hung for a moment, fingers gripping the top, feet feeling for the chain that stretched below. He swung along it. When he came to its end, he raised himself, caught the rail again and swung along that, swiftly hand over hand.

Now the mast was directly in front of him; he had reached the spot from which he planned to strike his first blow. He chinned himself, and streamed over the rail like a snake; lay flat against the bulwarks until breath came once more easily.

He was in plain sight of Gigi—and as he lay there Gigi's head came up with a jerk from his drum, his eyes stared straight into Kenton's own. The ugly face broke into a thousand wrinkles of amazement; then instantly became indifferent, immobile. He yawned, got upon his feet; then, hand over eyes, peered intently over the port side as though he had sighted something far away upon the sea.

"By Nergal, but Klaneth must know of this!" he said. He waddled over to the black cabin.

Kenton wriggled to the edge of the pit. He had glimpse of Zachel standing upon his platform stool, peering, searching for whatever it was that seemingly had so aroused the drummer's interest.

Kenton dropped into the pit. One leap he took and was beside the mast. The overseer turned sharply. He opened mouth to yell and swept hand down to belt where his poniard was sheltered.

The sword of Kenton hissed through air and through his neck.

The sheared head of Zachel leaped from his shoulders, mouth stretched open, eyes glaring. For three heartbeats the body of Zachel stood upright, blood spouting from the severed arteries, hand still gripping at the dagger.

The body of Zachel squattered.

The sleep horn fell from his girdle. Kenton snatched at it. The knees of Zachel's body crumpled down on it; crushed it.

From the benches of the oarsmen came no sound, no outcry; they sat, mouths agape, blades idle.

He groped in Zachel's belt for the overseer's keys, the keys that would free Sigurd. He found them, snatched them loose, tore the dagger from Zachel's stiffening fingers and raced down the narrow passage way to the Viking.

"Brother! I thought you gone! Sigurd forgotten . . ." the Norseman babbled. "By Odin what a blow! The dog's head leaped from his shoulders as though Thor had smitten him with his hammer. . . ."

"Quiet, Sigurd! Quiet!" Kenton was working with desperate haste among the keys, trying to find that which would fit the Viking's fetters. "We must fight for the ship . . . stand together, you and I. . . . Hell, damn these keys . . . which is the right one! If we can reach Klaneth's den before alarm is raised stand you between me and his priests. Leave Klaneth to me. Touch not Gigi nor Zubran the red beard. They cannot help us but they have given vow not to fight against us . . . remember, Sigurd . . . ah. . . ."

The manacles at Sigurd's wrists clicked and opened; the lock on the metal belt flew open. Sigurd shook his hands free of the chains, reached down and wrenched the cincture from his waist. He stood upright, flaxen mane streaming in the wind.

"Free!" he howled. "Free!"

"Close your jaws!" Kenton thrust his hands against the shouting mouth. "Do you want the pack down on us before we have chance to move!"

He pressed Zachel's dagger into the Viking's hand.

"Use that," he said, "until you have won a better weapon."

"That! Ho-ho!" laughed Sigurd. "A woman's toy! Nay, Kenton—Sigurd can do better than that!"

He dropped the dagger. He gripped the great oar; lifted it out of the thole pins. He bent forward sharply, bringing its shaft against the side of the port. there was a sharp crackling, a rending of wood. He drew back, bringing the oar against the opposite side of the port. There was another crackling, and Sigurd drew the oar in, broken squarely in the middle, a gigantic club all of ten feet long. He gripped it by the splintered end, whirled it round his head, the chains and the dangling manacles spinning like battle mace.

"Come!" barked Kenton, and stooped to pick up the dagger.

Now from all the pit came clamor; the slaves straining at their bonds and crying to be freed.

And from Sharane's deck came the shrilling of women. Out of the window poured her warrior maids.

No chance now to surprise the black priest. No chance but in battle—fang and claw. His sword and the club of Sigurd against Klaneth and his pack.

"Quick, Sigurd!" he shouted. "To the deck!"

"I first," grunted Sigurd. "Shield to you!"

He pushed Kenton aside, rushed past him. Before he could reach the foot of the stairway its top was filled with priests, white-faced, snarling, swords in their hands, and short stabbing spears.

Kenton's foot fell on something that rolled away from beneath it, sending him to his knees. He looked down into the grinning face of Zachel. His severed head it was that had tripped him. He lifted it by the hair, swung it round and hurled it straight at the face of the foremost priest at the stairway top. It caught the priest a glancing blow, fell among the others; rolled and bounced away.

They shrank back from it. Before they could muster again the Viking was up the steps and charging them, oar club flinging like a flail. And at his heels came Kenton, making for the black cabin's door.

There were eight of the black robes facing them. The Norseman's oar struck, shattering the skull of one like an egg shell. Before he could raise it again two of the priests had darted in upon him, stabbing, thrusting with their spears. Kenton's sword swept down, bit deep into the bone of an arm whose point was touching Sigurd's breast. With quick upward thrust he ripped that priest from navel to chin. The Viking dropped one hand from the oar, caught the half of the second spear, twisted it out of the black robe's grip and ran it through his heart. Down went another under bite of Kenton's blade.

Other priests came streaming from every passageway and corner of the black deck, armed with swords and spears and bearing shields. Out they streamed, screaming.

And out of the black cabin rushed Klaneth, roaring, a great sword in hand. Behind him were Gigi and the Persian. The black priest came straight on, charging like a bull through the half ring of his servitors. But Gigi and the Persian slipped over to the serpent drum, stood there watching.

For an instant the black priest stood towering over Kenton. Then he struck downward, a lightning blow designed to cleave Kenton from shoulder to hip.

But Kenton was not there when the blow fell. Swifter than the sword of Klaneth he had leaped aside, thrust out his own blade——

Felt it bite deep into the black priest's side!

The black priest howled and fell back. Instantly his acolytes streamed in between him and the besieged pair. They circled them.

"Back to back," shouted the Viking. Kenton heard the great club hum, saw three of the black robes mowed down by it as by giant flail. With sweep and thrust he cleared away the priests ravening at him.

Now the fighting had carried them close to the drum. He saw the Persian, scimitar unsheathed and held by rigid arm. And he was cursing, sobbing, quivering like a hound held in leash and held back from his quarry. Gigi, froth upon the corners of wide open mouth, face contorted, stood with long arms outstretched, hands trembling, shaking with that same eagerness.

Desire, Kenton knew, to join with him and Sigurd in that battle; both held back by vows not to be broken.

Gigi pointed downward. Kenton followed the gesture, saw a priest crawling, sword in hand, and almost within reach of the Viking's feet. One sweep of the sword against Sigurd's legs and he was done for; hamstrung. Forgetting his own defense, Kenton leaned forward, cut downward. The head of the creeping priest jumped from his shoulders, rolled away.

But as he straightened he saw Klaneth again above him, poised to strike!

"The end!" thought Kenton. He dropped flat, rolled away from the falling edge.

He had not counted on the Viking. Sigurd had seen that swift by-play. He swept his oar, held horizontally, in a gigantic punch. It crashed into Klaneth's chest.

The sword stroke fell short, the black priest was hurled backward, half falling for all his strength and massive bulk.

"Gigi! Zubran! To me!" he howled.

Before Kenton could rise, two priests were on him, clawing him, stabbing at him. He released his grip on his sword; drew the poniard of Zachel. He thrust upward; felt a body upon him stiffen, then collapse like a pricked balloon, felt too, the edge of a sword slice into his shoulder. He struck again, blindly; was drenched with sudden flood of blood. He heard a bubbling whispering and the second weight was gone.

He gripped his sword, staggered upright. Of all Klaneth's pack not more than half a dozen were on their feet. They had drawn back, out of reach of the Viking's club. Sigurd stood, drawing in great breaths. And the black priest was gasping too, holding his broad chest where the oar of Sigurd had struck. At his feet was a little pool of blood, dripping from where the sword of Nabu had pierced him.

"Gigi! Zubran!" he panted. "Take these dogs!"

The drummer leered at him.

"Nay, Klaneth," he answered. "There was no vow to aid you."

He bent over the tall drum, with heave of broad shoulders he hurled it over the side.

From the priests arose a groan. Klaneth stood, silent, struck dumb.

There came from the waves touching the ship a sound —sonorous and sinister.

A thunderous drumming, menacing, malignant—summoning!

Br-oom-rr-oom-oom!

The serpent drum swinging against the side of the ship! Lifted by the waves and by their arms beaten against the ship!

The Summoner of Nergal!

The ship trembled. A shadow fell upon the sea. Around Klaneth a darkness began to gather.

More angrily thundered the wave-beaten drum. The mists about the black priest thickened, writhed; beginning that hellish transmutation of Nergal's priest into the dread self of the Lord of the Dead.

"Strike!" howled Gigi. "Quick! Bite deep!"

He ran to the rail; dropped over it.

Kenton rushed straight upon that cloudy horror within which the black priest moved. His sword swept into it; struck. He heard a shriek, agonized, unbelieving. The voice of Klaneth. He struck again.

And striking realized that the drumming had ceased, that the voice of the drum was stilled. He heard Gigi's shout:

"Bite again, Wolf! Bite deep!"

The dark mist around Klaneth cleared. He stood there, dead eyes closed, hand holding an arm from which dark blood welled through clasping fingers.

And as Kenton raised his sword to strike again the black priest dashed into his eyes the blood from the hand that had held the wounded arm. Blinded, Kenton held his sword at mid-stroke. The black priest rushed upon him. Mechanically, through dimmed sight, he thrust out his blade to meet that rush; saw Sigurd driving down upon the remaining priests; heard the crack of bone as red stained oar met their bodies.

His sword struck against Klaneth's, and was beaten down.

Kenton's foot slipped on a gout of blood. He fell. The black priest crashed on him; his arms encircled him. Over and over they rolled. He saw Sigurd, whimpering with eagerness, striving to strike . . .

Suddenly Klaneth rolled over, Kenton on top of him; his grip relaxed; he grew limp; lay inert.

Kenton knelt upon him; looked up at the Norseman.

"Not yours," he gasped. "Mine!"

He sought for the dagger at his belt. The body of the black priest stiffened. Then, like a released spring, he leaped upon his feet, throwing Kenton away.

Before the Viking could raise his club Klaneth was at the rail.

He hurled himself over it into the sea!

A hundred feet away, the serpent drum floated, its top slit across by Gigi's knife. The head of Klaneth arose beside it, his hands gripped it. Under the touch the huge cylinder dipped to him with grotesque genuflection. From it came a dismal sound, like a lament.

Out of the silver haze a shadow moved. It darkened over black priest and drum. It shrouded them and withdrew. Where it had been was neither black priest nor Summoner! Man and drum—both had gone!

13

Master Of—Sharane!

BATTLE fury still in his veins, Kenton looked about him. The black deck was strewn with Klaneth's men; men crushed and broken under Sigurd's mace; men from whom his own sword had let out the life; men in twisted heaps; men—but not many—who still writhed and groaned.

He turned to Sharane's deck. Her women, white-faced, clustered at the cabin door.

And on the very verge of the barrier between the two decks stood Sharane. Proudly she faced him, but with misty eyes on whose long lashes tears still trembled. Diadem of shining crescent was gone; gone too that aura of the goddess which even when Ishtar was afar lingered like a splendor around this, her living shrine.

She was but a woman. Nay—only a girl! A girl all human, exquisite——

He was lifted high on the shoulders of Gigi and the Persian.

"Hail!" cried Gigi. "Hail! Master of the ship!"

"Master of the ship!" shouted the Persian.

Master of the ship!

"Put me down," he ordered. And when they had set him on his feet he strode from Klaneth's deck to Sharane's. He stood over her.

"Master of the ship!" he laughed. "And master of—you! Sharane!"

He gripped her slender wrists, drew her to him.

There was a cry from Gigi, a groan echoed by the Persian. Sharane's face paled. . . .

Out of the black cabin strode Sigurd, and in his arms was that dark statue of cloudy evil that had stood in Klaneth's shrine.

"Stop!" cried Gigi, and sprang. Before the Ninevite could reach him Sigurd had lifted the idol and cast it over into the waves.

"The last devil gone!" he shouted.

The ship trembled—trembled as though far beneath its keel a hand had risen and was shaking it.

It stopped. Around it the waters darkened.

Deep, deep down in those darkened waters began to glow a scarlet cloud. Deep, deep beneath them the cloud moved and widened as widens the thunderhead. It vortexed into a crimson storm cloud blotted with blacknesses. It floated up; ever growing, its scarlets deepening ever more angrily, its blacks shading ever more menacingly.

The lifting cloud swirled; from it shot out strangely ordered rays, horizontal, fan-shaped. From those slant-planed luminescences now whirling like a tremendous wheel in the abyss, immense bubbles, black and crimson, began to break. They arose, growing swiftly in girth as they neared the surface.

Within them Kenton glimpsed figures, misty figures; bodies of crouching men clad in armor that glimmered jet and scarlet.

Men within the bubbles!

Armored men! Men who crouched with heads on knees, clothed all in glittering scales. Warriors in whose hands were misty swords, misty bows, misty javelins.

Up rushed the bubble hosts, myriad after myriad. Now they were close to sea surface. Now they broke through.

The bubbles burst!

Out of their shattered sides the warriors sprang. All in their checkered mail, pallid-faced, pupilless eyes half closed and dead, they leaped out upon the darkened blue of the sea. From crest to crest of waves they vaulted. They ran over the waters as though over a field of withered violets. Silently they poured down upon the ship!

"Men of Nergal!" wailed Sharane. "Warriors of the Black One! Ishtar! Ishtar—help us!"

"Phantoms!" cried Kenton, and held high his blood stained sword. "Phantoms!"

And he knew in his soul that whatever they were—phantoms they were not!

The front rank poised themselves upon the tip of a curling wave as though upon a long land barrow. They thrust down bows no longer misty. To their cheeks they drew the tips of long arrows. Came a twang of strings, a pattering as of hail against the sides of the ship. A dozen shafts quivered along the side of the mast; one fell at his feet—serpent scaled, black and crimson, its head buried deep within the deck.

"Ishtar! Mother Ishtar! Deliver us from Nergal!" wailed Sharane.

As though in answer the ship leaped as if another hand had thrown it forward.

From the hosts still breaking through the bubbles arose a shouting. They raced after the flying ship. Another rain of arrows fell upon it.

"Ishtar! Mother Ishtar!" sobbed Sharane.

The hovering darkness split. For an instant out of it peered an immense orb circled with garlands of little moons. From it poured silver fire; living, throbbing, jubilant. The pulsing flood struck the sea nad melted through it. The shadows closed; the orb was gone.

The moon flames it had poured dropped down and down. Up to meet them sparkled other great bubbles all rosy, pearl and silver, shimmering with glints and glimmerings of tenderest nacre, gleamings of mother-of-pearl, cream of roses.

In each of them Kenton sensed a form, a body—wondrous, delicate and delicious; a woman's body from whose beauty the shining sides of the bubbles drew their glory!

Women within the bubbles!

Up rushed the spheres of glamour; they touched the surface of the wan sea. They opened.

Out of them flowed hosts of women. Naked, save for tresses black as midnight, silvery as the moon, golden as the wheat and poppy red, they stepped from the shimmering pyxes that had borne them upward.

They lifted white arms and brown arms, arms shell pink and arms pale amber, beckoning to the rushing, sea-born men-at-arms.

Their eyes gleamed like little lakes of jewels—sapphires blue, black and pale sapphires, velvet jet, sun stone yellow, witched amber; eyes gray as sword blades beneath winter moons.

Round hipped and slender hipped, high breasted and virginal, they swayed upon their wave crests, beckoning, calling to Nergal's warriors.

At their calling—dove sweet, gull plaintive, hawk eager, sweet and poignant—the scaled hosts wavered; halted. The bows that had been drawn dropped; swords splashed; javelins twirled through the deeps. Within their dead eyes a flame sprang.

The warriors shouted. They leaped forward . . . to the women. . . .

Wave crests on which mailed men raced met crests on which the wondrous women poised. Into the mailed arms the women were swept. For a breath, tresses brown and black, silver as the moon and golden as the wheat, swirled round mail ebon and scarlet.

Then warriors and women melted into the form behind the racing ship; became one with the jeweled and sparkling wake of it; a wake that rolled and sighed as though it were the soul of amorous seas.

"Ishtar! Mother Beloved!" prayed the Lady Sharane. "To Ishtar—homage!"

"To Ishtar—homage!" echoed Kenton, and bent his knee. Rising, he caught her to him.

"Sharane!" he breathed. Her soft arms wreathed his neck.

"My lord—I pray you forgiveness," she sighed. "I pray you forgiveness! Yet how could I have known—when first you lay upon the deck and seemed afraid and fled? I loved you! Yet how could I have known how mighty a lord you are?"

Her fragrance shook him; the softness of her against his breath closed his throat.

"Sharane!" he murmured. "Sharane!"

His lips sought hers and clung; mad wine of life raced through his veins; in the sweet fire of her mouth memory of all save this moment was burned away.

"I—give myself—to you!" she sighed.

He remembered. . . .

"You give nothing, Sharane," he answered her. "I—take! He lifted her in his arms; he strode through the rosy cabin's door; shut it with thrust of foot and hurled down its bar.

Sigurd, Trygg's son, came and sat at the threshold of the rosy cabin. He polished the black priest's sword, chanting low some ancient bridal lay.

Upon the black deck Gigi and Zubran moved, casting the bodies of the slain into the sea; ending the pain of those not yet dead; casting them then after the others.

One dove and then another fluttered down from the balcony of the little blossoming trees. The Viking watched them, still chanting. Quick after the first dropped others, twain upon twain. They cooed and bent inquisitive heads; they billed and murmured. They formed a half ring before the cabin's closed door.

The white breasted doves—red beaked, vermilion footed; the murmuring, the wooing, the caressing doves —they set their snowy seal upon the way to Kenton and Sharane.

The doves of Ishtar wedded them!

PART III
The Black Priest Strikes

14

"DEAR lord of mine—Kenton" whispered Sharane. "I think that even you do not know how greatly I love you!"

They sat within the rosy cabin, her head upon his breast.

It was a new Kenton who looked down upon the lovely face upturned to his. All that had been modern had fallen from him. He had gained in height, and brown as his face was the broad chest bared by open tunic. His blue eyes were clear and fearless, filled with a laughing recklessness; touched, too, with half fierce ruthlessness. Above the elbow of his left arm was a wide bracelet of thin gold, graven with symbols Sharane had cut there. Upon his feet were sandals that Sharane had embellished with woven Babylonian charms—to keep his feet upon a path of love that led to her and her alone.

How long had it been since that battle with the black priest, he wondered, as he drew her closer to him. Eternities it seemed—and but yesterday! How long?

He could not know—in that timeless world where eternities and yesterdays were as one.

And whether yester-moment or eternities ago, he had ceased to care!

On and on they had sailed. And ever as they slipped through the azure seas, memory of that other life of his had dwindled and sunk beneath the horizon of consciousness, as the land sinks behind the watcher on an outward bound ship. He thought of it, when at all, with a numbing fear that he might be thrust back into it again—that old life of his.

Away from the ship! Away from Sharane—never to return!

On and on they had sailed. The black cabin, swept clean of evil, housed now the Viking, Gigi and the Persian. Sigurd or Gigi handled the two great oars that, fastened to each side of the stern, steered the ship. Sometimes, in fair weather, maids of Sharane took their place at the rudder bars. The Viking had found an anvil in the hold under the black cabin; had made a forge and on it hammered out swords. One he had made for Gigi, full nine feet long, that the dwarf legged giant handled like a wand. Better, though, Gigi liked the mace that Sigurd had also made for him—long as the sword, with huge bronze ball studded with nails at its end. Zubran clung to his scimitar. But the Viking labored at his forge, beating out lighter brands for Sharane's warrior maids. He made them shields and taught them to use both sword and shield as they had been used on his dragons in the old Viking days.

Part fruit of that instruction, sword play with Sigurd, wrestling with Gigi, fencing with his own blade against the scimtar of Zubran, was Kenton now.

All this Gigi had encouraged.

"No safety while Klaneth lives!" he would croak. "Make the ship strong."

"We have done with Klaneth!" Kenton had said, a little boastfully.

"Not so," Gigi had answered. "He will come with many men. Sooner or later the black priest will come."

There had been recent confirmation of this. Soon after his battle Kenton had taken one of the blacks, a Nubian, and set him in Zachel's seat. But this had made them short one slave at the oars. They had met a ship, hailed it, and demanded an oarsman. Its captain had given them one— fearfully, quickly, and had sped away.

"He did not know that Klaneth was no longer here," chuckled Gigi.

But not long after this they had met another ship. Its captain would not halt when hailed and they had been forced to pursue and to fight. It was a small vessel, easily overhauled and easily captured. And that same captain had told them, sullenly, that Klaneth was at Emakhtila, High Priest of a temple of Nergal there, and one of the council of the House of Nergal in the temple of the Seven Zones. And more, the black priest was high in favor with one he called the Lord of the Two Deaths—the ruler, so they gathered, of Emakhtila.

Klaneth, said the captain, had sent forth word that the Ship of Ishtar was no longer to be feared, that it now held neither Nergal nor Ishtar but only men and women. It was to be sunk when met, but its men and women were to be saved. For them he offered a reward.

"And had my boat been but a little bigger and my men more, I would have claimed that reward," he had ended, bluntly.

They took what they wanted from him and let him go. But as the ship drew away, he shouted to them to take what joy of life they could at once, since Klaneth on a great ship and with many men was searching for them and their shift was apt to be short!

"Ho-ho!" grunted Gigi, and—"Oh-ho! Klaneth searches for us, does he? Well, I warned you he would, Wolf. What now?"

"Make for one of the isles, pick our vantage ground and let him come," answered Kenton. "We can build a fort, raise defenses. Better chance we would have against him than on the ship—if it be true that he pursues us in a great vessel with many soldiers."

They had found Kenton's word good, and they were sailing toward such an isle, Sigurd at the helm, Gigi and the Persian and the women of Sharane on watch, alert.

"Yea—dear lord of me—even you do not know how greatly I love you," whispered Sharane again, eyes worshipping, arms fettering his neck. His lips clung to hers. Even in the sweet fire of their touch he marvelled, blind to his own renaissance, at this changed Sharane—Love's changeling since that time he had carried her within her bower, disdaining her as gift, taking her by right of his two strong arms.

Swift memories shook him; of Sharane—conquered; of some unearthly wonder that had flamed over the shrine and with fingers of pure fire had woven his soul with hers in threads of flaming ecstasies!

"Tell me, lord of me—how much you love me," she murmured, languorously.

There came a shout from Sigurd:

"Waken the slaves! Drop oars! Storm comes!"

Imperceptibly, the cabin had darkened. He heard the shrilling of the overseer's whistle, a shouting and patter of feet. He unclasped Sharane's arms; gave her one kiss that answered her questioning better than words; passed out upon the deck.

Swiftly the sky blackened. There was a splintering flash of the prismatic lightning, a clashing of cymbaled thunder. A wind arose and roared. Down came the sail. Before the blast, held steady by the hands of Sigurd, the ship flew.

Then fell the rain. Through it scudded the ship, hemmed in by blacknesses which when the lightnings fell were threaded by myriads of multi-colored serpents of glass from sky to sea.

A tremendous gust of wind swept down upon the ship, careening her far over. It buffeted at Sharane's door; tore it open. Kenton staggered over to Gigi, shouted to the women to leave their watch, go inside. He watched them stumble in.

"Zubran and I will watch," he cried in Gigi's ear. "Go you and help Sigurd at the helm."

But Gigi had not gone a yard before the wind died as quickly as it had risen.

"To the right!" he heard Sigurd shout. "Look to the right!"

To the starboard rail the three ran. Within the darkness was a broad faint disk of luminescence, like a far away searchlight in a fog. Rapidly its diameter decreased, growing ever brighter as its size diminshed.

The disk burst out of the mists; it became a blazing beam that shot over the rushing waves and glared upon the ship. Kenton glimpsed double banks of oars that drove a huge bulk down upon them with prodigious speed. Beneath the light was a gleaming ram, lance tipped. It jutted out from the prow like the horn on a charging rhinoceros.

"Klaneth!" roared Gigi, and ran shouting to the black cabin, Zubran at his heels.

"Sharane!" shouted Kenton, and raced to her door.

The ship veered abruptly, careening until the sea poured over the port rail. Kenton's feet flew from under

91

him; he rolled head over heels to the bulwarks; struck and lay for an instant stunned.

Sigurd's manoeuvre could not save the ship. The *bireme* had changed course, swept down parallel with it to shear off its starboard bank of oars. The Viking had thought to escape the impact. But the attacking vessel's oarsmen were too many, its speed too great for the ship of Ishtar's single banks of seven. Down dipped the *bireme's* sweeps, checking its rush. It swung broadside on straight against the ship, crushing the starboard oars, like sticks!

Kenton reeled to his feet; saw Gigi leaping down to him, battle mace in hand; beside him Zubran, scimitar gleaming. And close behind them, the useless tiller abandoned, was Sigurd the Viking, shields under arm, his great sword held high.

They were beside him. His giddiness was gone. The Viking thrust him a shield. He drew his own sword.

"To Sharane!" he gasped. Forward they ran.

Before they could reach her door, defend it, a score of soldiers, chain mailed and armed with short swords, had poured down the side of the *bireme* and closed the way to the cabin. And behind them poured other scores.

Out whirled Gigi's giant mace, striking them down. Blue blade of Nabu, scimitar of Zubran, brand of Sigurd rose and fell, struck and thrust. In a breath were dripping red!

Yet not a step could they advance! For every soldier they slew, another took his place. And still the *bireme* rained men.

An arrow whistled, stood quivering in Sigurd's shield. Another flew and hung from Zubran's shoulder.

Came the bellowing of Klaneth:

"No arrows! Take the black-haired dog and yellow-hair alive! Slay the others—if you must—with swords!"

Now the fighting men from the *bireme* were all around them. Back to back in hollow square the four fought. Upon the deck the mail clad men fell. Steadily growing mounds of dead around them, they fought on. There was a sword gash across Gigi's hairy chest from which blood ran in little trickling streams. Sigurd was bleeding from a dozen cuts. But Zubran, save for the arrow wound, was untouched. He fought silently, but Sigurd chanted and howled as he struck and Gigi laughed as his giant mace crushed bone and sinew.

Yet still the barrier of the black priest's men held fast between them and Sharane!

What of Sharane! Kenton's heart sank. He cast a swift glance up at the balcony. She stood there with three of her warrior maids, swords in hands, battling against soldiers who crept two by two down a narrow bridge of planks that had been dropped from the *bireme's* deck.

But that glance had been no wise one. A sword bit into his unguarded side, paralyzing him. He would have fallen but for the Viking's hand.

"Steady, blood-brother!" he heard him say. "My shield is before you. Take breath!"

There came a triumphant shouting from the ship of Klaneth. Out from its deck two long poles had been thrust. There had been a tugging of ropes and from their ends a net had fallen—squarely over Sharane and her three women!

They were struggling to cut the meshes. They bound them, fettered them. The women beat against those meshes as helplessly as butterflies.

And suddenly the net tightened, was drawn together by cords. Slowly the poles began to lift carrying the net's burden upward to the deck of the attacking ship!

"Ho! Sharane!" mocked Klaneth, "Ho! Vessel of Ishtar! Welcome to my ship!"

"Christ!" groaned Kenton. Strength renewed by his fury and despair, he charged. Before his onslaught the warriors gave way. Again he rushed. Something whirled through, struck him upon the temple. He fell. The men of Klaneth swarmed upon him, clutching at his hands, his feet, smothering him.

They were hurled from him. The dwarf legs of Gigi were astride of him, his mace whistling, men dropping under its stroke. Dizzily he raised his head; saw Sigurd guarding him at right, Zubran at left and rear.

He looked upward. The net that held the struggling women was being dropped upon the *bireme's* deck.

Again he heard the bellow of Klaneth:

"Welcome, sweet Sharane! Welcome!"

He staggered up, broke from the Viking's grip, staggered forward—toward her.

"Seize him!" came the howl of the black priest. "His weight in gold to the men who bring him to me—alive!"

And now there was a ring of Klaneth's men around

93

him, sweeping him away. Between him and the three who had fought beside him eddied another stream of warriors, falling smitten by mace and sword and scimitar—but their places taken by others; others wedging in, widening steadily the distance between Kenton and his comrades.

He ceased to struggle. After all—this was what he wanted! This was best. They could take him—he would be with Sharane!

"Hold him up!" roared Klaneth. "Let the slut of Ishtar see him!"

He was lifted high in the hands of his captors. He heard a wail from Sharane. . . .

A dizziness seized him! It was as though he had been caught in some vortex and was being sucked away—away!

He had a vision of Sigurd, the Persian and Gigi staring at him, their faces incredulous bloody masks. And they had stopped fighting. There were other faces, scores of them, staring at him with that same incredulity—though now, it seemed, shaded with terror.

Now they were all staring at him as though over the edge of a prodigious funnel through which he had begun to drop!

And now clutching hands had melted away from him! The faces were gone.

"Gigi!" he called. "Sigurd! Zubran! Help me!"

He heard the howling of winds!

They changed into a trumpet note. The trumpeting changed. It became some familiar sound—some sound known in another life of his, ages and ages gone! What was it? Louder it grew, rasping, peremptory——

The shriek of an auto horn!

Shuddering, he opened his eyes.

He looked upon his own room!

There lay the shining jeweled ship—the ship of toys!

And there was a knocking at the door, agitated, frantic; the murmuring of frightened voices.

Then the voice of Jevins, faltering, panic stricken:

"Mr. John! Mr. John!"

15

Down The Rope Of Sound

KENTON fought back his faintness; reached out a trembling hand, and snapped on the electrics.

"Mr. John! Mr. John!"

The old servant's voice was sharp with terror; he rattled the door knob; beat against the panels.

Kenton steadied himself against the table; forced himself to speak.

"Why—Jevins—" he strove to lighten the dragging words, inject some naturalness into them—"What's the matter?"

He heard a little gasp of relief, another murmuring from the servants and then Jevins spoke again.

"I was passing and heard you cry out, sir. A dreadful cry! Are you ill?"

Desperately Kenton strove against the racking weakness; managed a laugh.

"Why, no—I fell asleep. Had a nightmare. Don't worry! Go to bed."

"Oh—it was that?"

The relief in Jevins' voice was greater, but the doubt was not altogether gone. He did not withdraw; stood there hesitating.

There was a mist before Kenton's eyes, a thin veil of crimson. His knees bent suddenly; barely he saved himself from falling. He stumbled to the couch and sank upon it. A panic impulse urged him to cry out to Jevins to bring help—to break down the door. Fast upon it came warning that he must not do this; that he must fight his battle out alone—if he were to tread the ship's deck again!

"Go, Jevins!" he cried harshly. "Hell, man—didn't I tell you I wasn't to be disturbed tonight? Get away!"

Too late he realized that never before had he spoken so to this old servant who loved him, he knew, like a son. Had he betrayed himself—crystallized Jevins' suspicions into certainty that within that room something was wrong indeed? Fear spurred his tongue.

"I'm all right!" He forced laughter into the words. "Of course, I'm all right!"

Damn that mist in front of his eyes! What was it? He passed a hand over them, brought it away wet with blood. He stared at it, stupidly.

"Oh, very well, Mr. John." There was no more doubt, nothing but affection in the voice. "But hearing you cry—"

God! Would the man never go! His eyes travelled from his hand up his arm. Crimson it was, red with blood to the shoulder. The fingers dripped.

"Only a nightmare," he interrupted quietly. "I won't sleep again until I'm done and go to bed—so run along."

"Then—good night, Mr. John."

"Good night," he answered.

Swaying he sat until the footsteps of Jevins and the others had died away. Then he tried to rise. His weakness was too great. He slid from the couch to his knees, crawled across the floor to a low cabinet, fumbled at its doors and drew down a bottle of brandy. He raised it to his lips and drank deep. The fiery stuff raced through him, gave him strength. He arose.

A sickening pang stabbed his side. He raised his hand to clutch the agony, covered it and felt trickle through his fingers a slow, warm stream!

He remembered—a sword had bitten him there—the sword of one of Klaneth's men!

Flashed before him pictures—the arrow quivering in the Viking's shield, the mace of Gigi, the staring warriors, the great net dropping over Sharane and her women, the wondering faces. . . .

Then—this!

Again he lifted the bottle. Half way to his mouth he stopped, every muscle rigid, every nerve taut. Confronting him was a shape—a man splashed red from head to foot! He saw a strong, fierce face from which glared eyes filled with murderous menace; long tangled elf locks of black writhed round it down to the crimson-stained shoulders. From hair edge to ear down across the forehead was a wound, from which blood dripped. Bare to the waist was this man and from the nipple of his left breast to mid-side ran a red wide-mouthed slash, open to the ribs!

Gory, menacing, dreadful in its red lacquer of life, a living phantom from some pirate deck of death it glared at him.

Stop! There was something familiar about the face—the eyes! His gaze was caught by a shimmer of gold on the right arm above the elbow. It was a bracelet. And he knew that bracelet——

The bridal gift of Sharane!

Who was this man? He could not think clearly—how could he—with numbness in his brain, the red mists before his eyes, this weakness that was creeping back upon him?

Sudden rage swept through him. He swung the bottle to hurl it straight at the wild fierce face.

The left hand of the figure swung up, clutching a similar bottle——

It was he, John Kenton, reflected in the long mirror on the wall. That ensanguined, fearfully wounded, raging shape was—himself!

A clock chimed ten.

As though the slow strokes had been an exorcism, a change came over Kenton. His mind cleared, purpose and will clicked back in place. He took another deep drink of the liquor, and without another look in the mirror, without a glance toward the jeweled ship, he walked to the door.

Hand on the key he paused, considering. No, that would not do. He could not risk going out into the hallway. Jevins might still be hovering near; or some of the other servants might see him. And if he had not known himself, what would be the effect of seeing him on them?

He could not go where water was to cleanse his hurts, wash away the blood. He must do with what is here.

He turned back to the cabinet, stripping the table of its cloth as he passed. His foot struck something on the floor. The blade of Nabu lay there, no longer blue but stained as was he from tip of blade to hilt. For the moment he left it lie. He poured spirits upon the cloth, made shift to cleanse himself with them. From another cabinet he drew out his emergency medical kit. There was lint there and bandages and iodine. Stiff-lipped with the torture of its touch, he poured the latter into the great wound in his side, daubed it into the cut across his forehead. He made compresses of the lint and wound the linen tapes around brow and chest. The blood flow stopped. The fiery agony

97

of the iodine diminished. He stepped again to the mirror and scanned himself.

The clock struck the half hour.

Half past ten! What had it been when he had clutched the golden chains of the ship—had summoned the ship and been lifted by those chains out of the room and into the mysterious world in which it sailed?

Just nine o'clock!

Only an hour and a half ago! Yet during that time in that other and timeless world he had been slave and conqueror, had fought great fights, had won both ship and the woman who had mocked him, had become—what now he was!

And all this in less than two short hours!

He walked over to the ship, picking up the sword as he went. He wiped the hilt clean of blood, the blade he did not touch. He drained the bottle before he dared drop his eyes.

He looked first on Sharane's cabin. There were gaps in the little blossoming trees. The door was down, flung broken on the deck. The casements of the window were shattered. Upon the roof's edge a row of doves perched, heads a-droop, mourning.

From the oar ports four sweeps instead of seven dipped on each side. And in the pit were no longer the eight and twenty rowers. Only ten were left, two to each of the stroke oars, one each to the other.

On the starboard side of the hull were gashes and deep dents—the marks of the *bireme's* combing of that ship of Ishtar now sailing somewhere on that unknown world from which he had been whirled.

And at the tiller bar a manikin stood—a toy steering the toy ship. A toy man, long haired, fair haired. At his feet sat two other toys; one with shining, hairless head, and apelike arms; the other red bearded, agate eyed, a shining scimitar across his knees.

Longing shook him, heartache, such homesickness as some human soul might feel marooned upon alien star on outskirts of space.

"Gigi!" he groaned. "Sigurd! Zubran! Bring me back to you!"

He bent over the three, touching them with tender fingers, breathing on them, as though to give them warmth of life. Long he paused over Gigi—instinctively he felt

98

that in the Ninevite more than the others dwelt the power
to help. Sigurd was strong, the Persian subtle—but in the
dwarf-legged giant ran tide of earth gods in earth's shouting youth; archaic, filled with unknown power long lost
to man.

"Gigi!" he whispered, face close—and again and again
—"Gigi! Hear me! Gigi!"

Did the manikin move?

Breaking his passion of concentration came a cry. News-
boys shouting some foolish happening of importance on
this foolish world on which he was cast away! It broke
the threads, shattered the fragile links that he had felt
forming between himself and the manikin. Cursing, he
straightened. His sight dimmed; he fell. Effort had told
upon him; the treacherous weakness crept back. He dragged
himself to the cabinet, knocked the head off a second
bottle, let half of it pour down his throat.

The whipped blood sang in his ears; strength flowed
through him. He snapped off the lights. A ray from the
street came through the heavy curtains, outlining the three
toy figures. Once more Kenton gathered himself for a
mighty effort of will.

"Gigi! It is I! Calling you! Gigi! Answer me! Gigi!"

The manikin stirred, its body trembled, its head raised!

Far, far away, thin and cold as tip of frost lance upon
glass, ghostly and unreal, coming from immeasurable distances, he heard Gigi's voice.

"Wolf I hear you! Wolf! Where are you?"

His mind clung to that thread of sound as though it
were a line flung to him over vast abysses.

"Wolf—come to us!" The voice was stronger.

"Gigi! Gigi! Help me to you!"

The two voices—that far flung, thin, cold one and his
own met and clung and knit. They stretched over that
gulf which lay between where he stood and the unknown
dimension in which sailed the ship.

Now the little figure no longer squatted! It was upright!
Louder rang Gigi's voice:

"Wolf! Come to us! We hear you! Come to us!"

Then as though it chanted words of power:

"Sharane! Sharane! Sharane!"

Under the lash of the loved name his will now streamed
fiercely.

"Gigi! Gigi! Keep calling!"

He was no longer conscious of his room. He saw the ship far, far beneath him. He was but a point of life floating high above it, yearning to it and calling, calling to Gigi to help him. The strand of sound that linked them strained and shook like a cobweb thread. But it held and ever drew him down.

And now the ship was growing. It was misty, nebulous; but steadily it grew and steadily Kenton dropped down that rope of sound to meet it. Strengthening the two voices came other sounds weaving themselves within their threads—the chanting of Sigurd, the calling of Zubran, the thrumming of the fingers of the wind on the harpstring of the ship's stays, the murmuring litany of the breaking waves telling their beads of foam.

Ever more real grew the ship. Striking through its substance came the wavering image of his room. It seemed to struggle against the ship, to strive to cover it. But the ship beat it back, crying out to him with the voices of his comrades and the voices of wind and sea in one.

"Wolf! We feel you near! Come to us—Sharane! Sharane! Sharane!"

The phantom outlines leaped into being; they enclosed him.

The arms of Gigi reached out to him, gripped him, plucked him out of space!

And as they gripped, he heard a chaotic whirling, a roaring as of another world spinning from under him and lashed by mighty winds.

He stood again upon the ship.

He was clasped tight to Gigi's hairy chest. Sigurd's hands were on his shoulders. Zubran was clasping and patting Kenton's own hands clutching Gigi's back, singing in his joy strange intricate Persian curses.

"Wolf!" roared Gigi, tears filling the furrows of his wrinkled face. "Where did you go? In the name of all the gods—where have you been?"

"Never mind!" sobbed Kenton. "Never mind where I've been, Gigi! I'm back! Oh, thank God, I'm back!"

16

How The Ship Was Manned

FAINTNESS conquered him. The wounds and the effort of will had sapped his strength to its limit. When he came back to consciousness he was on the divan in Sharane's raped cabin. His bandages had been replaced, his wounds redressed. The three men and four of Sharane's maids were looking down upon him. There was no reproach on any of their faces—only curiosity, tempered with awe.

"It must be a strange place to which you go, Wolf," Gigi said at last. "For see! The slash across my chest is healed, Sigurd's cuts, too—yet your wounds are as fresh as though made but a moment ago."

Kenton looked and saw that it was so; the slash across Gigi's breast was now only a red scar.

"Also it was a strange way to leave us, blood-brother," rumbled the Viking.

"By the fire of Ormuzd!" swore the Persian. "It was a very good way! A good thing for us that you left as you did. Cyrus the King taught us that it was a good general who knew how to retreat to save his troops. And that retreat of yours was a masterly one, comrade. Without it we would not be here now to welcome you."

"It was no retreat! I could not help but go!" whispered Kenton.

"Well," the Persian shook a dubious head, "whatever it was, it saved us. One instant there you were lifted on the paws of the black priest's dogs. Another instant you had faded into a shadow. And then, lo, even the shadow was gone!"

"How those dogs who had held you shrieked and ran," laughed Zubran. "And the dogs who were biting at us ran too—back to their kennels on the *bireme* they ran, for all Klaneth's cursing. They had great fear, comrade— and so in fact for a moment had I. Then down went

101

their oars, and away sped their ship with Klaneth's cursing still sounding even after they had gotten safely out of sight of us."

"Sharane!" groaned Kenton. "What did they do to her? Where have they taken her?"

"To Emakhtila, or Sorcers' Isle, I think," answered Gigi. "Fear not for her, Wolf. The black priests want you both. To torture her without your eyes looking on, or to slay you without hers beholding your agonies would be no revenge for Klaneth. No—until he lays hands on you Sharane is safe enough."

"Not comfortable, perhaps, nor happy, but assuredly safe enough," confirmed the Persian.

"Three of her maids they took with her in the nets," said Sigurd. "Three they slew. These four they left when you vanished."

"They took Satalu, my little vessel of joy," mourned Gigi. "And for that Klaneth shall also pay when reckoning comes."

"Half the slaves were killed when the *bireme* crashed against us," went on the Viking. "Oars crushed in ribs, broke backs. Others died later. The black-skin we put in Zachel's place is a man! He fought those who dropped into the pit and slew his share. Only eight oars have we now instead of twice seven. The black-skin sits at one of them—unchained. When we take new slaves he shall be overseer again and honored."

"And I remember now," it was Gigi, dropping back to his first thought, "that when I dragged you up the side of Klaneth's cabin that day you fought his priests, you still bled from the bites of Sharane's girls. Yet with us there had been time and time again for them to have healed. And here you are once more with old wounds fresh. It must be a strange place indeed, that you go to, Wolf— is there no time there?"

"It is your own world," he answered. "The world from whence all of you came."

And as they stared at him, he leaped up from the divan.

"Sail to Emakhtila! At once! Find Sharane! Free her! How soon, Gigi? How soon?"

He felt the wound in his side open, fell back, his spurt of strength exhausted.

"Not till your wounds are healed," said Gigi, and began to unfasten the reddening bandages. "And we must make

102

the ship strong again before we take that journey. We must have new slaves for the oars. Now lie quiet, until you heal. Klaneth will do Sharane no harm as long as there is hope of taking you. I, Gigi, tell you this. So set your heart at ease."

And now began for Kenton a most impatient time of waiting. To be chained here by his wounds when, despite Gigi's assurances, the black priest might be wreaking his ultimate vengeance upon Sharane! It was not to be borne. Fever set in. His wounds had been more serious than he had known. Gigi nursed him.

The fever passed, and as he grew stronger he told him of that lost world of theirs; what had passed there during the centuries they had sailed on the timeless ship; of its machinery and its wars, its new laws and its customs.

"And none now go Viking!" mused Sigurd. "Clearly then I see that there is no place for me there. Best for Sigurd, Trygg's son, to end his days where he is."

The Persian nodded.

"And no place for me," he echoed. "For a man of taste such as I, it seems no world at all to live in. I like not your way of waging wars, nor could I learn to like it—I who seem to be a soldier of an old, old school, indeed."

Even Gigi was doubtful.

"I do not think I would care for it," he said. "The customs seem so different. And I notice, Wolf, that you were willing to risk chains and death to get out of that world—and lose no time getting back to this."

"The new gods seem so stupid," urged Zubran. "They do nothing. By the Nine Hells, the gods of this place are stupid enough—still they do something. Although perhaps it is better to do nothing than to do the same stupid things over and over," he ruminated.

"I will make me a steading on one of these islands," said Sigurd, "after we have carried away Kenton's woman and slain the black priest. I will take me a strong wife and breed many younglings. I will teach them to build ships. Then we shall go viking as I did of old. Skoal! Skoal to the dragons slipping through Ran's bath with the red ravens on their sails and the black ones flying overhead!" shouted Sigurd.

"Say, blood-brother," he turned to Kenton, "when you have your woman back will you make a steading beside mine? With Zubran taking wives and he and Gigi—if he is not too old—breeding young, and with those who will join us—by Odin, but we could all be great Jarls in this world!"

"That is not to my liking," replied the Persian promptly. "For one thing it takes too long to rear strong sons to fight for us. No—after we have finished our business with Klaneth I will go back to Emakhtila where there are plenty of men already made. It will be strange if I find there no discontented ones, men who can be stirred to revolt. If there be not enough of them—well, discontent is the easiest thing in the world to breed; much easier than sons, Sigurd. Also I am a great soldier. Cyrus the King himself told me so. With my army of discontented men I shall take his nest of priests and rule Emakhtila myself! And after that—beware how you raid my ships, Sigurd!"

Thus they talked among themselves, telling Kenton things of their own lives as strange to him as his own tales must have been to them. Steadily, swiftly his wounds healed until they were at last only red welts, and strength flowed back in his veins.

Now for many sleeps, while he grew well, they had lain hidden within a land-locked cove of one of the golden isles. Its rock-jawed mouth had been barely wide enough for them to enter. Safe enough this place seemed from pursuit or prying eyes. Nevertheless they had drawn the ship close against a high bank whose water side dropped straight down to the deep bottom. The oars had been taken in. The branches of the feathery trees drooped over the craft, covered it.

The time came when Kenton, awakening, felt full tide of health. He walked back to the rudder bar where Sigurd, Gigi and the Persian were stretched out talking. He paused for the hundredth time beside the strange compass that was the helmsman's guide in this world, where there was neither sun nor moon nor stars, no east or west, north or south. Set within the top of a wooden standee was a silver bowl covered with a sheet of clear crystal. Around the lip of this bowl were inlaid sixteen symbols, cuneiform, scarlet. Attached to a needle rising vertically from the bowl's bottom were two slender pointers, serpent shaped, blue. The larger, he knew, pointed always toward Emakhtila, that land to which, were Gigi right, Sharane had been carried by the black priest. The smaller pointed toward the nearest land.

As always, he wondered what mysterious currents stirred them in this poleless world; what magnetic flow from the scattered isles pulled the little one; what constant flow from Emakhtila kept the big one steady? Steadier far than compass needles of earth pointed to the north.

And as he looked it seemed to him that the little blue needle spun in its scarlet pool and lay parallel with the greater one—both pointing to the Isle of Sorcerers!

"An omen!" he cried. "Look, Sigurd! Gigi—Zubran—look!"

They bent over the compass. but in the instant between his call and their response the smaller needle had shifted again; again pointed to the isle where they lay moored!

"An omen?" they asked, puzzled. "What omen?"

"Both the needles pointed to Emakhtila!" he told them. "To Sharane! It was an omen—a summons! We must go! Quick, Gigi—Sigurd—cast loose! We sail for Emakhtila!"

They looked at him, doubtfully; down at the compass once more; at each other covertly.

"I saw it, I tell you!" Kenton repeated. "It was no illusion—I am well! Sharane is in peril! We must go!"

"Sh-h-h!" Gigi held up a warning hand, listened intently, parted the curtains of the leaves and peered out.

"A ship," he whispered, drawing back his head. "Bid the maids get arrows and javelins. Arm—all of you. Quiet now—and speed!"

They could hear the drop of oars; voices; the low tapping of a hammer, beating the stroke for the rowers. The maids of Sharane silently ranged themselves along the port rail near the bow, bows standing, arrows at strings, beside them their stabbing javelins, their swords, too; their shields at feet.

The four men crouched, peeping out through the trees. What was coming? Questing ship of Klaneth that had nosed them out? Hunters searching the sea for them spurred on by the black priest's promises of reward?

Through the narrow entrance to the hidden harbor drifted a galley. Twice the length of the ship of Ishtar, it was single tiered, fifteen oars to the side and double banked—two men to each sweep. There were a dozen or more men standing on the bow deck; how many others

105

not visible there was no knowing. The galley crept in. It nosed along the shore. When less than two hundred feet away from the hidden watchers grapnels were thrown over the side and the boat made fast.

"Good water here, and all we need," they heard one say.

Gigi put his arms around the three, drew them close to him.

"Wolf," he whispered, "now do I believe in your omen. For lo! close upon its heels follows another and better one. A summons indeed. There are the slaves we must have for our vacant oars! And gold too, I'll warrant, that we shall want when we reach Emakhtila."

"Slaves and gold, yes," muttered Kenton; then sardonically as half a dozen more men came up from below and joined the group on the bow—"only remains to find the way to take them, Gigi."

"Nay, but that will be easy," whispered Zubran. "They suspect nothing, and men surprised are already half beaten. We four will creep along the bank until we are just opposite their bow. When we have been away for as long as Zala there—" he motioned to one of the warrior maids—"can count two hundred, the maids shall pour their arrows into that group, shooting fast as they can but taking careful aim and bringing down as many as they can. Then we will leap aboard and upon those left. But when the maids hear us shout they must shoot no longer at the bow, lest we be struck. Thereafter let them keep any others from joining those forward. Is it a good plan? I'll warrant we shall have their ship in less time than it has taken me to tell it."

A qualm shook Kenton.

"Now by the gods!" came the voice, evidently of the captain of the galley. "Would that cursed Ship of Ishtar had been here. Had it been—well, I think none of us would need go faring out of Emakhtila again. Gods! If we might only have crept upon her here and won Klaneth's reward!"

Kenton's compunction fled; here were the hunters, and delivered into the hands of the hunted.

"Right, Zubran," he whispered fiercely. "Beckon Zala to us and tell her the plan."

And when that had been done he led them over to the side of the ship into the covert. There was a ledge that helped them in their going and it seemed to Kenton, watching hungrily the craft which, won, might mean Sharane, that the maids' arrows would never fly.

At last they came, buzzing like bees and swarming among the cluster of men on the strange ship. And the maids were aiming straight. Of the near score fully half were down, spitted, before they broke for shelter, crying crazily. Kenton shouted and leaped upon the deck, cutting with his sword, while the mace of Gigi struck, and the blade of Sigurd, the scimitar of Zubran took toll. Beaten ere they could raise a hand, those left alive knelt and cried for mercy. A little band running to their aid from the stern met an arrow storm from the maids, threw down their arms, raised hands of submission.

They herded their captives together, disarmed them and thrust them into the forward cabin. They locked them in, first making sure there were no weapons there and no way for them to escape. They took the keys to the rowers' chains. The Viking went down into the pit, picked out nineteen of the sturdiest slaves, loosed and drove them two by two over to the ship. He manacled them to its empty oars.

Much gold they found, too, and other things that might prove useful in Emakhtila—clothes of seamen in the fashion of the place, long robes to cover them and make them less open to detection.

Arose then the question of what was to be done with their prize—and the men aboard her. Gigi was for putting them all to the sword. The Persian thought that it would be best to bring back the slaves, leave their ship where she was, and after killing all those on the captive galley, put forth to Emakhtila on her. There was much in his plan to be commended. The Ship of Ishtar was a marked vessel. There was no mistaking her. This other craft would arouse no suspicion in the minds of those who saw it sailing. And once landed at Emakhtila, and what lay before them done, they could sail back on it and recover their own.

But Kenton would not have it. And the upshot was that the captain was called out for questioning and told that if he answered truthfully his life and those of the others would be spared.

There was little he could tell them—but that little was enough to quicken Kenton's heart—bring new dread to it also. Yes, there had been a woman brought to

107

Emakhtila by Klaneth, the Priest of Nergal. He had won
her in a fight, Klaneth had said, a sea battle in which
many men had been slain. He had not said where, or
with whom this battle had taken place, and his soldiers
had been warned to be silent. But it began to be whispered that the woman was the woman of the Ship of
Ishtar. The priestesses of Ishtar had claimed her. But
Klaneth who had great power had resisted them, and as
a compromise the Council of Priests had made her
priestess of the God Bel and placed her in Bel's Bower
on top of the Temple of the Seven Zones.

"I know that Temple and the Bower of Bel," Sigurd
had nodded. "And why its priestess must live there," he
had whispered, looking askance at Kenton.

This woman appeared now and then, heavily veiled,
attending certain ceremonies to the God Bel, the captain went on. But she seemed to be a woman in a dream.
Her memory had been taken from her—or so it was re-
ported. Beyond that he knew nothing—except that Klaneth
had doubled his reward for three of them—he pointed to
Gigi, Zubran and the Persian; and had trebled it for him—
he pointed to Kenton.

When they were done with him they unloosed the remaining slaves and sent them ashore. They hailed the
ship and the Nubian brought her over. They watched the
captain and his men pass over the side of the galley and
disappear among the trees.

"Plenty of water and food," grumbled Gigi. "They
fare far better at our hands than we would have fared
at theirs."

They hitched the captured galley to the ship; slowly
pulled it out of the harbor through the rock-lipped mouth.
And after they had gone a mile or so Sigurd dropped into
it, did a few things with an axe, and climbing back
cut it loose. Rapidly the galley filled and sank.

"Now," cried Kenton, and took the rudder bar, steering
the ship straight to where the long blue arrow pointed.
Pointed to Emakhtila and to Sharane——
Sharane!

17

They Seek Sorcerers' Isle

Luck clung to them. The silver mists hung close about the ship, shrouding her so that she sailed within a circle not more than double her length. Ever the mists hid her. Kenton, sleeping little, drove the slaves at the oar to point of exhaustion.

"There is a great storm brewing," warned Sigurd.

"Pray Odin that it may hold back till we are well within Emakhtila," answered Kenton.

"If we but had a horse I would sacrifice it to the All-Father," said Sigurd. "Then he would hold that storm till our needs called it."

"Speak low, lest the sea horses trample us!" warned Kenton.

He had questioned the Viking about that interruption of his when the captain of the captured galley had said that the captured woman was Priestess of Bel's Bower.

"She will be safe there, even from Klaneth—so long as she takes no other lover than the god," Sigurd had said.

"No other lover than the god!" Kenton had roared, hand dropping to sword and glaring at Sigurd. "She shall have no lover but me—god or man, Sigurd! What do you mean?"

"Take hand from sword, Wolf," Sigurd had replied. "I meant not to offend you. Only—gods are gods! And there was something in that captain's talk about your woman walking in dream, memory withdrawn from her—was there not? If that be so—blood-brother—you are in those memories she has lost!"

Kenton winced.

"Nergal once tried to part a man and a woman who loved," he said, "even as Sharane and I. He could not. I do not think Nergal's priest can succeed where his master failed."

"Not well reasoned, Wolf." It was Zubran who had

come quietly upon them. "The gods are strong. Therefore they have no reason for subtlety or cunning. They smite —and all is done. It is not artistic, I admit—but it is unanswerable. And man, who has not the strength of the gods, must resort to cunning and subtlety. That is why man will do worse things than the gods. Out of his weakness he is forced to it. The gods should not be blamed—except for making man weaker than they. And therefore Klaneth is more to be feared by you than Nergal, his master."

"He cannot drive me out of Sharane's heart!" Kenton cried.

The Viking bent his head down to the compass.

"You may be right," he muttered. "Zubran may be right. All I know is that while your woman is faithful to Bel, no man may harm her!"

Vague as he might be on that one point, the Viking was direct and full of meat upon others. The Norseman had been observant while slave to the priests of Nergal. He knew the city and the Temple of the Seven Zones intimately. Best of all he knew a way of entering Emakhtila by another road than that of its harbor.

This was indeed all important, since it was not within the bounds of possibility that they could enter that harbor without instant recognition.

"Look, comrades," Sigurd scratched with point of sword a rude map on the planks of the deck. "Here lies the city. It is at the end of a fjord. The mountains rise on each side of it and stretch in two long spits far out to sea. But here"—he pointed to a spot in the coast line close to the crotch where the left hand mountain barrier shot out from the coast—"is a bay with a narrow entrance from the sea. It is used by the priests of Nergal for a certain secret sacrifice. Between it and the city a hidden way runs through the hills. That path brings you out to the great temple. I have traveled the hidden way and have stood on the shores of that bay. I went there with other slaves, bearing priests in litters and things for the sacrifice. While it would take two good sleeps for a ship to make the journey from Emakhtila to this place, it is by the hidden way only half so far as a strong man could walk in my own land between the dawn and noon of a winter day. Also there are many places there where the ship can be hidden. Few galleys pass by and

110

no one lives near—which is why the priests of Nergal picked it.

"Also I know well the Temple of the Seven Zones —since long it was my home," went on Sigurd. "Its height is thirty times the ship's mast."

Kenton swiftly estimated. That would make the temple six hundred feet—a respectable height indeed.

"Its core," said the Viking, "is made up of the sanctuaries of the gods and the goddess Ishtar, one upon each other. Around this core are the quarters of the priests and priestesses and lesser shrines. These secret sanctuaries are seven, the last being the house of Bel. From Bel's House a stairway leads up into his Bower. At the base of the temple is a vast court with altars and other shrines where the people come to worship. Its entrances are strongly guarded. Even we four could not enter—there!

"But around the temple, which is shaped thus"—he scratched the outline of a truncated cone—"a great stone stairway runs thus"—he drew a spiral from base to top of cone. "At intervals, along that stairway, are sentinels. There is a garrison where it begins. Is this all clear?"

"What is clear," grunted Gigi, "is that we would need an army to take it!"

"Not so," the Viking answered. "Remember how we took the galley—although they outnumbered us? We will row the ship into that secret harbor. If priests are there we must do what we can—slay or flee. But if the Norns decree that no priests be there, we will hide the ship and leave the slaves in care of the black-skin. Then the four of us, dressed as seamen in the clothes and the long cloaks we took from the galley, will take the hidden way and go into the city.

"For as to that stairway—I have another plan. It is high walled—up to a man's chest. If we can pass without arousing the guards at its base, we can creep up under shadow of that wall, slaying the sentinels as we go, until we reach the Bower of Bel and entering, bear Sharane away.

"But not in fair weather could we do this," he ended. "There must be darkness or storm that they see us not from the streets. And that is why I pray to Odin, that this brewing tempest may not boil until we have reached the city and looked upon that stairway. For in that

111

storm that is surely coming we could do as I have said and swiftly."

"But in all this I see no chance of slaying Klaneth," growled Zubran. "We creep in, we creep up, we creep out again with Sharane—if we can. And that is all. By Ormuzd, my knees are too tender for creeping! Also my scimitar itches to scratch itself on the black priest's hide."

"No safety while Klaneth lives!" croaked Gigi, playing upon his old tune.

"I have no thought of Klaneth now," rumbled the Viking. "First comes Kenton's woman. After that—we take up the black priest."

"I am ashamed," said Zubran. "I should have remembered. Yet in truth, I would feel easier if we could kill Klaneth on our way to her. For I agree with Gigi—while he lives, no safety for your blood-brother or any of us. However—Sharane first, of course."

The Viking had been peering down into the compass. He looked again, intently, and drew back, pointing to it.

Both the blue serpents in the scarlet bath were parallel, their heads turned to one point.

"We head straight to Emakhtila," said Sigurd. "But are we within the jaws of that fjord or out of them? Wherever we are we must be close."

He swung the rudder to port. The ship veered. The large needle slipped a quarter of the space to the right between the red symbols on the bowl edge. The smaller held steady.

"That proves nothing," grunted the Viking, "except that we are no longer driving straight to the city. But we may be close upon the mounts. Check the oarsmen."

Slower went the ship, and slower, feeling her way through the mists. And suddenly they darkened before them. Something grew out of them slowly, slowly. It lay revealed as a low shore, rising sharply and melting into deeper shadows behind. The waves ran gently to it, caressing its rocks. Sigurd swore a great oath of thankfulness.

"We are on the other side of the mounts," he said. "Somewhere close is that secret bay of which I told you. Bid the overseer drive the ship along as we are."

He swung the rudder sharply to starboard. The ship turned; slowly followed the shore. Soon in front of them

112

loomed a high ridge of rock. This they skirted, circled its end and still sculling silently came at last to another narrow strait into which the Viking steered.

"A place for hiding," he said. "Send the ship into that cluster of trees ahead. Nay—there is water there, the trees rise out of it. Once within them the ship can be seen neither from shore nor sea."

They drifted into the grove. Long, densely leaved branches covered them.

"Now lash her to the tree trunks," whispered Sigurd. "Go softly. Priests may be about. We will look for them later, when we are on our way. We leave the ship in charge of the women. The black-skin stays behind. Let them all lie close till we return——"

"There would be better chance for you to return if you cut off that long hair of yours and your beard, Sigurd," said the Persian, and added: "Better chance for us, also."

"What!" cried the Viking, outraged. "Cut my hair! Why, even when I was slave they left that untouched!"

"Wise counsel!" said Kenton. "And Zubran—that flaming beard of yours and your red hair. Better for you and us, too, if you shaved them both—or changed their color."

"By Ormuzd, no!" exclaimed the Persian, as outraged as Sigurd.

"The fowler sets the net and is caught with the bird!" laughed the Viking. "Nevertheless, it is good counsel. Better hair off face and head than head off shoulders!"

The maids brought shears. Laughing, they snipped Sigurd's mane to nape of neck, trimmed the long beard into short spade shape. Amazing was the transformation of Sigurd, Trygg's son, brought about by that shearing.

"There is one that Klaneth will not know if he sees him," grunted Gigi.

Now the Persian put himself in the women's hands. They dabbled at beard and head with cloths dipped in a bowl of some black liquid. The red faded, then darkened into brown. Not so great was the difference between him and the old Zubran as there was between the new and old Sigurd. But Kenton and Gigi nodded approvingly —at least the red that made him as conspicuous as the Norseman's long hair was gone.

Remained Kenton and Gigi. Little could be done for

113

either of them. There was no changing Gigi's frog slit of a mouth, the twinkling beady eyes, the bald pate, the immense shoulders.

"Take out your earrings, Gigi," bade Kenton.

"Take off that bracelet on your arm," replied Gigi.

"Sharane's gift! Never!" exclaimed Kenton, as outraged as had been both the Norseman and the Persian.

"My earrings were put there by one who loved me as much as she does you." For the first time since Kenton had known Gigi there was anger in his voice.

The Persian laughed softly. It broke the tension. Kenton grinned at the drummer, somewhat guiltily. Gigi grinned back.

"Well," he said. "It seems that we must all make our sacrifices—" he began to unscrew the earrings.

"No, Gigi!" Kenton could not bring himself to break that golden band upon which Sharane had graven the symbols of her love. "Leave them be. Rings and bracelet —both can be hidden."

"I do not know—" Gigi paused doubtfully. "It seems to me to be better. That idea of sacrifice—it grows stronger."

"There is little sense in what you say," said Kenton stubbornly.

"No?" mused Gigi. "Yet many men must have seen that bracelet of yours that time you fought the black priest's men and lost Sharane. Klaneth must have seen it. Something whispers to me that token is more perilous than the rings in my ears."

"Well, nothing whispers to me," said Kenton, shortly. He led the way into what had been Klaneth's cabin and began stripping to clothe himself in the sailors' gear they had taken from the captured galley. He slipped on a loose shirt of finely tanned, thin leather whose loose sleeves fastened around his wrists.

"You see," he said to Gigi, "the bracelet is hidden."

Next came loose hose of the same material drawn tight by a girdle around the waist. He drew on high, laced buskins. Over the shirt he fastened a sleeveless tunic of mail. On his head he placed a conical metal covered cap from whose padded sides dropped, shoulder deep, folds of heavy oiled silk.

The others dressed with him in similar garments. Only the Persian would not leave off his own linked mail. He knew its strength, he said, and the others were new to

114

him. It was an old friend, often tried and always faithful, he said; he would not cast it off for new ones whose loyalty was still untried. But over it he drew one of the shirts and a tunic. And Gigi, after he had set the cap upon his head, drew close the folds of silk so that they hid his ears and their pendants. Also he fastened around his neck another long fold of silk, binding the others fast and hiding his mouth.

And when they had covered themselves with the long cloaks they scanned each other with lightened hearts. The Viking and the Persian were true changelings. Little fear of recognition there. Changed enough by his new garb, it seemed to them, was Kenton. The cloak hid Gigi's stumpy legs and the cloths around his face, the close fitting, conical cap altered it curiously into one not easily recognziable.

"It is good!" murmured the Viking.

"It is very good!" echoed Kenton.

They belted themselves and thrust into the belts both their own swords and short ones of Sigurd's forging. Only Gigi would take neither that nine foot blade the Norseman had made for him nor the great mace. The latter was too well known; the other too cumbersome for their journey; impossible, like the mace, to hide. He took two swords of average length. Last he picked up a long, thin piece of rope, swiftly spliced to it a small grappling hook. He coiled the rope around his waist, hanging the grapple to his belt.

"Lead, Sigurd," said Kenton.

One by one they dropped over the ship's bow, waded through shallow water and stood upon the shore while Sigurd cast about for his bearings. The mists had grown thicker. The golden leaves, the panicles of crimson and yellow blooms were etched against them as though upon some ancient Chinese screen. In the mists Sigurd moved, shadowy.

"Come," the Viking joined them. "I have found the way."

Silently they followed him through the mists, under the silver shadows of the trees.

PART IV
In the Sorcerers' City

18

THERE was a hidden way, in truth. How Sigurd followed it in the glimmering fog, by what signs led, Kenton could not tell. But the Viking walked along, unhesitant.

Between high rocks covered with the golden ferns the narrow road ran, and through thickets where the still air was languorous with the scent of myriads of strange blossoms; through dense clumps of slender trunks which were like bamboo stems all lacquered scarlet, and through groves where trees grew primly in parklike precision and under which the tarnished silver shadows were thick. Their steps made no sound on the soft moss. They had long lost the murmur of the sea. Sound of any kind around them there was none.

At the skirt of one of the ordered groves the Viking paused.

"The place of sacrifice," he whispered. "I go to see if any of Nergal's black dogs are about. Wait for me here."

He melted into the mists. They waited, silent. Each felt that something evil lay sleeping within those trees and if they spoke or moved it would awaken, draw them to it. And out of it, as though the sleeping evil breathed, pulsed the sickly sweet and charnel odor that had hung in Klaneth's cabin.

Silently as he had gone, Sigurd returned.

"No black robes there," he said. "Yet—something of their dark god dwells in that grove always. Eager am I to pass this place. Go softly and quickly."

They pushed on. At last Sigurd paused, exhaled a vast sigh of relief.

"We have passed," he told them.

He led them with increased speed. And now the way began to climb steeply. They passed through a long and deep ravine in which the glimmering, misty light was hardly strong enough for them to pick their way over the boulders that strewed it.

They passed out of it between two huge monoliths— and halted. Abruptly the silence that had enveloped them had been broken. Before them was nothing but the wall of the mists, but from them and far, far below came a murmuring, a humming of a great city, the creaking of masts, the rattle of gear, the splashing of oars and now and then a shouting, darting up like a kite from the vague clamor.

"The harbor," said Sigurd, and pointed downward to the right. "Emakhtila lies beneath us—close. And there," —he pointed again downward and a little to the left— "there is the temple of the Seven Zones."

Kenton followed the pointing finger. A mighty mass loomed darkly in the silvery haze, its nebulous outlines cone-shaped, its top flattened. His heart quickened.

Down they went, and down. The murmuring of the city came to them ever louder and louder. Ever the great bulk of the temple grew plainer, climbing higher and higher into the heavens as they descended. And ever the mists hid the city from them.

They came to a high stone wall. Here Sigurd turned and led them into a grove of trees, thick, heavily shadowed. Through the trees they slipped, following the Viking who now went on with greater caution.

At last he peered out from behind an enormous trunk, beckoned them. Beyond the trees was a deep rutted, broad roadway.

"A road into the city," he said. "A free road on which we can walk without fear."

They clambered down a high bank and took that road, walking now side by side. Soon the trees gave way to fields, cultivated as far as the mists would let them see; fields filled with high plants whose leaves were shaped

117

like those of the corn, but saffron yellow instead of green and instead of ears long panicles of gleaming white grains; rows of bushes on whose branches shone berries green as emeralds; strange fruits; three-stemmed vines from which fell star-shaped gourds.

They saw houses, two-storied; block-like with smaller cubes for wings like those a child makes. They were painted startlingly—both in colors and patterns; façades striped with alternate vertical, yard wide bands of blue, and yellow façades of dull blue through which darted scarlet zigzags like the conventionalized lightning bolt; broad horizontal bands of crimson barred with stripes of green.

The road narrowed, became a thoroughfare paved with blocks. The painted houses became thicker. Men and women passed them, brown faced and black, clad alike in one sleeveless white garment cut short just below the knees. On the right wrist of each of these was a bronze ring from which fell a half dozen links of chain. They carried burdens—jugs, baskets of the fruits and gourds, loaves of bread colored ruddy brown, flat cakes a foot across. They glanced at the four curiously as they passed.

"Slaves," said Sigurd.

Now the painted houses stood solidly, side by side. These were galleried and on the galleries were flowering trees and plants like those upon the rosy cabin of the ship. From some of them women leaned and called out to them as they went by.

They passed out of this street into a roaring avenue thronged with people. And here Kenton halted in sheer amazement.

At its far end loomed the huge bulk of the terraced temple. Its sides were lined with shops. At their doors stood men crying out their wares. Banners fell from them on which in woven silk ran the cuneiform letters that told their goods.

Past him walked Assyrians, men of Nineveh and Babylon with curled heads and ringleted beards; hook nosed, fierce eyed Phoenicians; sloe-eyed, muslin skirted Egyptians; Ethiopians with great golden circles in their ears, almond lidded, smiling yellow men. Soldiers in cuirasses of linked mail, archers with quivers on back and bows in hand strode by; priests in robes of black and crimson and blue. Stood in front of him for an instant a ruddy

118

skinned, smooth muscled warrior who carried upon one shoulder the double bladed ax of ancient Crete. Over his other shoulder lay the white arm of a sandalled woman in oddly modern pleated and patterned skirt, snake girdled and with high, white breasts peeping from her opened and as oddly modern blouse. A Minoan and his mate he knew the pair to be, two who had perhaps watched youths and maids who were Athen's tribute to the Minotaur go through the door of the labyrinth to the lair where the monstrous man-bull awaited them.

And there went a cuirassed Roman, gripping a short sword of bronze that might have helped cut out the paths the first Cæsar trod. Behind him strode a giant Gaul with twisted locks and eyes as coldly blue as Sigurd's own.

Up and down along the center of the thoroughfare rode men and women in litters borne on the shoulders of slaves. His eyes followed a Grecian girl, long limbed and lithe, with hair as yellow as the ripened wheat. They followed, too, a hot eyed Carthaginian lovely enough to be a bride of Baal who leaned over the side of her litter and smiled at him.

"I am hungry and I thirst," grunted Sigurd. "Why do we stand here? Let us be going."

And Kenton realized that this pageant of past ages could be no strange thing to these comrades who were also of that past. He nodded assent. They swung into the crowd and stopped before a place wherein men sat eating and drinking.

"Better for us to enter two by two," said Gigi. "Klaneth seeks four men and we are four strangers. Wolf, go you in first with Sigurd. Zubran and I will follow—but do not notice us when we enter."

The shopkeeper set food before them and high beakers of red wine. He was garrulous; he asked them when they had made harbor, if their voyage had been a good one.

"It is a good time to be off the sea," he gossiped. "Storm comes—and a great one. I pray to the Dispenser of Waters, that he hold it until Bel's worship is ended. I close my shop soon to see that new priestess they talk so much about."

Kenton's face had been bent over, his cap veils hiding it. But at this he raised it and stared full into the man's face.

The shopkeeper blanched, faltered, stared back at him with wide eyes.

Had he been recognized? Kenton's hand sought stealthily his sword.

"Pardon!" gasped the shopkeeper, "I knew you not—" Then he peered closer, straightened and laughed. "By Bel! I thought you were—another—Gods!"

He hurried away, Kenton looked after him. Was his departure a ruse? Had he recognized him as the man Klaneth sought? It could not be. His fright had been too real; his relief too sincere. Who was it then that Kenton so resembled to bring forth this fright and relief?

They finished their food quickly, paid from the gold they had taken from the galley; passed out into the street. Almost at once Gigi and the Persian joined them.

Two by two they passed down the street, not hurrying, like men just in from a long voyage. But as they went Kenton, with an ever growing puzzlement and apprehension, saw now one and now another glance at him, pause as though in wonder and then, averting eyes go swiftly by. The others saw it, too.

"Draw the cap cloths about your face," said Gigi, uneasily. "I like not the way they stare."

Briefly Kenton told him of the shopkeeper.

"That is bad," Gigi shook his head. "Now who can it be you so resemble that those who look at you grow frightened? Well—hide your face as best you can."

And this Kenton did, keeping his head bent as he walked. Nevertheless heads still turned.

The street entered a broad park. People were strolling over its sward, sitting on benches of stone, and gigantic roots of trees whose trunks were thick as the sequoia and whose tops were lost in the slowly thickening mists. And when they had gone a little way Sigurd turned off the highway into this park.

"Wolf," he said. "Gigi is right. They stare at you too much. It comes to me that it will be better for all if you go no further. Sit upon this bench. Bow your head as though asleep or drunken. There are few here and they will be fewer as the temple court fills. The mists hide you from those who pass along the street. The three of us will go on to the temple and study that stairway. Then we will return to you and we will take counsel."

Kenton knew the Viking was right. Steadily his own

120

unease had grown. And yet—it was hard to stay behind, not to see for himself that place where Sharane lay captive, leave to others the chance of finding way to her.

"Courage, brother," said Sigurd as they left him. "Odin has held off the storm for us. Odin will help us get your woman."

Now for a time, a long, long time, it seemed to him, he sat upon that bench with face covered by hands. Stronger and stronger grew that desire to see for himself Sharane's prison, study its weaknesses. After all, his comrades were not as interested as he; their eyes not sharpened by love. He might succeed where they would fail; his eyes see what theirs would miss. And at last the desire mastered him. He arose from the bench, made his way back to the thronged street. When it was a few steps away, he turned and went along through the park, paralleling the street but not going out on it.

And in a short while he came to the end of the park and stood, half hidden, looking out.

Directly before him, not fifty yards away, arose the immense bulk of the Temple of the Seven Zones.

It blocked his vision like a Cyclopean cone. The great stairway coiled round it like a serpent. For a hundred feet up from its base the temple shone like burnished silver. There a circular terrace bit into the cone. Above that terrace for another hundred feet the surface was covered with some metal of red gold color, rich orange. Another terrace and above that a façade of jet black, dull and dead. Again a terrace. The mists hid the walls above this last, but he thought that through them he could see a glint of flaming scarlet and over it a blue shadow.

His eyes followed the girdling stairway. He stepped forward that he might see a little better. Broad steps led up from its base to a wide platform on which stood many men on armor. That, he realized, was the garrison which they must either trick or overcome. His heart sank as he counted the soldiers that guarded it.

He looked beyond them. The rise of the stairway from the platform of the guards was gradual. About five thousand feet away the park came close to the side of the temple. There was a clump of high trees whose branches almost touched the stairway at that point.

Gigi's rope and grapple! Ah, wise had been the Ninevite, anticipating some such chance. Kenton was lightest of the

121

four—he could climb those trees, drop to the stairway, or if that were not possible, cast the grapple over the wall of it, swing in and climb up the rope and over!

Then he could drop that rope for the three to swarm it. It could be done! And if in such a storm as Sigurd prophesied, with certainty of giving no alarm to the garrison below.

Suddenly he had the sense of being watched. He saw that the space between him and the temple was empty of people; saw an officer of the garrison standing at the base of the steps staring.

Kenton turned; swiftly skirted the street until he was back to the bench. He seated himself on it as he had been before—bent over, face in hands.

And as he sat there some one dropped down beside him.

"What is the matter, sailor?" came a voice, roughly kind. "If you are sick why not go home?"

Kenton spoke huskily, keeping his face covered.

"Too much of Emakhtila wine," he answered. "Leave me be. It will pass."

"Ho!" laughed the other, and gripped an arm about the elbow. "Look up. Better seek home before the tempest breaks."

"No, no," said Kenton, thickly. "Never mind the tempest. Water will help me."

The hand dropped from his arm. For a time, whoever it was beside him, was silent. Then he arose.

"Right, sailor," he said heartily. "Stay here. Stretch out on the bench and sleep a little. The gods be with you!"

"And with you," muttered Kenton. He heard the footsteps of that brief companionship retreating. Cautiously he turned his head, looked in their direction. There were several figures walking there among the trees. One was an old man in a long blue cloak; another an officer dressed like the one who had watched him from the base of the great stairway; a sailor; a hurrying citizen. Which had it been?

The man who had sat beside him had gripped his arm, gripped it where Sharane's bracelet bound! And that officer—the watching soldier of the garrison! Had it been he? Had he been followed?

He sat bolt upright, clapped his right hand on the sleeve of the leather shirt. His hand touched—the bracelet! The sleeve had been slit by a knife to reveal it!

Kenton leaped to his feet—to run. Before he could take a step there was a rustling behind him, a trampling. A heavy cloth was thrown over his head like a bag. Hands clutched his throat. Other hands wound strand after strand of rope around his arms, pinioning them to his sides.

"Take that cloth off his face—but keep your hands around his throat," said a cold dead voice.

His head was freed. He looked straight into the pale eyes of Klaneth!

Then from the double ring of soldiers around him came a gasp of amazement, a movement of terror. An officer stepped forward, stared at him incredulously.

"Mother of the Gods!" he groaned, and knelt at Kenton's feet. "Lord—I did not know——" He leaped up, set knife to his bonds.

"Stop!" Klaneth spoke. "It is the slave! Look again!"

Trembling, the officer studied Kenton's face, lifted the cap veils; swore.

"Gods!" he exclaimed, "but I thought he was——"

"And he is not," interposed Klaneth smoothly. His eyes gloated over Kenton. He reached down into his belt, drew from it the sword of Nabu.

"Hold!" the officer quietly took it from him. "This man is my prisoner until I deliver him to the King. And till then I keep his sword."

The feral light in the pupils of the black priest glowed.

"He goes to Nergal's House," he rumbled. "Best beware, captain, how you cross Klaneth."

"Cross or no cross," replied the officer, "I am the King's man. His orders I obey. And you know as well as I do that he has commanded all prisoners to be brought before him first—no matter what even high priests may say. Besides," he added slyly, "there is that matter of the reward. Best to get this capture a matter of record. The King is a just man."

The black priest stood silent, fingering his mouth. The officer laughed.

"March!" he snapped. "To the temple. If this man escapes—all your lives for his!"

In a triple ring of the soldiers walked Kenton. On one side of him strode the officers; on the other the black priest, gloating gaze never leaving him; Klaneth, licking his merciless lips.

Thus they passed through the wooded park, out into the street and at last through a high archway, and were swallowed up within a gateway of the temple.

19

The Lord Of The Two Deaths

THE KING of Emakhtila, Lord of the Two Deaths, sat, legs crooked, on a high divan. He was very like Old King Cole of the nursery rhyme, even to that monarch's rubicund jollity, his apple round, pippin red cheeks. Merriment shone in his somewhat watery blue eyes. He wore one loose robe of scarlet. His long, white beard, stained here and there with drops of red and purple and yellow wine, wagged roguishly.

The judgment chamber of the King of Emakhtila was some hundred feet square. His divan rested on a platform five feet high that stretched from side to side like a stage. The chequered floor raised in a sharp concave curve to build it. The curved front was cut through by a broad flight of low wide steps ascending from the lower floor and ending about five feet from the divan of the king.

Two and ten archers in belted kirtles of silver and scarlet stood on the lowest step, shoulder to shoulder, bows at stand, arrows at strings, ready on the instant to be raised to ears and loosed. Four and twenty archers knelt at their feet. Six and thirty shafts of death were leveled at Kenton, black priest and the captain.

Out from each side of the steps and along the curved wall to where it met the sides of the chamber another file of bowmen stretched, scarlet and silver, shoulder to shoulder, arrows alert. The twinkling eyes of the king could see the backs of the heads ranged over the edge of his stage like footlights.

Along the other three walls, shoulder to shoulder, arrows at strings, eyes fixed on the King of Emakhtila, ran an unbroken silver and scarlet frieze of archers. They

124

stood silent; tense as automatons tightly wound and waiting for touch upon some hidden spring.

The chamber was windowless. Pale blue tapestries covered all its walls. A hundred lamps lighted it with still, yellow flames.

Twice a tall man's height away from the king's left hand a veiled shape stood, motionless as the bowmen. Even through its thick veils came subtle hints of beauty.

At the same distance from the king's right hand another veiled shape stood. Nor could its veils check hint of horror seeping forth from what they covered.

One shape set the pulses leaping.

One shape checked them.

On the floor, at the king's feet, crouched a giant Chinese with a curved and crimson sword.

Close to each end of the divan stood, fair and young and naked to their waists. Six to this side—six to that. They held ewers filled with wine. At their feet were great bowls of wine, red and purple and yellow, in larger bowls of snow.

At the right hand of the Lord of the Two Deaths knelt a girl with golden cup on outstretched palms. At his left hand another knelt, a golden flagon on her palms. And the king to drink used equally well his left hand and his right, raising cup or flagon, setting them to his lips, putting them back. Whereupon at once they were refilled.

Through many passages the captain and the black priest had hurried Kenton to this place. And now the king drank deep, set down his cup and clapped his hands.

"The King of Emakhtila judges!" intoned the Chinese, sonorously.

"He judges!" whispered the bowmen ranged along the walls.

Kenton, black priest and captain stepped forward until their breasts touched the foremost arrow points. The king leaned, merry eyes twinkling on Kenton.

"What jest is this, Klaneth?" he cried in a high, thin treble. "Or have the Houses of Bel and Nergal declared war upon each other?"

"They are not at war, lord," answered Klaneth. "This is the slave for whom I have offered great reward and whom I now claim since I have taken——"

"Since *I* have taken, Mighty One," interrupted the captain, kneeling as he spoke. "And so have earned Klaneth's reward, O Just One!"

"You lie, Klaneth!" chuckled the king. "If you are not at war why have you trussed up——"

"Look again, lord," interrupted Klaneth. "I do not lie."

The watery eyes peered closer at Kenton.

"No!" laughed the king. "You are right. He is what the other man would be were he half as much a man. Well, well——"

He raised the flagon; before he had half lifted it to his lips he paused and looked into it.

"Half full!" giggled the king. "Only half full!"

He glanced from the flagon to the girl who stood closest to the kneeling girl at his left. His round face beamed on her.

"Insect!" chuckled the king. "You forgot to fill my flagon!"

He raised a finger.

A bow string sang along the left wall, an arrow shrilled. It struck the trembling girl in the shoulder on the right side. She swayed, eyes closed.

"Bad!" the king cried merrily, and again held up a finger.

From the frieze along the right wall another bow string sang; an arrow whistled across the room. The shaft cleft the heart of the first archer. Before his body touched the floor the same bow sang once more.

A second shaft leaped into sight deep within the left side of the wounded girl.

"Good!" laughed the king.

"Our lord has granted death!" chanted the Chinese. "Praise him!"

"Praise him!" echoed the bowmen and the cup maidens.

But Kenton, mad with swift rage at that heartless killing, leaped forward. Instantly the bow strings of the six and thirty archers before him were drawn taut, arrow shafts touched ears. Black priest and captain caught him, threw him down.

The Chinese drew a small hammer and struck the blade of his sword. It rang like a bell. Two slaves came out on the dais and carried the dead girl away. Another girl took her place. The slaves dragged off the dead archer. Another slipped through the curtains and stood where he had been.

"Let him up," crowed the king—and drained his filled flagon.

"Lord—he is my slave." All the black priest's will could not keep the arrogant impatience out of his voice. "He has been brought before you in obedience to your general command. You have seen him. Now I claim my right to take him to his place of punishment."

"Oh-ho!" the king set down his cup, beamed at Klaneth. "Oh-ho! Sh-so you won't let him up? And you will take him away? Oh-ho!

"Toe nail of a rotting flea!" he shrilled. "Am I King of Emakhtila or am I not? Answer me!"

From all around the chamber came the sigh of tight drawn bow strings. Every arrow of the silver and scarlet frieze of bowmen was pointed at the black priest's great body. The captain threw himself down beside Kenton.

"God's!" muttered that shoulder. "Hell take you and the reward. Why did I ever see you!"

The black priest spoke, voice strangled between rage and fear—

"King of Emakhtila you are!"

He knelt. The king waved his hand. The bow strings dropped loose.

"Stand up!" cried the king. The three arose. The King of Emakhtila shook a finger at Kenton.

"Why were you so angered," he chuckled, "by my boon of death to those two? Man—how many times, think you, will you beeseech death to come, and pray for my swift archers before Klaneth is done with you?"

"It was slaughter," said Kenton, eyes steady on the watery ones.

"My cup must be kept filled," answered the king gently. "The girl knew the penalty. She broke my law. She was slain. I am just."

"Our lord is just!" chanted the Chinese.

"He is just!" echoed the archers and the cup maidens.

"The bowman made her suffer when I meant painless death for her. Therefore he was slain," said the king. "I am merciful."

"Our lord is merciful!" chanted the Chinese.

"He is merciful!" echoed the bowmen and the cup maidens.

"Death!" the king's face wrinkled jovially. "Why, man —death is the first of boons. It is the one thing out of

127

which the gods cannot cheat us. It is the one thing that is stronger than the fickleness of the gods. It is the only thing that is man's own. Above the gods, heedless of the gods, stronger than the gods—since even gods in their due time must die!

"Ah!" sighed the king—and for a fleeting instant all King Cole jocundity was gone. "Ah! There was a poet in Chaldea when I dwelt there— a man who knew death and how to write of it. Maldronah, his name. None here knows him———"

And then softly:

> " 'Tis better be dead than alive, he said—
> But best is never to be!"

Kenton listened, interest in this strange personality banishing his anger. He too knew Maldronah of ancient Ur; had run across that very poem from which the king had quoted while going through some of the inscribed clay tablets recovered by Heilprecht in the sands of Nineveh —back in that old life, half forgotten. And involuntarily he spoke the beginning of the last macabresque stanza:

> "Life is a game, he said;
> Its end we know not—nor care,
> And we yawn ere we come to its end———"

"What!" the king cried. "You know Maldronah! You———"

Old King Cole again, he shook with laughter.

"Go on!" he ordered. Kenton felt the bulk of Klaneth beside him tremble with wrath. And Kenton laughed, too —meeting the twinkling eyes of the king; and while the Lord of the Two Deaths beat time with cup and flagon he finished Maldronah's verse, with its curious jigging lilt entangled in slow measure of *marche funerale*:

> "Yet it pleases to play with the snare,
> To skirt the pit, and the peril dare,
> And lightly the gains to spend;
> There's a door that has opened, he said,
> A space where ye may tread—
> But the things ye have seen and the things ye have done,
> What are these things when the race is run

And ye pause at the farthest door?
As though they never had been, he said—
Utterly passed as the pulse of the dead!
Then tread on lightly with nothing to mourn!
Shall he who had nothing fear for the score?
Ah—better be dead than alive, he said—
But best is ne'er to be born!"

Long sat the king in silence. At last he stirred, raised his flagon and beckoned one of the maidens.

"He drinks with me!" he said, pointing to Kenton.

The archers parted; let the cup maiden pass. She stood before Kenton; held the flagon to his lips. He drank deep; lifted head and bowed thanks.

"Klaneth," said the king, "no man who knows Maldronah of Ur is a slave."

"Lord," answered the black priest, stubbornly. "Yet this man is my slave."

The king again sat silent, drinking now from cup and now from flagon; eyes now on Kenton, now at Klaneth.

"Come here," he ordered at last—and pointed with one finger at Kenton, with another at the side of the Chinese.

"Lord!" said Klaneth, more uneasily yet as stubbornly. "My slave stays beside me."

"Does he?" laughed the king. "Ulcer on a gnat's belly! Does he?"

All around the chamber the bow strings sighed.

"Lord," panted Klaneth, with bowed head. "He goes to you."

As he passed him, Kenton heard the black priest's teeth grate; heard him sob as does a man after a long race. And Kenton, grinning, stepped through the opened space of archers; stood before the king.

"Man who knows Maldronah," smiled the king. "You wonder how I, alone, have greater power than these priests and all their gods? Well—it is because in all Emakhtila I am the only one who has neither gods nor superstitions. I am the one man who knows there are only three realities. Wine—which up to a certain point makes man see more clearly than the gods. Power—which being combined with man's cunning makes him superior to the gods. Death—which no god can abolish and which I deal at will."

"Wine! Power! Death!" chanted the Chinese.

"These priests have many gods—each of them jealous

129

of all the others. Ho! Ho!" laughed the king. "I have no gods. Therefore I am just to all. The just judge must be without prejudice; without belief."

"Our lord is without prejudice!" chanted the Chinese.

"He has no beliefs!" intoned the bowmen.

"I am on one side of the scales," nodded the king. "On the other side are many gods and priests. There are only three things that I am sure are real. Wine, power, death! Those who try to outweigh me have beliefs many times three. Therefore I outweigh them. If there were but one god, one belief opposite me—lo, I would be outweighed! Yea—three to one! That is paradox—also it is truth."

"The Lord of Emakhtila speaks truth!" whispered the bowmen.

"Better three straight arrows in your quiver than three-score crooked ones. And if there should arise one man in Emakhtila with but one arrow and that arrow straighter than my three—that man would soon rule in my place," beamed the king.

"Archers—hear ye the king!" chanted the Chinese.

"And so," the king said, briskly, "since all the gods and all the priests are jealous of each other, they make me—who gives not a curse for any god or priest—king of Emakhtila—to keep peace among them and hold them back from destroying each other! And this, since I now have ten bowmen to every one of theirs, and twenty swordsmen to each swordman of the priests, I do very well. Ho! Ho!" laughed the king. "That is power."

"Our lord has power!" cried the Chinese.

"And having power I can get drunk at will," chuckled the king.

"Our lord is drunken!" whispered the archers, all around the chamber.

"Drunken or sober—I am King of the Two Deaths!" tittered the ruler of Emakhtila.

"The Two Deaths!" whispered the archers, nodding to each other.

"To you—man who knows Maldronah—I unveil them," said the king.

"Bowmen at sides and back—bend your heads!" shouted the Chinese. The heads of the archers along three sides of the living frieze dropped immediately upon their breasts.

The veils fell from the shape upon the left hand of the king.

There, looking at Kenton with deep eyes in which were tenderness of the mother, shyness of the maid, passion of the beloved mistress, stood a woman. Her naked body was flawless. In it, harmonies of mother, maid and mistress flowed in one compelling chord. From her breathed all springtides that ever caressed earth. She was the doorway to enchanted worlds, the symbol of everything that life could offer both of beauty and of joy. She was all the sweetnesses of life, its promises, its ecstasies, its lure and its reason. Looking on her Kenton knew that life was something to be held fast. That it was dear and filled with wonders. Exquisite—not to be let go!

And that death was very dreadful!

He had no desire toward her. But she fanned to roaring flame desire for life in full continuance.

In her right hand she held a strangely shaped instrument, long, with sharp fangs and rows of tearing claws.

"To her," chuckled the king, "I give only those whom I greatly dislike. She kills them slowly. Looking upon her, they cling to life; fiercely, terribly they cling to it. Each moment of life that she draws from them with those claws and teeth is an eternity through which they battle against death. Slowly she draws them out of life—wailing, clinging to it, turning stubborn faces from death! And now—look!"

The veils fell from the shape at his right hand.

There crouched a black dwarf, misshapen, warped, hideous. He stared at Kenton out of dull eyes that held every sorrow and sadness and disillusionment of life; held all of life's uselessness, its weariness, its empty labor. And looking at him, Kenton forgot that other shape—knew that life was dreadful, not to be borne.

And that death was the one good thing!

In his right hand the dwarf held a slender sword, rapier thin, needle pointed. Kenton fought increasing desire to hurl himself upon that point—die upon it!

"To him," laughed the king, "I give those who have greatly pleased me. Swift is their death and a sweet cup to their lips."

"You there—" the king pointed to the captain who had trapped Kenton. "Not too pleased am I with you for taking this man who knows Maldronah, even if he be Klaneth's slave. Go up before my left hand death!"

Face bloodless white, the captain marched to the steps;

131

rigid he marched through the archers, marched without pause until he stood before the woman. The Chinese struck his sword. Two slaves entered, heads bent low, carrying a lattice of metal. They stripped the captain of his armor, strapped him naked to the grate. The woman leaned over him, tenderness, love, all life's promise in her wondrous face. She thrust the fanged instrument against his breast—so lovingly!

From his lips came a shrieking, anguished, despairing; prayers and curses; the wailing of the newly damned.

Still the woman leaned over him, smiling, tender, her eyes brooding upon his.

"Let be!" giggled the king. She lifted the thing of torment from the soldier's breast; bent to her veils and threw them over her. The slaves unbound the captain; dressed his shaking body. Sobbing, he staggered back, sank on knees at the black priest's side.

"I am displeased," said the king, merrily. "Yet you did your duty. Therefore—live for a while, since that is your desire. I am just."

"Just is our lord," echoed the chamber.

"You—" he pointed to the archer who had slain cup maiden and a fellow bowman—"I am much pleased with you. You shall have your reward. Come to my right hand death!"

Slowly at first the archer stepped forward. Faster he moved as the dull eyes of the dwarf met his and clung to them. Faster and faster—he raced up the steps, hurling the archers aside and leaped upon the slender sword!

"I am generous," said the king.

"Our lord is generous," intoned the Chinese.

"Generous!" whispered the bowmen.

"I am thirsty," laughed the king. He drank deep from left hand and right. His head nodded; he swayed a bit; quite drunkenly.

"My command!" he opened and closed one twinkling eye after the other. "Hear me, Klaneth! I am sleepy. I will sleep. When I was awaken—bring this man who knows Maldronah to me again. Let no harm come to him before then. It is my command. Also he shall have a guard of bowmen. Take him away. Keep him safe. It is my command!"

He reached for his cup. It dropped from his lax hand.

"By my Deaths!" he whimpered. "What shame that casks can hold so much and man so little!"

He sank upon the divan.

The Lord of the Two Deaths snored.

"Our lord sleeps!" chanted the Chinese, softly.

"He sleeps!" whispered the bowmen and cup maidens.

The Chinese arose, bent over the king. He raised him on his shoulders like a child. The Two Deaths followed him. The two and ten archers upon the lowest step turned, marched up and circled the four. The four and twenty turned, marched and circled them. The bowmen beside the curved wall swung round and six abreast marched up the steps. The living frieze of scarlet and silver swung six by six out from their walls and followed them.

The double ring stepped forward, passed through the curtains at the rear. After them strode the bowmen.

Six fell out of the ranks, ranged themselves beside Kenton.

The cup maidens picked up ewers and bowls. They tripped through the curtains.

One of the six bowmen pointed to the lower floor. Kenton walked down the steps.

Black priest on one side of him, white faced captain on the other, three archers marching before them, three after them, he passed out of the judgment chamber of the king.

20

Behind The Wall

THEY LED Kenton to a narrow room in whose high walls were slitted windows. Its heavy door was solid bronze. Around its sides ran stone benches. In its center was another bench. The bowmen sat him on it, tied his ankles with leathern thongs, threw cloaks on its top and pressed him down upon them. They seated themselves two by two on three sides of the room, eyes fixed on black priest and captain, now ready.

The captain tapped the black priest on the shoulder.

"My reward?" he asked. "When do I get it?"

"When the slave is in my hands and not before," answered Klaneth, savagely, "If you had been—wiser, you would have had it by now."

"Much good it would be doing me, with an arrow through my heart or—" he shuddered—"wailing even now at the feet of the king's left hand death!"

The black priest looked at Kenton evilly; bent over him.

"Put no hope in the king's favor," he muttered. "It was his drunkenness that was speaking. When he awakens he will have forgotten. He will give you to me without question. No hope there!"

"No?" sneered Kenton, meeting the malignant eyes steadily. "Yet twice have I beaten you—you black swine."

"But not a third time," spat Klaneth. "And when the king awakens I will have not only you but that temple drab you love! Ho!" rumbled the black priest as Kenton winced, "that touches you, does it? Yes, I will have you both. And together you shall die—slowly, ah, so slowly, watching each other's agonies. Side by side—side by side until slowly, slowly, my torturers have destroyed the last of your bodies. Nay, the last of your souls! Never before has man or woman died as you two shall!"

"You cannot harm Sharane," answered Kenton. "Carrion eater whose filthy mouth drips lies! She is Bel's preistess and safe from you."

"Ho! You know that do you?" grunted Klaneth; then bent, whispering close to Kenton's ear so softly that no one but him could hear. "Listen—here then is a sweet thought to carry you while I am away. Only while the priestess is faithful to the god is she beyond my reach. Now listen—listen—before the king awakes your Sharane shall have taken another lover! Yea! Your love shall lie in the arms of an earthly lover! And he will not be—you!"

Kenton writhed, striving to break his bonds.

"Sweet Sharane!" whispered Klaneth leering. "Holy Vase of Joy! And mine now to break as I will—while the King sleeps!"

He stepped back to the soldier who had taken Kenton. "Come," he said.

"Not I," answered the soldier, hastily. "By the gods, I prefer this company. Also if I lose sight of this man—I might forever lose sight of that reward you owe me for him."

"Give me his sword," ordered Klaneth, reaching toward the blade of Nabu which the officer had retained.

"The sword goes with the man," answered the captain, setting it behind him; he looked at the archers.

"That is true," the bowmen nodded to each other. "Priest, you cannot have the sword."

Klaneth snarled; his hands flew out. Six bows bent, six arrows pointed at his heart. Without word, the black priest strode out of the cell. An archer arose, dropped into place a bar, sealing the door. A silence fell. The officer brooded; now and then he shivered as though cold, and Kenton knew he was thinking of that Death who with smiling, tender eyes had pressed teeth of torture in his breast. The six bowmen watched him unwinkingly.

And at last Kenton closed his own eyes—fighting to keep back the terror of Klaneth's last threat against his beloved; fighting against despair.

What plot had the black priest set going against her, what trap had he laid, to make him so sure that so soon he would have her in his hands—to break! And where were Gigi and Sigurd and Zubran? Did they know how he had been taken? A great loneliness swept over him.

How long his eyes were closed, or whether he had slept —he never could tell. But he heard as though from infinite distances away a still, passionless voice.

"Arise!" it bade him.

He opened his lids; lifted his head. A priest stood beside him, a priest whose long blue robes covered him from head to foot. Nothing could he see of the priest's face.

He knew that his arms and ankles were free. He sat up. Ropes and thongs lay on the floor. On the stone benches the bowmen leaned one against the other asleep. The officer was asleep.

The priest pointed to his sword, the sword of Nabu lying across the sleeping soldier's knees. Kenton took it. The priest pointed to the bar that held the door. Kenton lifted it and swung the door open. The blue priest glided through the doorway, Kenton close behind.

The blue priest drifted along the corridor for a hundred paces or so and then pressed against what, to Kenton's sight, was a blank wall. A panel opened. Now they stood in a long corridor, dimly lighted. Along it they went in a great curve. It came to Kenton that this hidden passage followed the huge arc of the temple, that it ran behind the temple's outer wall.

Now a massive bronze door closed the way. The blue priest seemed only to touch it. Yet it swung open; it closed behind them.

Kenton stood in a crypt some ten feet square. At one end was the massive door through which he had come; at the other was a similar one. At his left was a ten-foot slab of smooth, pallid stone.

The blue priest spoke—if indeed it were he speaking, since the passionless, still voice Kenton heard seemed, like that which had bidden him arise, to come from infinite distance.

"The mind of the woman you love—sleeps!" it said, "She is a woman walking in dream—moving among dreams that another mind has made for her. Evil creeps upon her. It is not well to let that evil conquer—Yet the issue rests on you—on your wisdom, your strength, your courage. When your wisdom tells you it is the time— open that farther door. Your way lies through it. And remember—her mind sleeps. You must awaken it—before the evil leaps upon her."

Something tinkled on the floor. At Kenton's feet lay a little wedge shaped key. He stooped to pick it up. As he raised his head he saw the blue priest beside the far door.

The blue priest seemed but a wisp of wind-drawn smoke that, even as he looked, faded through the bronze and vanished!

Kenton heard the murmur of many voices, muffled, vague. He slipped from door to door, listening. The voices were not within the passage. They seemed to seep through the slab of pallid smooth stone. He placed an ear against it. The sounds came to him more distinctly, but still he could distinguish no words. The stone must be exceedingly thin here, he thought, that he could hear at all. He saw at his right a little shining lever. He drew it down.

A three-foot wide, misty disc of light began to glow within the stone. It seemed to eat through the stone; it flashed out dazzlingly. Where the disc had been was a circular opening, a window. Silhouetted against it were the heads of a woman and two men. Their voices came now as clearly to his ears as though they stood beside him; over them came the wavelike murmur of a multitude. He drew

136

back, fearing to be seen. The little lever snapped back into place. The window faded; with its fading the voices muted. He stared again at the smooth, pale wall.

Slowly he drew down the lever; once more he watched the apparent burning out of the solid stone; saw the three heads reappear. He had his free hand over the visible wall to the edge of the circle; higher he lifted it, into the disc itself. And ever he touched cold stone. Even that which was to his eyes an opening was to the questing fingers—stone!

He understood—this was some device of the sorcerers—the priests. A device to give them a peeping place, a listening post, within the crypt. Some knowledge of the properties of light not yet learned by the science of Kenton's own world, control of a varying vibration that made the rock transparent from within but not from without. Whatever the secret, the stone was made as porous to the aerial waves of sound as to the etheric waves of light.

Keeping his grip upon the handle, Kenton peered out between the heads and over the shoulders of those so close to and still so unconscious of him.

21

Before The Altar Of Bel

THE MISTS had lifted. They had become dense lurid clouds pressing down almost upon the top of the Zoned Temple. In front of him was a huge court paved with immense octagons of black and white marble. Trooping down upon this court like a forest of faëry, halting in a wide semicircle around it, were hosts of slender pillars, elfin shafts all gleaming red and black whose tapering tops were crowned with carven, lace-tipped fronds glistening like gigantic ferns wet with dew of diamonds and sapphires. Upon the black and scarlet columns shone mysterious symbolings in gold and azure, in emerald and vermilion and silver. In halted myriads these pillars reached up toward the sullen, smouldering sky.

Hardly a hundred feet away was a golden altar, guarded by crouching Kerubs, man-headed, eagle-winged, lion-bodied, carven from some midnight metal. They watched at each corner of the altar with cruel, bearded faces set between paws and as alert as though alive. From the tripod on the altar a single slender crimson flame lifted, lance tipped and motionless.

In a vast crescent, a dozen yards in the van of the columns stood a double ring of bowmen and spearmen. They held back a multitude; men and women and children pouring out of the ordered grove of pillars and milling against the soldiers like wind driven leaves against a well. Score upon score of men and women and children plucked from their own times and set down in this timeless world.

"The new priestess—they say she is very beautiful?" One of the men in front of Kenton had spoken. He was thin, white faced, a Phrygian cap over his lank hair. The woman was of a bold and blown comeliness, black tressed, black eyed. The man at her right was an Assyrian, bearded, wolf visaged.

"She was a princess, they say," the woman spoke. "They say she was a princess in Babylon."

"Princess in Babylon!" echoed the Assyrian, wolf face softening, homesickness in his voice—"Oh, to be back in Babylon!"

"The Priest of Bel loves her—so they say," the woman broke the silence.

"The priestess?" whispered the Phrygian; the woman nodded. "But that is forbidden," he muttered. "It is—death!" The woman laughed again.

"Hush!" it was the Assyrian, cautioning.

"And Narada—the God's Dancer—loves the Priest of Bel!" the woman went on, unheeding. "And so—as always one must speed to Nergal!"

"Hush!" whispered the Assyrian.

There was a rumbling ruffle of drums, the sweet piping of a flute. Kenton sought the sounds. His gaze rested on half a score of temple girls. Five crouched beside little tambours upon whose heads rested their rosy thumbs; two held to red lips pierced reeds; three bent over harps. Within their circle lay what at first seemed to him a mound of shimmering spider web spun all of threads of jet, in which swarms of golden butterflies were snared. The mound quivered, lifted.

138

The sable silken strands had meshed a woman, a woman so lovely that for a heartbeat Kenton forgot Sharane. Dark she was, with the velvety darkness of the midsummer night; her eyes were pools of midnight skies in which shone no stars; her hair was mists of tempests snared in nets of silken gold. Sullen indeed was that gold, and in all of her something sullen that menaced the more because of its sweetness.

"There is a woman!" the bold eyes turned to the Assyrian. "She'll have what she wants—my bed on it!"

There came a voice from beside her, wistful, dreamy, worshipping:

"Ah, yes! But the new priestess—she is no woman! She is Ishtar!"

Kenton craned his neck, looking for the speaker. He saw a youth, hardly more than nineteen, saffron robed and slight. His eyes and face were those of a beautiful dreaming child.

"He is half mad," the dark woman whispered to the Assyrian. "Ever since the new priestess came, he haunts this place."

"We are going to have a storm. The sky is like a bowl of brass," muttered the Phrygian. "The air is frightened."

The Assyrian answered:

"They say Bel comes to his house in the storm. Perhaps the priestess will not be alone tonight."

The woman laughed, slyly. Kenton felt desire to take her throat in his hands. There came a low clashing of thunder.

"Perhaps that is he, rising," said the woman, demurely.

There was a throbbing of the harp-strings, a complaining from the tambours. A dancing girl sang softly:

> "Born was Nala for delight,
> Never danced there feet so white;
> Every heart on which she trod.
> Dying owned her heel its god;
> Loose her girdle day or night—
> Born was Nala for delight!"

The brooding eyes of Narada flashed angrily.

"Be quiet!" Kenton heard her whisper. There was a ripple of laughter among the girls; the two with the pipes trilled them softly; the drums murmured. But she who had sung sat silent over her harp with downcast eyes.

The Phrygian asked:

"Is this priestess then really so beautiful?"

The Assyrian said:

"I do not know. No man has ever seen her unveiled."

The youth whispered:

"When she walks I tremble! I tremble like the little blue lake of the temple when the breeze walks on it! Only my eyes live, and something grips my throat."

"Peace!" a brown eyed girl with kindly face and babe in arms spoke. "Not so loud—or it will be a bowstring."

"She is no woman! She is Ishtar! Ishtar!" cried the youth.

The soldiers nearby turned. Through them strode a grizzled officer, short sword in hand. Before his approach the others drew back; only the youth stood motionless. Right and left the sword carrier peered beneath bushy brows. Ere he could fix gaze on the youth a man in sailor's cap and tunic of mail had walked between the two, gripped the youth's wrist, held him hidden behind him. Kenton caught a glimpse of agate eyes, black beard——

It was Zubran!

Zubran! But would he pass on? Could Kenton make him hear if he called? If his body could not be seen from without, could his voice penetrate the stone?

The sword bearer scanned the silent group, uncertainly. The Persian saluted him gravely.

"Silence here!" grunted the officer at last, and passed back among his men.

The Persian grinned; pushed the youth from him; stared at the dark woman with eyes bolder than her own. He jostled the Phrygian from his place; laid a hand upon the woman's arm.

"I was listening," he said. "Who is this priestress? I am newly come to this land and know nothing of its customs. Yet by Ormuzd!" he swore and dropped his arm around the woman's shoulders. "It was worth the journey to meet *you!* Who is this priestess that you say is so beautiful?"

"She is the keeper of Bel's Bower," the woman nestled close to him.

"But what does she there?" asked Zubran. "Now if it were—you—I could understand without asking. And why does she come here?"

"The priestess lives in Bel's Bower upon the top of the temple," the Assyrian spoke. "She comes here to worship at his altar. When her worship is done she returns."

"For such beauty as you say is hers," remarked Zubran, "her world seems small indeed. Why, if she is so beautiful, is she content to dwell in so small a world?"

"She is the god's," answered the Assyrian. "She is the keeper of his house. If the god entered he might be hungry. There must be food for him in his house and a woman to serve it. Of he might be amor——"

"And so there must be a woman there," interrupted the bold eyed wench, smiling up at him.

"We have something like that in my country," the Persian drew her closer. "But the priestesses seldom wait alone. The priests see to that—Ho! Ho!"

God! Would Zubran never come close enough to the wall? So close that Kenton might call to him? And yet— if he did! Would not those others hear him also——? And then——

"Have any of these priestesses who—wait—" Zubran's voice purred—"Have any of these waiting priestesses ever —ah, entertained—the god?"

The youth spoke: "They say the doves speak to her— the doves of Ishtar! They say she is more beautiful than Ishtar!"

"Fool!" whispered the Assyrian. "Fool, be still! Will you bring bad luck upon us? No woman can be more beautiful than Ishtar!"

"No woman can be more beautiful than Ishtar," sighed the youth. "Therefore she is—Ishtar!"

The Phrygian said: "He is mad!"

But the Persian stretched out his right arm, drew the youth to him.

"Have any of these priestesses ever held the god?" he asked.

"Wait," murmured the woman. "I will ask Narodach the archerer. He comes sometimes to my house. He knows. He has seen many priestesses." she held the Persian's arm fast about her girdle, leaned forward—"Narodach! Come to me!"

An archer turned; whispered to the men on each side of him; slipped from between them. They closed up behind him.

"Narodach," asked the woman. "Tell us—have any of the priestesses ever held—Bel?"

The archer hesitated, uneasily.

"I do not know," slowly he answered at last. "They tell many tales. Yet *are* they but tales? When first I came here there was a priestess in Bel's house. She was like the crescent moon of our old world. Many men desired her."

"Ho, archer," rumbled the Persian. "But did she—hold the god?"

Narodach said: "I do not know. They said so—they said that she had been withered by his fires. The wife of the charioteer of the Priest of Ninib told me that her face was very old when they took away her body. She was a date tree that had withered before it had borne fruit, she said."

"If I were a priestess—and so beautiful—I would not wait for a god!" the woman's eyes clung to Zubran. "I would have a man. Yea—I would have many men!"

"There was another who followed," said the archer. "She said the god had come to her. But she was mad—and being mad, the priests of Nergal took her."

"Give me men, I say!" whispered the woman.

Said Narodach the archer musing: "One there was who threw herself from the Bower. One there was who vanished One there was——"

The Persian interrupted: "It seems that these priestesses who wait for Bel are not—fortunate."

Said the woman with intense conviction:

"Give me—men!"

There was a nearer clashing of thunder. In the lurid, ever-darkening sky, the clouds began a slow churning.

"There will be a great storm," muttered the Phrygian.

The girl Narada had rebuked thrummed against her harp strings; she sang half maliciously, half defiantly:

> "Every heart that sought a nest,
>   Flew straightway to Nala's breast—
>   Born was Nala for delight——"

She checked her song. From afar came the faint sound of chanting; the tread of marching feet. Bowman and spearmen raised bows and spears in salute. Behind them the milling multitudes dropped to their knees. The Persian drew close to the wall. And his was now the only head in the circular window whose pane was stone.

"Zubran!" called Kenton, softly.

The Persian turned startled face to the wall, then leaned against it, cloak tight around his face.

"Wolf!" he whispered. "Are you safe? Where are you?"

"Behind the wall," whispered Kenton. "Speak softly."

"Are you hurt? In chains?" muttered the Persian.

"I am safe," answered Kenton. "But Gigi—Sigurd?"

"Searching for you," the Persian said. "Our hearts have been well-nigh broken——"

"Listen," said Kenton. "There is a clump of trees—close to the stairway above the garrison——"

"We know," answered Zubran. "It is from them we make the steps and scale the temple. But you——"

"I will be in the Bower of Bel," said Kenton. "Soon as the storm breaks—go there. If you do not find me—take Sharane, carry her back to the ship. I will follow."

"We will not go without you," whispered Zubran.

"I hear a voice speaking through the stone." It was the Assyrian, kneeling. Zubran dropped from Kenton's sight.

The chanting had grown louder; the marching feet were close. Then from some secret entrance of the temple there swept out into the open space a company of archers and a company of swordsmen. Behind them paced as many shaven, yellow robed priests, swinging smoking golden censers and chanting as they walked. The soldiers formed a wide arc before the altar. The priests were silent upon a somber chord. They threw themselves flat on the ground.

Into the great court strode a single figure, tall as Kenton himself. A robe of shining gold covered him and a fold of this he held on raised left arm, completely covering his face.

"The Priest of Bel!" whispered the kneeling woman.

There was a movement among the temple girls. Narada had half risen. Never had there been such yearning, such bittersweet desire as that in her midnight eyes as the Priest of Bel passed her, unheeding. Her slender fingers gripped the cobwebs that meshed her; their webs were lifted by the swelling breast of her; shuddered with the sighs that shook her.

The Priest of Bel reached the golden altar. He dropped the arm that held the shrouding fold. And then Kenton's stiff fingers almost loosed the shining lever.

He looked, as in a mirror, into his own face!

143

22

How Narada Danced

BREATHLESSLY Kenton stared at this strange twin. There was the same square jaw, firm-lipped dark face, the same clear blue eyes.

His mind groped toward the black priest's plot. Was this to be—Sharane's lover? Some flash of understanding half illumined his mind—too brief to be more than half caught. It left him groping again.

Through the stone he heard the Persian cursing. Then——

"Wolf, are you behind me?" he muttered. "Are you truly behind me, Wolf?"

"Yes," he whispered. "I am here, Zubran. That is not I! It is some sorcery."

His gaze flew back to the Priest of Bel; began now to take note of subtle differences in their two faces. The lips were not so firm, the corners of the mouth drew down, there was hint of indecision about them and the chin. And the eyes were strained, shadowed with half wild, half agonized longing. Silent, tense, the Priest of Bel stared over the lifted head of Narada, her lithe body as rigid as his own, unheeding her, intent upon that hidden portal through which he had come.

The lanced, crimson flame upon the altar flickered; swayed.

"The gods guard us!" he heard the bold-eyed woman say.

"Be silent! What is the matter?" said the Assyrian.

The woman whispered: "Did you see the Kerubs? They glared at the priest! They moved toward him!"

The woman with the babe said: "I saw it! I am frightened!"

The Assyrian said: "It was the light on the altar. It flickered."

Said the Phrygian low: "Perhaps it was the Kerubs. Are

144

they not Bel's messengers? Did you not say the priest loved Bel's woman?"

"Silence there!" rang the voice of the officer from behind the double ring. The priests began a low chanting. In the eyes of the priest a fire began to glow; his lips quivered; his body bent forward as though drawn by an unseen cord. Across the wide place walked a woman—alone. She was cloaked from neck to feet in purple; her head was swathed in golden veils.

Kenton knew her!

His heart leaped toward her; his blood raced. He quivered under such shock of longing that it seemed as though his leaping heart must break beneath it.

"Sharane!" he called, forgetting; and again—"Sharane!"

She glided through the opened ranks of the men-at-arms kneeling to her as she passed. Straight to the altar she paced and stood silent, motionless beside the Priest of Bel.

There was a louder rolling of the metallic thunder. As it died away the priest turned to the altar, lifted his hands high. From his attendants droned a long, sustained humming upon a single deep note. Up and out swept the priest's arms; seven times he bowed low before the crimson flame. He stood upright. Down upon their knees dropped archers and spearmen; with a rustling of bows, a muffled beating of spear shafts.

Still to that weird humming the Priest of Bel began his invocation:

> "Oh merciful among the gods!
> O bullnecked among the gods!
> Bel Merodach, king of the heavens and the worlds!
> Heavens and earths are thine!
> Breather of life art thou!
> Thy house is prepared for thee!
> We worship and await."

Kenton heard a whisper—tremulous, golden—"I worship and await!"

Sharane's voice! The golden voice of Sharane playing upon every taut nerve of him like myriads of little fingers over stretched harp strings!

Again the Priest of Bel:

> "O begetter! O self-begotten!

145

O beautiful one who givest life to the babe!
O merciful one who givest life to the dead!
King art thou of Ezida! Lord of Emakhtila!
A resting place for the King of Heaven is thy house!
A resting place for the Lord of Worlds is thy house!
We worship and await thee!"

And once more Sharane—tremulous—"I worship and await Thee!" The priest intoned:

"Lord of the Silent Weapon!
Look favorably on thy house, O Lord of Rest!
May Ezida speak peace to thee in thy house!
May Emakhtila speak rest to thee in thy house!
We worship and await thee!"

And again Sharane: "I worship and await Thee!"
Now Kenton saw the priest make toward the altar a gesture in which lurked an inexplicable defiance. He turned and faced Sharane. His voice rang loudly, jubilantly:

"Full of delight is thy supremacy!
Opener of the lock of morning art thou!
Opener of the lock of evening art thou!
To open the lock of the Heavens is thy supremacy!
I worship and await thee!"

At the first words the humming of the priests ceased; Kenton saw them stir, glance at each other uncertainly; saw a ripple pass through kneeling soldiers and worshippers as their heads raised; heard murmuring, astonished, uneasy.

Beneath him the kneeling Assyrian muttered: "That was not in the ritual!"

The Persian asked: "What was not in the ritual?"

The woman said: "That the priest cried last. It is not Bel's. It belongs to Our Lady Ishtar!"

The youth whispered: "Yes! Yes—he knows her too! She is Ishtar!"

The woman with the babe sobbed: "Did you see the Kerubs stretch their claws? I am frightened. I am frightened, and it is not good for the child's milk. The light on the altar is like spilled blood!"

146

Said the Assyrian, uneasily: "I do not like it! It was not of Bel's ritual! And the storm is coming fast!"

Narada arose, abruptly. Her handmaids bent over drums and harps; set their pipes to lips. A soft and amorous theme beat up from them, delicate, clinging—like the beating of the wings of countless doves, the clinging of countless little soft arms, the throbbing of countless little rosy hearts. Under it the body of Narada swayed like a green reed at the first touch of roving winds of spring. The multitude looked, sighed once and was still.

But Kenton saw that the priest's eyes never left Sharane, standing like a woman asleep beneath her veils.

Louder the music sounded; quicker, throbbing with all love longing, laden with all passion; hot as the simoon. To it, as though her body drank in each calling, imperious note, turned it into motion, made it articulate in flesh, Narada began to dance.

In the midnight eyes that had been so sorrowful, many little leaping joyous stars danced. The scarlet mouth was a luring, honeysweet flame promising unknown raptures; and the swarms of golden butterflies meshed within her gossamer nets of jet hovered, swept down, clung to and caressed the rose and pearl of her body as though she were some wondrous flower. They were clouds of golden butterflies darting upon her, covering with kisses all her loveliness, gleaming within the cloudy nets that swirled about her, yet hiding no single exquisite contour. Maddening, breathless, grew dance and music, and in music and dance Kenton watched mating stars, embracing suns, moons swollen with birth. Gathered in them he sensed all passion, all desire of all women under stars and suns and moons. . . .

The music slowed, softened; the dancer was still; from all the multitude a soft sighing arose. He heard Zubran, his voice hoarse:

"Who is that dancer? She is like a flame! She is like the flame that dances before Ormuzd on the Altar of Ten Thousand Sacrifices!"

The woman jealously: "She danced the wooing of Bel by Ishtar. She has danced it many times. Nothing new in that."

The Phrygian said, maliciously: "He asked who she is?"

The woman said, spitefully: "Gods! That dance is no new thing, I tell you. Many women have danced it."

The Assyrian said: "She is Narada. She belongs to Bel."

The Persian said wrathfully: "Are all the fair women in this country Bel's? By the Nine Hells—Cyrus the King would have given ten talents of gold for her!"

"Hush!" whimpered the Assyrian; and the other two echoed him—"Hush!"

Narada had begun once more to dance. The music grew louder. But now it was languourous; dripping sweetness; distilling the very dew of desire.

The blood hammered hot in Kenton's veins——

"She dances the surrender of Ishtar to Bel!" It was the Assyrian, gloating.

The Persian stood upright.

"Aie!" he cried. "Cyrus would have given fifty talents of gold for her! She is a flame!" cried Zubran, and his voice was thick, clogged. "And if she is Bel's—why then does she look so upon the priest?"

None heard him in the roaring of the multitude; soldiers and worshippers, none of them had eyes or ears for anything but the dancer.

Nor had Kenton!

Then witchery of the midnight woman was gone; raging at himself he beat against the stone. For the tranquillity of Sharane had broken. Her white hand thrust aside the shrouding purple folds. She turned; moved swiftly away toward that hidden entrance from which she had come.

The dancer stopped; the music died; again came the uneasy movement of the multitude; a louder murmuring.

"That was not in the ritual!" The Assyrian sprang to his feet. "The dance is not yet finished."

There was a clashing of thunder almost overhead.

"She grows impatient for the god," the woman said, cynically.

"She is Ishtar! She is the moon hiding her face behind a little cloud!" The youth took a step toward the men-at-arms guarding the priestess.

The bold-eyed woman arose, caught his arm; spoke to the soldiers.

"He is mad! He lives at my house. Do not hurt him! I will take him away!"

But the youth broke away from her; thrust her aside. He darted through the guards and raced across the square to meet the advancing priestess. He threw himself at her hurrying feet. He hid his face in the hem of her cloak.

148

She paused, regarding him through her veils. Instantly Bel's priest was at her side. He thrust a foot against the youth's face; sent him rolling a yard away.

"Ho! Alrac! Druchar! Take this man!" he shouted. Two officers came running to him, swords drawn; the attendant priests clustered, whispering; all the multitude was silent.

The youth twisted, sprang upon his feet, faced the priestess.

"Ishtar!" he cried. "Show me your face. Then let me die!"

She stood silent, as though she neither heard nor saw. The soldiers seized him, drew back his arms. And then, visibly, strength flowed into the youth's slight frame. He seemed to expand, to grow in height. He threw the soldiers from him; he struck the Priest of Bel across the eyes. He gripped the veils of the priestess.

"I will not die until I see your face, O Ishtar!" he cried—and so crying tore the veils away. . . .

Kenton looked upon the face of Sharane.

But not the Sharane of the ship—vital, filled with the fire of life.

Here was a Sharane of wide, unseeing eyes; upon whose white brows dream sat throned; a mind that floated through linked labyrinths of illusion.

The Priest of Bel's voice shrilled:

"Slay that man!"

The swords of the two captains bit through the youth's breast.

He fell, still holding tight the veils. Sharane looked down upon him, unconcerned.

"Ishtar!" he gasped. "I have seen you—Ishtar!"

His eyes glazed. Sharane tore the veils from his stiffening hands; threw the tattered remnants over her face. She swept on to the temple—was gone from Kenton's straining sight.

From the multitude a clamor arose. Archers and spearmen began to push back the throng through the forest of the slender, lacquered pillars; sifted among them; vanished with those they herded. Past the Priest of Bel went his soldiers and acolytes; and after them slipped the harpers, the pipers and the drum girls of Narada.

Within that vast court circled by the elfin shafts remained only dancer and priest. The lurid sky darkened steadily. The slow, churning movement of the clouds had become more rapid. The lanced flame on the altar of Bel shone brighter—angrily; like a lifted, scarlet sword. Around the crouching Kerubs the shadows thickened. The metallic thundering had become continuous, marching closer.

With the passing of Sharane, Kenton would have opened that other door of bronze. Something counselled him that the time had not yet come; that a little longer he must wait. And as he waited dancer and priest drifted to that strange window through which he peered.

Close to him they paused.

PART V
Dancer and Priest

23

"BEL should be pleased with his worship, priest!" Kenton heard the dancer say.

The priest asked, dully: "What do you mean?"

Narada drew closer to him; her hands fluttered out to him.

"Shalamu," she whispered. "Did I dance for the god? You know I danced for—you. And whom did you worship, Shalamu? The god? No—the priestess. And whom, think you, did she worship?"

"She worshipped Bel! Our Lord Bel who has—all," the priest answered, bitterly.

Said the dancer, mockingly: "She worshipped herself, Shalamu!"

He repeated, stubbornly, wearily: "She worshipped Bel."

Closer came Narada, touched him with fluttering, yearning hands.

"Does any woman worship a god, Shalamu?" she asked. "Ah—no! I am a woman—and I know. This priestess would be a god's woman—no man's. She holds herself too high, too precious, for man. She loves herself. She worships herself. She would bow down to herself as a god's woman. Women make gods of men and then love them. But no woman loves any god she has not made, Shalamu!"

The priest said, sullenly: "Well—I worshipped her!"

The dancer said: "As she worshipped—herself! Shalamu —does she long to give joy to Bel? To our Lord Bel who has Ishtar? Can we give joy to the gods—to the gods who have all? The lotus rises to the sun—but is it to give joy to the sun that she rises? No! It is to give joy to herself. So the priestess! I am a woman—and I know."

Her hands were on his shoulders; he took them in his own: "Why do you say these things to me?"

"Shalamu!" she murmured. "Look in my eyes. Look on my mouth—my breasts. Like the priestess I am the god's. But I give myself to you—beloved!"

He said, dreamily: "Yea—you are beautiful!"

Her arms were round his neck, her lips close to his.

"Do I love the god?" she whispered. "When I dance is it to delight his eyes? It is for you I dance—beloved. It is for you I dare Bel's wrath——" Softly she drew his head down on her breast—"Am I not fair? Fairer than this priestess who is Bel's and worships herself nor will ever give herself to you? Are not my perfumes pleasing? No god possesses me—beloved!"

Dreamily he answered her again: "Yea—you are very fair."

"I love you—Shalamu!"

He thrust her from him: "Her eyes are like the Pools of Peace in the Valley of Forgetfulness! When she comes near me the doves of Ishtar beat their wings above my head! She walks upon my heart!"

Narada drew back, scarlet lips pale, brows a menacing straight line:

"The priestess?"

"The priestess," he answered. "Her hair is like the cloud that veils the sun at dusk. The wave of her robe scorches me as the wind from the desert noon scorches the palm. The wave of her robe makes me cold as the wind of the desert night makes cold the palm."

She said:

"That youth was bolder far than you, Shalamu."

Kenton saw the red rush through the priest's face.

"What do you mean?" he snarled.

"Why did you have the youth slain?" coldly as before come her voice.

He answered, hotly: "He did sacrilege. He——"

She stopped him, contemptuously: "Because he was

bolder than you. Because he dared to tear the veils from her. Because you knew yourself the coward. This is why you had him slain!"

His hands twitched to her throat: "You lie! You lie! I would dare!"

Again she laughed: "You did not even dare to slay him—yourself!"

His hands were at her throat; she thrust them carelessly aside.

"Coward!" she said. "He dared to lift the veil from what he loved. He dared the wrath both of Ishtar and of Bel!"

The priest cried brokenly: "Would I not dare? Do I fear death? Do I fear Bel?"

Her eyes mocked him.

"Hai! You love so greatly!" she taunted. "The priestess awaits the god—in his lonely house! Perhaps he is not in the storm! Perchance he tarries with another maid—Oh, fearless one! Bold lover—take his place!"

He shrank back from her.

"Take—his—place!" he whispered.

"You know where the armor of the god is hidden. Go to her as the god!" she said.

For a long moment the priest stood, quivering. Then Kenton saw irresolution fly; decision take its place. He strode to the altar—down went the lanced flame; wavered; died. In the sudden dark the crouching Kerubs seemed monstrously to take wing.

There came a flash of the weird lightning.

By its irised flare he saw the Priest of Bel passing swiftly along that way Sharane had come and gone; saw Narada lying huddled in her nets of jet, the sipping flocks of golden butterflies at rest upon her; heard a low, heartbroken wailing.

Slowly Kenton's hand began to slip from the lever. Now was the time to use that key, pass on where the blue priest had pointed. His hand froze upon the lever.

A shadow, blacker than the dusk without, had passed the window; stood over the dancer; a huge and unwieldly bulk—familiar.

Klaneth!

"Good!" rumbled the black priest, and touched her with his foot. "Now soon neither he nor Sharane shall

153

trouble you more. And you have well earned that reward I promised you."

Narada looked up at him with white and piteous face, stretched shaking hands out to him.

"If he had loved me," she wailed, "never would he have gone. If he had loved me but a little—never would I have let him go. But he angered me—he shamed me, throwing back to me the love I offered him. Not for you, black snake, despite our bargain, did I send him to her—and to death!"

The black priest stared at her, then laughed.

"Whatever your reason—you sent him," he said. "And Klaneth pays his debts."

He dropped a handful of flashing jewels into her outstretched palms. She screamed, opened fingers as though the gems burned her; they fell and rolled about the chequered stones.

"If he had loved me! If he had loved me but a little!" sobbed Narada—and crouched again, a huddled heap, among her butterflies.

Kenton, to him now clear all the black priest's plot, let the lever go; raced to the farther door of bronze, thrust the wedged key into it; slipped past the slowly opening edge, and ran down the passageway it had barred. Two flames burned in him as he raced along that passage—white flame of love for his woman, black flame of hate against Klaneth. He knew that wherever the Priest of Bel was bound there must be Sharane. The end—unless Kenton could reach the Bower of Bel in time and conquer—inevitable.

Narada had repeated—but too late! The black priest had gambled—and the black priest had won!

Kenton cursed as he ran. If Sharane, meshed in ensorcelled dream, saw the Priest of Bel as the god himself —still would she have taken earthly lover! Her innocence could not save her. Klaneth would see to that.

And if Sharane should awaken—God! Would she not in the dawn of that awakening take the Priest of Bel for him—for Kenton!

But either way—the presence of priest and priestess in Bel's Bower would be enough to damn them both. Yes— Klaneth would see to that.

He crossed a traverse passage: ran blindly down a sloping corridor along whose sides glared guarding chimeræ;

stopped in front of a wide portal from which hung, motionless and rigid, folds that seemed carved from solid silver. Caution whispered to him; he put out a hand, parted the metallic curtainings, peered within. . . .

He looked into his own room.

There it lay before him, his old room in his old world!

He saw the jeweled ship, glimmering, glittering—but as though he saw it through a fog; through a mist of fiery particles, half veiling it. The long mirror glinted behind that same luminous vapor. Infinitely small, in infinite numbers, the sparkling atoms hung between him and that room of his—back in New York!

And he—here in this strange world!

Misty was the room, nebulous, quivering now into plainer sight; now withdrawing into indefiniteness.

And as he stared at it, incredulous, the old bleak despair clutching him, he felt within his hands the curtains grow light as silken gauze, stiffen back into metal—alternately; slip from his hands, strengthen within them as his room steadied in the sparkling mist, dissolved within it into phantom outlines!

Yet ever as his room swung inward clearer, swung back dimmer, the outlines of the jeweled ship hardened, crystallized, shone forth brighter—summoning him, dragging him back!

24

The Gods—And Man's Desire

KENTON braced himself; he held tight to the curtains. He fought with all his will to check their melting. The curtains were like bars between his old world and this of his great adventure.

A force, a pull like a strong undertow, dragged him forward each time they melted in his hands and the nebulous outlines of his room crisped into steadiness. Plainly he could pick out every detail of that room, the long mirror, the cabinets, the divan—the stains of his blood still wet upon the floor.

And always, whether room were melting mist or clear outline, the jeweled ship shining steadily—watchful.

Now he swung out and over that room; the ancient Chinese rug on its floor was below him—at once close and infinite distances away. He heard the first voices of those shrieking winds of space!

In that brief instant he realized that it was the shining toy itself drawing him back!

Something was reaching up and out to him from the dark deck of the ship! Something malignant and mocking —dragging him, dragging him to it!

Darker grew the black deck—stronger its pull——

"Ishtar!" he prayed, gaze upon the rosy cabin. "Ishtar!" Did the cabin flash as though filled with sudden light?"

The outlines of his room melted; again the curtains were heavy in his hands; he stood once more on firm feet at the threshold of the House of the Moon God.

Once, twice, thrice more the room pulled back—but each time less real, more spectral. And against each pulse Kenton set his will; closed eyes and thrust away the vision of it with all his strength.

His will won. The room vanished; in that envanishment a finality not to be mistaken. The spell was broken, the subtle links snapped.

Caught by the reaction he clung to the curtains, knees weak and shaking. Slowly he found himself, resolutely parted the folds.

He looked now into a vast hall filled with mist of argent light; still was this mist, yet palpable—as though the rays that formed it were woven. Interlaced and luminous, the webbed mist made of the chamber a home of immensities, of tremendous distances. He thought, but was not sure, that there was motion within these silver webs—shadowy shapes half appearing, vanishing, never quite coming into full sight. Far away he caught another movement; a figure was coming forward; steadily, inexorably. It drew closer, slowly; it swam into sight—a man, golden-helmeted, over his shoulder a short cloak of gold shot through with scarlet, in his hand a golden sword; head bent, pushing on as though against some strong current.

It was the Priest of Bel clad in the raiment of his god!

Scarce breathing, Kenton watched him. The eyes so like his own were black with dread and awe—yet filled with will and purpose; indomitable. The mouth was set, the lips white, and in all the priest's body Kenton sensed a tremor, a shuddering—deep as the priest's soul. Whether real or but phantoms, he knew the terrors of this place were realities to this strange double of his.

The Priest of Bel passed, and Kenton, waiting until he was half hidden in the shining mists, slipped through the curtains, followed him.

Now Kenton heard a voice; a still voice, passionless as that which had bidden him arise from his bed of stone; and like that voice neither was it in the place wherein he trod nor within him. It was as though borne to him out of farthest space . . .

The voice of Nabu, God of Wisdom!

Listening, he felt himself not one man, but three—a single purposed Kenton who followed the priest and would follow him through hell so he led to Sharane; a Kenton who, tied by some inexplicable link to the mind of the priest, felt and saw and heard, suffered and feared even as he; and a Kenton who hearkened to the words of Nabu as coldly, as dispassionately as they were uttered, watched as coldly, as detachedly, all they pictured.

"The House of Sin!" the voice rang. "Chief of the Gods! Nannar! Begetter of Gods and men! Lord of the Moon! Lord of the Brilliant Crescent! Great of Horns! Nannar Perfect of Form! Decreer of Destiny! Self Created! Whose House is the first of the Zones and Whose Color is Silver!

"He passes through the House of Sin!

"He goes by the altars of chalcedon and of sard which are set with the great moonstones and with rock crystals, the altars where burn the white flames from which Sin the Fashioner created Ishtar! He sees the pale and shining serpents of Nannar writhe toward him and from the silver mists that veil the crescented horns of sin he sees the winged white scorpions dart upon him!

"He hears the sound of the tramping of myriads of feet, the feet of all the men to be born beneath the Moon! And he hears the sound of the sobbing of myriads of women, the sobbing of all the women to be born and to bear! He hears the clamor of the Uncreate!

"And he passes!

"For lo! Not the Begetter of Gods nor the awe of him may stand before man's desire!"

So the voice rang—and was silent. And Kenton saw all these things, saw the shimmering white serpents writhe through the silver mists and strike at the priest; saw the winged scorpions dart upon him; visioned within the mists a vast and awful shape upon whose clouded brows the crescent of the moon was bound. In his own ears he heard the tramping of armies of the unborn, the sobbing of worlds of women yet unborn, the clamor of the Uncreate! Saw and heard—even, he knew, as did the Priest of Bel!

And followed.

The golden helm flashed high above him. Kenton paused at the base of a winding stairway whose broad steps circled upward, changing as they arose from pallid silver to glowing orange. He waited until the priest—never hastening, never looking back—had ascended; he passed into the place to which the stairway led; slipped after him.

He looked into a temple filled with crocused light even as that through which he had just come had been filled with webs of moonbeams. A hundred paces away marched the priest, and as Kenton moved on the still voice resumed its whispering:

"The House of Shamash! Offspring of the Moon! God of the Day! Dweller in the House of Luster! Banisher of Darkness! King of Judgment! Judge of Mankind! On Whose Head Resteth the Crown with the High Horns! In Whose Hands are Life and Death! Who cleanseth Man with His Hands like a Tablet of Burnished Copper! Whose House is the Second of the Zones and Whose Color is Orange!

"He passes through the House of Shamash!

"Here are the altars of opal set with diamonds and the altars of gold set with amber and the yellow sunstones. Upon the altars of Shamash burn sandalwood and cardamon and verbena. He goes by the altars of opal and of gold; and he goes by the birds of Shamash whose heads are wheels of flame and who guard the wheel that turns within the House of Shamash and is a potter's wheel upon which all the souls of men are shaped.

"He hears the noise of myriads of voices, the wailing

158

of those who have been judged and the shouting of those who have been judged!

"And he passes!

"For lo! Not the King of Judgment nor the fear of him may stand before man's desire!"

Again Kenton saw and heard all these things; and following the priest came to a second stairway whose steps merged from glowing orange into ebony black. And still following he stood, at last, in a great hall of gloom, the name of whose dread master he knew even before the still voice came murmuring to him out of hidden, secret space:

"The House of Nergal! The Mighty One of the Great Dwelling Place! King of the Dead! He who Scattereth the Pestilence! He Who Ruleth over the Lost! The Dark One without Horns! Whose House is the Third of the Zones and Whose Color is Black!

"He passes through the House of Nergal!

"He goes by Nergal's altars of jet and of bloodstone! He goes by the red fires of civet and of bergamot that burn thereon! He goes by the altars of Nergal and the lions that guard them! The black lions whose eyes are as rubies and whose claws are blood red, the red lions whose claws are as black iron and whose eyes are as jet; and he passes the sable vultures of Nergal whose eyes are as carbuncles and whose heads are the fleshless heads of women!

"He hears the whimpering of the People of the Great Dwelling Place and he tastes the ashes of their passion!
"And he passes!

"For lo! Not the Lord of the Dead nor the dread of him may swerve man from his desire!"

Now the steps of the stairway by which Kenton ascended from the House of Nergal faded from ebon into crimson, and fiery, wrathful scarlet was the light that filled the place in which he stood, watching the Priest of Bel go steadily on.

"The House of Ninib!" whispered the voice. "Lord of Spears! Lord of the Battle! Master of the Shields! Master of the Hearts of Warriors! Ruler of the Strife! Destroyer of Opposition! Breaker of the Lock! The Smiter! Whose Color is Scarlet, Whose House is the Fourth of the Zones!

"Of shields and of spears are builded the altars of Ninib and their fires are fed with the blood of men and the tears of women, and upon the altars of Ninib burn the gates of fallen cities and the hearts of conquered kings! He goes by the altars of Ninib. He sees threaten him the crimson fangs of the boars of Ninib whose heads are wreathed with the right hands of warriors, the crimson tusks of the elephants of Ninib whose feet are ankleted with the skulls of kings, and the crimson tongues of the snakes of Ninib which lick up the cities!

"He hears the clashing of spears, the smiting of swords, the falling of walls, the crying of the conquered!

"And he passes!

"For lo! Since ever man was, the altars of Ninib have been fed with the fruits of man's desire!"

Upon the fourth stairway he set his feet; ascended steps that ran from the vermilion of licking flame to the clear serene blue of untroubled skies, stood within a chamber all filled with calm, azure light. Closer now seemed the voice.

"The House of Nabu! Lord of Wisdom! Bearer of the Staff! Mighty One of the Waters! Lord of the Fields Who Openeth up the Subterranean Streams! The Proclaimer! He who Openeth the Ears of Understanding! Whose Color is Blue and Whose House is the Fifth of the Zones!

"The altars of Nabu are of blue sapphire and of emerald and from them shine clear amethysts! The flames that burn on the altars of Nabu are blue fires in whose light only the truth has shadow! And the flames of Nabu are cold flames nor is there any scent over his altars! He passes by the altars of sapphire and of emerald and their cold fires! He passes the fishes of Nabu which have women's breasts but silent mouths! He passes the seeing eyes of Nabu which look forth from behind his altars and he touches not the staff of Nabu which holdeth up with wisdom the feet!

"Yea—he passes!

"For lo!—when did Wisdom stand before man's desire!"

Up from the blue of Nabu's House went the priest, and behind him on a stairway that merged from sapphire into rosy pearl and ivory climbed Kenton. Little, caressing tendrils of incense reached out to him as he went and all about him beat little languorous, linked notes of amorous sound; coaxing, calling, infinitely alluring, perilously sweet. Slowly, slowly Kenton followed him, listening to the voice, yet half heeding it, half forgetful of his quest, struggling with a vast desire to heed the calling, linked and amorous music; surrender to the spirit of this ensorcelled chamber —go no further—forget—Sharane!

"The House of Ishtar!" came the voice. "Mother of the Gods and of Men! The Great Goddess! Lady of the Morning and of the Evening! Full Bosomed! The Producer! She who Hearkeneth to Petition! The Mighty Weapon of the Gods! She who Slays and She Who Creates Love! Whose Color is Rose—pearl. And the House of Ishtar is the Sixth of the Zones!

"He passes through the House of Ishtar! Of white marble and of rose coral are her altars and the white marble is streaked with blue like a woman's breast! Upon her altars burn ever myrrh and frankincense, attar and ambergris! And the altars of Ishtar are set with pearls both white and rose, with hyacinths and with turquoise and with beryls!

"He goes by the altars of Ishtar, and, like the pink palms of maidens desirous, the rose wreaths of the incense steal toward him. The white doves of Ishtar beat their wings about his eyes! He hears the sound of the meeting of lips, the throbbing of hearts, the sighs of women, and the tread of white feet!

"Yet he passes!

"For lo! Whenever did Love stand before man's desire!"

From that chamber of amorous witcheries the stairway climbed, reluctant; shifting from its rosy pearl to flaming, flashing gold. And scaling it he stood within another vast place radiant as though it were the heart of the sun. Faster and faster the priest of Bel moved onward as though here all his terrors were concentrated, were crowding upon his hurrying heels!

"The House of Bel!" Rang the voice. "Merodach! Ruler of the Four Regions, Lord of the Lands! Child of the Day! Bull Necked! Elephant Thewed! Mighty One! Conqueror of Tiamat! Lord of the Igigi! King of Heavens and of Earth! Bringer of Things to Completeness. Lover of Ishtar.

"Bel-Merodach, Whose House is the Seventh of the Zones, and Whose Color is Golden!

"Swiftly he passes through the House of Bel!

"The altars of Bel are of gold and rayed like the sun! On them burn the golden fires of the summer lightnings and the smoke of the incense hangs over them like the clouds of the thunderstorm! The Kerubs whose bodies are lions and whose heads are eagle heads, and the Kerubs whose bodies are bulls and whose heads are the heads of men guard the golden altars of Bel, and both are winged with mighty wings! And the altars of Bel are reared upon thews of elephants and are held upon the necks of bulls and the paws of lions!

"He goes by them! He sees the fires of the lightnings sink and the altar shake! In his ears is the sound of worlds crushed by the fist of Bel; of worlds breaking beneath the smiting of Bel!

"Yet he passes!

"For lo! Not even the Might of God may crush the desire of man!"

The voice ceased, it seemed to retreat to those far regions whence it had come. In its withdrawal Kenton sensed finality; knew it would sound no more for him there; that now he was thrown on his own wit and strength; must captain his own way henceforward.

Out from one side of the House of Bel jutted a squared buttress, perpendicular, fifty feet or more wide. It thrust itself into this temple within a temple like the gigantic pier of a bridge. Its top was hidden.

Down its smooth façade darted a broad and angled streak of gold that Kenton for an instant took to be a colossal ornament, a symboling of the darting lightning bolt of Bel. Closer he came to it, following the priest. And now he saw that the golden streak was no ornament. It was a stairway, fashioned to represent the leaping levin but—a stairway. A stepped stairway of sharply angled flights that, clinging to the mighty buttress wall, climbed from the floor of the House of Bel up to—what?

At the foot the priest of Bel faltered; for the first time he looked behind him; seemed half moved to retreat. Then with the same despairing gesture of defiance with which he had turned from the altar, he began to creep cautiously, silently up the angled stairs.

And Kenton, waiting again until he was but a shadow in the shining mists, followed.

25

In The Bower Of Bel

THE TEMPEST had struck. Kenton, climbing, heard thunderings like the clashing of armied shields; clanging of countless cymbals, *tintamarre* of millions of gongs of brass. Ever louder grew the clangor as he ascended; with it mingled now the diapason of mighty winds, staccato of cataracts of rain.

The stairway climbed the sheer wall of the buttress as a vine a tower. It was not wide—three men might march abreast up it; no more. Up it went, dizzily. Five sharp angled flights of forty steps, four lesser angled flights of fifteen steps he trod before he reached its top. Guarding the outer edge was only a thick rope of twisted gold supported by pillars five feet apart.

So high was it that when Kenton neared its end and looked down he saw Bel's house only as a place of golden mists—as though he looked from some high mountain ledge upon a valley whose cloudy coverlet had just been touched by rays of morning sun.

The clinging stairway's last step was a slab some ten feet long and six wide. Upon it a doorway opened—a narrow arched portal barely wide enough for two men to pass within it side by side. The doorway looked out, over the little platform, into the misty space of the inner temple. The hidden chamber into which it led rested upon the head of the gigantic buttress.

One man might hold that stair end against hundreds.

The doorway was closed by a single fold of golden curtains as heavy and metallic as those which had covered the portal of the Moon God's Silver House. Involuntarily he shrank back from parting them—remembering what the parting of those argent hangings had revealed to him. He mastered that fear; drew a corner of them aside.

He looked into a quadrangular chamber, perhaps thirty feet square, filled with the dancing peacock plumes of the lightnings. He knew it for his goal—Bel's place of pleasance where Kenton's love waited, fettered by dream.

He glimpsed the priest crouched against the further wall, rapt upon a white veiled woman standing, arms stretched wide, beside a deep window close to the chamber's right hand corner. The window was closed by one wide, clear crystal pane on which the rain beat and the wind lashed. With thousands of brushes dipped in little irised flame the lightnings limned the loves of Bel broidered on hangings on the walls.

In the chamber were a table and two stools of gold; a massive, ivoried wooded couch. Beside the couch was a wide bellied brazier and a censer shaped like a great hour glass. From the brazier arose a tall yellow flame. Upon the table were small cakes, saffron colored, in plates of yellow amber and golden flagons filled with wine. Around the walls were little lamps and under each lamp a ewer filled with fragrant oil for their filling.

Kenton waited, motionless. Danger was gathering below him like a storm cloud with Klaneth stirring it in wizard's caldron. Perforce he waited, knowing that he must fathom this dream of Sharane's—must measure the fantasy in which she moved, mind asleep, before he could awaken her. The blue priest had so told him.

To him came her voice:

"Who has seen the beatings of his wings? Who has heard the tramplings of his feet like the sound of many chariots setting forth for battle? What woman has looked into the brightness of his eyes?"

There was a searing flash, a clashing of thunder—within the chamber itself it seemed. When his own sight had cleared he saw Sharane, hands over eyes, groping from the window.

And in front of the window stood a shape, looming gigantic against the flickering radiance, and helmed and bucklered all in blazing gold—a god-like shape!

Bel-Merodach himself who had leaped there from his steeds of storm and still streaming with his lightnings!

So Kenton for one awed instant thought—then knew it to be the Priest of Bel in the stolen garments of his god.

The white figure, that was Sharane, slowly drew hands from eyes; as slowly let them fall, eyes upon that shining form. Half she dropped to her knees, then raised herself proudly; she searched the partly hidden face with her wide, green dreaming eyes.

"Bel!" she whispered, and again: "Lord Bel!"

The priest spoke: "O beautiful one—for whom await you?"

She answered: "For whom but thee, Lord of the Lightnings!"

"But why await you—me?" the priest asked, nor took step toward her. Kenton, poised to leap and strike, drew back at the question. What was in the mind of the Priest of Bel that he thus temporized?

Sharane spoke, perplexed, half-shamed:

"This is thy house, Bel. Should there not be a woman here to await thee? I—I am a king's daughter. And I have long awaited thee!"

The priest said: "You are fair!" His eyes burned upon her—"Yes—many men must have found you fair. Yet I—am a god!"

"I was fairest among the princesses of Babylon. Who but the fairest should wait for thee in thy house? I am fairest of all—" So Sharane, all tranced passion.

Again the priest spoke:

"Princess, how has it been with those men who thought you fair? Say—did not your beauty slay them like swift, sweet poison?"

"Have I thought of men?" she asked, tremulously.

He answered, sternly. "Yet many men must have thought of you—king's daughter. And poison, be it swift and sweet, must still bear pain. I am—a god! Yet I know that!"

There was a silence; abruptly he asked: "How have you awaited me?"

She said: "I have kept the lamps filled with oil; I have prepared cakes for thee and set out the wine. I have been handmaiden to thee."

The priest said: "Many women have done all this—for men, king's daughter—I am a god!"

She murmured: "I am most beautiful. The princes and the kings have desired me. See—O Great One!"

The irised lightnings caressed the silver wonder of her body, hardly hidden in the nets of her red gold hair unbound and fallen free.

The priest leaped from the window. Kenton, mad with jealousy that another should behold that white beauty,

darted through the curtains to strike him down. Halfway
he stopped short, understanding, even pity for the Priest
of Bel holding him back.

For the priest's soul stood forth naked before his inner
sight—and that soul was even as his own would have been,
he knew, had he been priest and the priest been Kenton.

"No!" cried Bel's priest, and tore the golden helm of
his god from his head, hurled sword away, ripped off
buckler and cloak—

"No! Not one kiss for Bel! Not one heart beat for Bel!
What—shall I pander for Bel? No! It is the man you shall
kiss—I! It is a man's heart that shall beat against yours—
mine! I—I! No god shall have you."

He caught her in his arms, set burning lips to hers.

Kenton was upon him.

He thrust an arm under the priest's chin; bent back the
head until the neck cracked. The priest's eyes glared up
into his; his hands left Sharane and battered up at Kenton's face; he twisted to break the latter's grip. Then his
body became limp; awe and terror visibly swept away his
blind rage. For now the priest's consciousness had taken in
Kenton's face—saw it as his own!

His own face was looking down upon him and promising him—death!

The god he had defied, betrayed—had struck! Kenton
read his thoughts as accurately as though they had been
spoken. He shifted grip, half lifted, half swung the priest
high above the floor and hurled him against a wall. He
struck; crashed down; lay there twitching.

Sharane crouched—veils caught up, held fast to her by
rigid hands—on the edge of the ivoried couch. She stared
at him, piteously; her wide eyes clung to his, bewildered;
deep within her he sensed grapple of awakening will
against the webs of dream.

One great throb of love and pity for her pulsed through
him; in it no passion; to him at that moment she was no
more than child, bewildered, forsaken, piteous.

"Sharane!" he whispered, and took her in his arms.
"Sharane—beloved! Beloved—awaken!"

He kissed her on the cold lips, the frightened eyes.

"Kenton!" she murmured. "Kenton!"—and then so low
he could barely hear— "Ah yes—I remember—you were
lord of me—ages—ages—ago!"

"Wake, Sharane!" cried Kenton, and again his lips met

166

and clung to hers. And now her lips warmed and clung to his!

"Kenton!" she whispered. "Dear lord—of me!"

She drew back, thrust into his arms little fingers that clutched like ten slow closing fingers of steel; in her eyes he saw the dream breaking as break the last storm clouds before the sun; in her eyes the dream lightened and darkened; lightened—became but cloudy, racing wisps.

"Beloved!" cried Sharane, and all awake, freed from all dream, threw arms around his neck, pressed lips all alive to his: "Beloved one! Kenton!"

"Sharane! Sharane!" he whispered, the veils of her hair covering him as she drew his face to her cheeks, her throat, her breast.

"Oh, where have you been, Kenton?" she sobbed. "What have they done to me? And where is the ship—and where have they taken me? Yet—what does it matter since you are with me!"

"Sharane! Sharane! Beloved!" was all he could say, over and over again, his mouth on hers.

Hands gripped his throat, strong hands, shutting off his breath. Choking, he glared into the mad eyes of the Priest of Bel. Broken, Kenton had thought him—and broken he had not been!

He threw right leg behind the priest's; hurled himself back against the priest with all his strength. The priest fell, dragging Kenton with him. His hands relaxed just enough to let Kenton thrust one of his own between the strangling fingers and his throat. Like a snake the priest slid from under him, threw him aside, sprang to his feet. Quick as he, Kenton leaped up. Before he could draw sword the Priest of Bel was upon him again, one arm around him prisoning his right arm, the other with the elbow fending off Kenton's left arm and tearing at his throat.

Far below, through the drumming of the blood in his ears, Kenton heard the faint throb of another drum, awakening, summoning, menacing—as though it had been a beat of the *ziggurat's* own heart, alarmed and angry!

And far below Gigi, swinging with long apelike arms from the grapnel he had cast over the outer stairway's edge, hears it, too; swarms with frantic speed up the rope, and with the same tremendous speed follow him first Zubran and close behind him the Viking.

"Alarm!" mutters Sigurd, and draws them under the protection of the skirting wall that they may hear him. "Pray Thor that the sentinels have not heard! Swift now!"

Hugging the wall, the three climb up and around the silver terrace of Sin, the Moon God. The lightnings have almost ceased, but the rain sweeps down in stinging sheets and the winds roar. The stairway is a rushing torrent half knee deep. Blackness of the great storms shrouds them.

Breasting wind and rain, stemming the torrent, they climb—the three.

About Bel's high bower reeled Kenton and the priest, locked tight in each other's arms, each struggling to break the other's hold. Around them circled Sharane, the priest's stolen sword in hand, panting, seeking opening to strike; finding none, so close were the two locked, so swiftly did back of priest, back of lover swirl before her.

"Shalamu! Shalamu!" the dancer of Bel stood at the golden curtains—whipped up through the terrors of the secret shrines by love, remorse, despair! White faced, trembling, she clung to those curtains.

"Shalamu!" shrilled the dancer. "They come for you! The Priest of Nergal leads."

The priest's back was toward her, Kenton facing her. The priest's head was bent forward, straining to sink teeth in his neck, tear out the arteries; deaf; blind to all but the lust to kill, his ears were closed to Narada.

And Narada, seeing Kenton's face in the fitful light of the brazier, thought it that of the man she loved.

Before Sharane could move she had sped across the room.

She drove her dagger to the hilt in the back of the Priest of Bel!

Huddled for shelter in an alcove cut for them in the *ziggurat*'s wall, the sentinels of the silver zone feel arms thrust out of the storm. Two fall with necks snapped by Gigi's talons, two fall under swift thrusts of Sigurd's sword, two drop beneath the scimitar of the Persian. In that niche now lie only six dead men.

"Swift! Swift!" Sigurd leads the way past the silver zone. They round the orange zone of Shamash the Sun God.

Three deaths reach out of the void, and the sentinels of the orange zone lie dead behind the hurrying feet of the three.

They sense a deeper darkness at their left—the black walls of the zone of Nergal, God of the Dead——

"Swift! Swift!"

The Priest of Bel slid from Kenton's opening arms; he dropped to his knees; he fell backward, dying eyes staring into those of the dancer.

"Narada!" he gasped, through bloody froth. "Narada—you—" The froth turned to a red stream.

The Priest of Bel was dead.

One look the dancer gave him, gave Kenton, and knew——

"Shalamu!" she wailed—and wailing flew at Kenton, dagger poised to strike. Before he could draw sword, before he could raise hands to beat her off, even before he could fall back, she was upon him. Down swept the blade, straight for his heart. He felt the bit of its point——

The point swerved, ripped down through the skin over his ribs. In that same instant Sharane had sprung, had caught the dancer's hand, had wrested the dagger from it and driven it deep into Narada's breast.

Like a young tree at the ax's last blow the dancer stood for a heartbeat, shuddering, then down she dropped, prone upon the priest. She moaned and with the last flare of life flung arms around his head and laid lips to his.

Dead lips now on lips of the dead!

They stared at each other—Sharane with red blade in hand, Kenton with red rune on chest written by that blade —they stared down at the Priest of Bel and at Bel's dancer; there was pity in Kenton's eyes; there was no pity in Sharane's.

"She would have killed you!" she whispered, and again: "She would have killed you!"

A blinding flash filled the chamber; fast on its heels chaotic shatterings. The lightnings had begun afresh. Kenton ran to the doorway; parted the curtains; listened. Below him the House of Bel lay tranquil in its misty aureate glow. He heard nothing—and yet, had there been sound could he have heard it in the tumult of the thunderings? He saw nothing, heard nothing—and yet——

He sensed that danger was close; stealing up to them; perhaps even now creeping up the zigzags of those steps whose base was hidden. Torment and death for Sharane and for him—creeping, stealing, ever closer.

He ran back to the window. Gigi—Sigurd—Zubran! Where were they? Had they failed to make the outer stairway? Or were they marching up to him, cutting their way through the sentries? Were close?

Could they not meet them—Sharane and he?

The window was deep. Three feet of masonry stretched between the inner sill and the yard wide, single pane that closed it. He drew himself in; saw that the pane was thick, transparent crystal held by a circle of metal, kept shut by levers thrust into niches within the casement of stone. One by one he lifted the levers. The window flew open; he was half pushed, half washed back into the chamber by the wind and rain volleying through. He battled forward against them; looked down over the outer sill——

The steps of the great stairway were full forty feet below him!

Between window and steps fell an almost perpendicular wall, streaming with storm, impossible to descend, equally as impossible to be scaled.

He peered on each side and above him.

The Bower of Bel was a huge cube set on the top of the conical temple. The window through which he peered was close to the edge of a side of this cube. Not more than a yard from his right hand was a corner of that cube; for twenty feet to his left its black wall stretched; its top was twenty feet above him.

He felt Sharane beside him; knew that she was trying to tell him something. Could not hear her in the shrieking of the tempest.

Set within the breast of a lightning flare the sentinels of Nergal see three silhouettes of doom spring out of the blackness. Swords bite among them. One shrieks and tries to flee. His cry is torn to tatters by the roaring gale; he is caught by long arms, long talons snap his neck; he goes whirling with the wind over the stairway's wall.

And now the red zone's sentries are dead within their niche.

And now the three pass by the blue zone of Nabu, the God of Wisdom and find no guards to challenge them; nor are there sentries before Ishtar's white house, and none outside the golden zone of Bel.

And here the curving stairway abruptly ends!

Now they take counsel there, the three, scanning the smooth masonry rising above them without break. A wail that not even the tempest can still shudders past them—the heartbroken wailing of Bel's dancer as she hurls herself on Kenton.

"That cry came from there!" Thus Sigurd, pointing outward where the window of Bel's bower, hidden to them, faces the lightnings. And now they see that the wall of the great stairway merges into the side of the topping structure close to its corner. But the wall's slope is such that none may stand upon it to peer round that corner; nor can one standing on the highest step see round that corner's edge.

"Use for your long arms, Gigi," grunts the Viking: "Stand close as you can to stair wall end. Here! Grip me by knees and thrust me outward. My back is strong and I can twist round that corner."

Gigi takes him by the knees, lifts him; throws one muscle gnarled dwarf leg over the wall for balance; thrusts Sigurd out with mighty arms.

And Sigurd, held against the side by the wind like a leaf, looks straight into the face of Kenton little more than a foot from him!

"Wait there!" howls the Viking, and signals Gigi with kick of foot to draw him back.

"The Wolf!" he tells them. "There—in a window so close he can draw me through to him! Lift me again, Gigi. When I kick—let me go! Then let Zubran follow by the same road. Stay you here, Gigi—for without you to draw us back there will be no return. Stay where you are with arms outstretched, ready to bear in to you whatever you touch. Quick now!"

Again he is swung outward; his wrists are caught in Kenton's grip. Gigi loosens him. For an instant he swings in space and then is drawn up to the sill and over.

"Zubran comes!" he shouts to Kenton and runs to the doorway where Sharane stands, sword in hand.

And now the Persian, held by Gigi's long arms, swings

round the bower's edge, is caught by Kenton; stands beside him.

Fanned by the gale rushing through the open window the brazier flamed like a torch; the heavy golden curtains were bellying; the little lights along the wall all blown out. The Persian leaned back, found the levers and snapped enough of them to hold the window shut. He gave Kenton's hand one swift clasp; looked curiously at the bodies of priest and dancer.

"Gigi!" cried Kenton. "Is he safe there? Did none follow you?"

"None," answered the Persian, grimly. "Or if they did —their hands are too shadowy to hold swords, Wolf. Gigi is safe enough. He waits to swing us to him as we crawl from the window—all except one of us," he added, under his breath.

Kenton, thoughts on Gigi, the way to freedom, did not hear that last odd phrase. He leaped to the door on one side of which stood watchful Sharane, on the other tense Sigurd. He drew her to him in fierce caress; loosed her and peered through the curtains. Far below him were dull gleamings, reflection from armored caps and coats of mail, glints of swords. A quarter of the way up the angled stair that led from Bel's House to his Bower they were—soldiers, moving slowly, cautiously, silently; creeping to surprise, as they thought, Bel's priest in dreaming Sharane's arms!

There was time, minutes still, for him to put in action the thought swift-born within his brain. He set the golden helm of Bel on his head, fastened buckler, threw the scarlet threaded mantle over his shoulders.

"Sigurd!" he whispered—"Zubran! Those who come must believe that here are only Sharane and—that man who lies there. Else before we could pass the middle terrace they will have given the alarm, soldiers will be pouring up the outer stairway and—we are done! Therefore when those below are close upon the door Sharane and I will leap out on them with swords. They will not try to slay us—only capture us. They will be confused—fall back. Then take Sharane swiftly and pass her out to Gigi. We will follow—"

"The first part of the plan is good, Wolf," interrupted

the Persian, smoothly. "But not the last. Nay—one must remain here until the others are safely away from the temple. Else when they had entered here, quickly will the black priest's wit tell him what has happened. And there will be a ring around the place through which a regiment could not break. Nay—one must remain; stay behind for —a time."

"*I* will stay," said Kenton.

"Beloved!" whispered Sharane. "You go with me—or I go not at all!"

"Sharane—" began Kenton.

"Dear lord of mine—" she stayed him, serenely. "Do you think that ever again I will let you go from me—be parted from you? Never! In life or death—never!"

"Nay Wolf—I stay," said the Persian. "Sharane will not go without you. So that bars you—since go she must. Gigi cannot well remain—since he cannot get here to remain. That you will admit? Good! And Sigurd must go to show us the road back, since none but him knows it. Who is left? Zubran! The gods have spoken. Their argument is unanswerable."

"But how will you get away? How find us?" groaned Kenton. "You say yourself that without Gigi's help you cannot swing from the window!"

"No," answered Zubran. "But I can make me a rope out of these bed coverings and the hangings. I can slip down that rope to the steps I glimpsed beneath me. And one may escape where five could not. I remember the road through the city and that road we took when we came out of the trees. Wait you there for me."

"They are very close, Kenton!" called Sharane softly.

Kenton ran to the doorway. A dozen steps below crept the soldiers, a score of them, treading noiselessly two by two, small shields ready, swords in hands; behind them a little knot of priests, yellow robed and black robed and among the black robes—Klaneth.

Crouched against the wall at Sharane's right was Sigurd, hidden but set for swift guarding of her. The Persian dropped at Kenton's left, pressed close to the wall where those who came forward might not see him.

"Cover the brazier," whispered Kenton. "Put it out. Best have no light behind us."

The Persian took it, but he did not touch the cover that would have killed the fires within. Instead, he shook it, covered the flame with embers, set it in a corner where the faint glow of the coals could not be seen.

The feet of the first pair of soldiers were almost on the top step, their hands reached out to draw aside the coverings of the narrow door.

"Now!" breathed Kenton to Sharane. He tore the curtains down. They stood, she in her white robes of priestess, he in the golden panoply of the god, confronting the soldiers. And they, paralyzed by that unexpected apparition, gaped at the twain.

Before they could recover from surprise Sharane's blade flashed, Kenton's sword struck like bolt of thin blue lightning. Down went the two leaders. Ere the man he had slain could fall, Kenton had snatched the shield from his arm, passed it to Sharane; slashed down again at the warriors behind.

"For Ishtar!" he heard Sharane cry—and saw her sword bite deep.

"The woman! The priest! Take them!" came the roar of Klaneth.

Down bent Kenton, raised a fallen soldier in his arms and hurled him straight into the pack. The body flailed them—as though alive! Down they went before it—rolling, cursing; down the flight they fell, soldiers and priests. Some there were who crashed into the slender railing, tore gaps in it, dropped and plunged like plummets through the mists to be broken on the floor of Bel's House so far below.

Back Kenton leaped; caught Sharane in his arms, tossed her to Sigurd.

"To the window!" he bade. "Give her to Gigi!"

He darted before them; opened the pane. Far away now the lightnings glimmered; blackness had given way to darkest twilight; the rain still hissed in sheets driven by the howling wind. In that dark twilight he saw the dripping arms of Gigi stretched out round the Bower's corner. He dropped back. The Viking slid past him, Sharane in his grip. For an instant she hung in air; she was caught by Gigi. She was drawn from sight.

There was a shouting from the inner stairway. The soldiers had rallied; were rushing up. Kenton saw Sigurd and the Persian lifting the heavy couch, throwing off its coverings, tilting it. They rocked it to the doorway, shoved it through, sent it crashing down the steps. There was an-

174

other shouting, cries of agony, groanings. The bed had swept the men before it as a well hurled ball does the wooden pins. It had swept and crushed them—had swung across the stairway at turn of the highest lesser angled ledge and had jammed there against the golden roped rail —a barricade.

"Go Sigurd," cried Kenton. "Wait for us by the woods. I fight here with Zubran."

The Persian looked at him, a light of affection such as Kenton had never before seen there softening the agate eyes. He nodded to Sigurd.

As though it had been a signal prearranged, the Viking's arms were instantly around Kenton. Strong as he had grown, Kenton could not break their grip. And Zubran whisked the golden helm of Bel from his head and set it on his own; tore loose the golden buckler, dropped his own coat of mail and fastened it in its place; took the scarlet threaded mantle of the god and wrapped it half around his mouth, hiding his beard.

Then Kenton was carried like a struggling child to the window; was thrust out of it; was caught by Gigi and dropped beside the weeping Sharane.

The Viking turned and folded the Persian in his arms.

"No waiting, Northman! No sentiment now!" Zubran snapped, breaking away. "There can be no escape for me —you know that, Sigurd. The rope? Words—to satisfy the Wolf! I love him. The rope? Why, they would slide down it behind me like snakes. Am I a trembling hare to lead the hounds to the hiding places of my kind? Not I! Now go, Sigurd—and when you have gotten clear of the city tell them. And make for the ship as quickly as you can."

Said the Viking, solemn: "Shield maidens are close! Odin takes the hero, no matter what his race! You sup with Odin All-Father in Valhalla soon, Persian!"

"May he have dishes that I have never tasted," jested the Persian. "Out of the window, Norseman!"

And Zubran holding his knees, the Viking crawled out, and was caught by Gigi.

Then down the terraces, Sigurd leading, Sharane covered by Gigi's great cloak, Kenton cursing still, flew the four of them.

26

The Passing Of Zubran

THE PERSIAN did not close the window after them. He let the wind stream through. He swaggered back through Bel's Bower.

"By all the Dævas!" swore Zubran, "never have I known such feeling of freedom as now! Lo—I am all alone—the last man in the world! None can help me, none can counsel me, none can weary me! Life is simple at last—all there is to it is for me to slay until I am slain. By Ormuzd —how my spirit stands on tiptoe——"

He peered around the doorway.

"Never has that couch given man such trouble to mount!" he chuckled as he watched the soldiers below working to clear away the barrier.

Turning, he piled in the middle of Bel's Bower the silken coverings of the bed. He ripped down the wall hangings and threw them on the heap. One by one he took the lamps and emptied them on the pyre; the oil in the ewers beneath them he poured upon it.

"That old world of mine," mused the Persian as he worked, "how it wearied me! And this world has wearied me—by the Flame of Sacrifice, but it has! And I am sure that new world of the Wolf's would weary me most of all. I am done with the three of them."

He picked up the body of the Priest of Bel, carried it to the window.

"It will puzzle Klaneth more to find you outside than within," he laughed, and slid the body over the sill.

He stood over the dancer.

"So beautiful!" whispered Zubran, and touched her lips, her breasts. "I wonder how you died—and why. It must have been amusing—that! I had no time to ask the Wolf. Well—you shall sleep with me, dancer. And perhaps when we awaken—if we do—you shall tell me."

He stretched Narada out upon the oil soaked pile. He

took the smoking brazier and placed it close beside her. . . .

There was a roaring from below; a trampling of feet on the stairway. Up streamed the soldiers, stronger now by scores. An instant Zubran showed himself at the doorway, Bel's golden mantle twisted round his neck, half hiding his face.

"The priest! The priest!" they cried—and Klaneth's voice bellowed over all——

"The priest! Slay him!"

The Persian stepped back to the cover of the wall, smiling. He picked up the shield Sharane had dropped.

Through the narrow doorway a soldier leaped, a second on his heels.

The scimitar hissed twice, swift as swiftest snake. The two fell under the feet of those pressing from behind, tripping them, confusing them.

And now up and down, thrusting, ripping, slashing, danced Zubran's blade until its red sweat dyed his arm from hand to shoulder. In front of him grew a barricade of the dead.

Two by two only could they set foot upon the Bower's threshold—and two by two steadily they fell, blocking that threshold from side to side with a steadily rising wall of bodies. At last their swords glinted toward him no more; he heard the forward ranks cry out behind the barrier; leaping upon the slain he saw them turn and press back those who marching upward tried to sweep them on.

The Persian flexed the weary muscles of his arm; laughed as he heard the voice of Klaneth:

"There is but one man there! Kill him—and bring me the woman. Ten times her weight in gold for him who takes her!"

They mustered; they rushed up the stairway like a racing snake; they clambered over the wall of the dead. The red drip of Zubran's scimitar became a running rivulet——

An agony bit deep into his side, above the groin. A fallen swordsman had raised himself, thrust up his blade.

The Persian knew the wound was mortal!

He cut down at the grinning face, leaped again upon the dead, cleared the doorway with storm of strokes. He thrust his shoulder against the wall of bodies, threw them out. They spewed upon the steps, rolled down. They fell upon the climbing men, tripped them; pitched them off the rail-

177

less edge of the stairway; sent them hurtling down through the mists, clutching at the air.

For twenty steps the stairway was clear!

An arrow whistled.

It cut through the twisted mantle around Zubran's neck; pierced him where helm and gorget met. He drank the salt blood pouring down his throat.

The Persian staggered to the silken pile on which lay Narada. He caught a leg of the brazier and overturned its coals upon the oil soaked cloths.

Thin flames arose. The blast from the opened window caught them and turned them into roaring fans of fire.

Through them Zubran crept; stretched himself out beside the body of the dancer; twisted, and gathered her in his arms.

"A clean death," he whispered. "At the last . . . like all men. . . . I return to the . . . gods of my fathers. A clean death! Take me—O Fire Immortal!"

A flame shot up beside him. It hovered, then bent.

The tip of the flame broadened.

It became a cup of fire filled with wine of flames!

Into that cup the Persian dipped his lips; he drank of its wine of fire; he breathed its incense.

His head fell back, unmarred; the dead face smiling. His head dropped upon Narada's breasts.

The flames made a canopy over them; the flames tented them.

27

How They Fared Back To The Ship

Now the four for whose freedom the Persian had died were far away. Safely they had passed the terraces; the dead sentries lay as they had fallen. But as they went the four heard a humming begin inside the *ziggurat* like that of a disturbed and colossal hive, heard the great drum resume its throbbing and sped faster under cover of the wall

178

of stone to where the grapnel of Gigi hung. One by one they slipped down its rope and into the sheltering trees. The tempest scourged them—but it shielded them. None was on the wide street to challenge their going. Emakhtila lay within its painted houses hiding from the storm.

When the cup of flame had dipped to the Persian's lip they were well along the other way upon which opened the hidden path back to the ship.

When the soldiers had at last mustered courage to swarm the stairs once more, and with the black priest on their heels had poured within the silent Bower, the four were far beyond the clustered houses, stumbling through the deep mud of the farmside, the Viking at lead, Kenton guarding the rear—and watching, ever watching, for Zubran.

And back in that chamber where Zubran's ashes lay mixed with the dancer's, the black priest stood, mazed and with something of fear touching his wicked heart—until his wandering gaze caught gleam of the butterflies in Narada's veils that had slipped from her when the Persian had lifted her, caught, too, the trail of blood that led to the open window. Staring out that window the black priest saw in the livid dusk the crumpled body of Bel's priest—dead, white face raised to his own, forty feet below.

The priest! Then whose were the charred bodies on the pyre? Who had been the man fighting in golden helm and buckler, face hidden in the god's mantle? So swift had been the sword play, so much had that man been hidden by the soldiers, so much by cover of the wall, that Klaneth watching from below had caught few glimpses of him; had taken it for granted that he was Bel's priest.

Back ran the black priest; kicked savagely at the ashes of the pyre and what still lay among them.

Something clanged upon the floor—a broken scimitar! He knew that hilt—Zubran's, the Persian!

Something glittered at his feet—a buckle, gems undulled by their bath of fire! He knew that, too—the buckle of Narada's girdle!

Why then—these blackened forms were the Persian—the dancer!

Sharane had been freed!

The black priest stood rigid, face so dreadful that the

soldiers shrank back from him, threw themselves against the walls, out of his way.

Then Klaneth plunged howling out of Bel's Bower, down the angled stairway, through the secret shrines, on and on until he reached that cell where he had left Kenton with the six archers. He threw open the door, saw archers and officer deep in sleep and Kenton—gone!

And shrieking curses, staggered out of the cell, roaring for men to go forth to search the city for the temple drab and the slave; offering all he owned for them—all, all! If only they brought their pair back to him alive!

Alive!

By now the four had left the road and had halted in that wood where the hidden path began and where the Persian, in his craft, had bade them wait for him. And here Sigurd told them of Zubran's sacrifice and why that sacrifice had been necessary. And Sharane wept and Kenton's throat ached with sorrow and Gigi's beady black eyes grew soft and his tears ran down the furrows of his wrinkles.

"What's done—is done," said Sigurd. "He sups, by now, with Odin and the heroes!"

Brusquely he shouldered by them and took the way.

On they went and on. The rain drenched them, the wind beat them. When storm lightened they went swiftly; when it darkened so that the Viking could no longer see the trail, they halted. On and on—beating back to the ship.

Now Sharane faltered and fell, nor could she rise again; and the three, clustering round her, saw that her thin sandals were in rags and that her slim feet were bare and bleeding and that for long each step must have been an agony. So Kenton took her in his arms and carried her, and when he tired Gigi took her; and Gigi was untiring.

And at last they came to where the ship lay hid. They hailed her and found the warrior maids on watch. To them they gave Sharane and they carried their mistress into her cabin and ministered to her.

Now arose discussion as to whether they should stay hid until the tempest had abated. At last they decided that they would not; that it was better to push out to sea than stay so close to Emakhtila and Nergal's haunted place. So the chains were unshackled from the trees, the ship drawn out of shelter, her bow warped round and pointed to harbor's mouth.

Then up came the hook; down dipped the oars. Slowly the ship gathered speed. She swung out round the point of rocks and, Sigurd at the steering oar, shot into the eye of the wind, breasted the roaring combers and leaped like a racer out into the open ocean.

Kenton, utterly spent, dropped where he stood. To him came Gigi, lifted and carried him into the black cabin.

Long squatted Gigi beside him, wide awake, though weary as he was, peering here and there with bright eyes; listening, watchful. For it seemed to Gigi that the black cabin was not as it had been when they had left it; it seemed to Gigi that he heard a whispering, ghosts of whispers, coming and going.

And now Kenton moaned and muttered in his deep sleep, gasped as though hands sought his throat. Gigi, pressing paw on Kenton's heart, stilled him.

But after a time the watchful eyes of Gigi dulled, their lids dropped, his head nodded.

In the empty niche where the idol of Nergal had stood above the bloodstone slab of worship a darkness gathered, a cloudy shape of curdled shadows.

The shape darkened. Within it began to form the semblance of a face, a face that brooded upon the sleeping pair, hate filled, menacing——

Again Kenton groaned and fought for breath against nightmare terror. And the drummer threshed out long arms, leaped to his feet, glared about him——

Swiftly as it had come, before Gigi's sleep-heavy eyes could open, the shadowy face had vanished—the niche was empty.

28

The Vision Of Kenton

WHEN Kenton awakened, it was the Viking and not Gigi who lay beside him, stripped and snoring. He must

181

have slept long, for the drenched garments the Ninevite had taken off him were dry. He put on clout and tunic, slipped feet in sandals, threw over his shoulders a short cloak and softly opened the door. Blackness and dark twilight had given way to a pallid dusk that turned the sea a sullen grey. The rain had ceased, but all the world of the ship vibrated to the steady roar of a mighty wind pouring over it.

Before that wind the ship was flying, riding like a gull on the crests of giant waves; slipping back, as the swells passed, through smoothly onrushing floors of water like liquid slate; rising to fly again upon the crest of the next racing wave.

Kenton struggled up to the steersman's place, the spindrift stinging his face like sleet. To one of the rudder oars clung Gigi, at the other were two slaves from the rowers' pit. The Ninevite grinned at him; pointed to the compass. He looked and saw that the needle which held constant to Emakhtila pointed straight astern.

"Far behind us now is that den!" shouted Gigi.

"Go below!" cried Kenton in a pointed ear, and would have taken the oar from him. But Gigi only laughed, shook his head and pointed toward the cabin of Sharane.

"That is your course," he roared. "Steer it!"

And buffeting the gale Kenton came to the door of the rosy cabin; opened it. Sharane lay asleep, cheek cradled in one slim hand, tresses covering her like a silken net of red gold. Two maids, watchful, crouched at her bedside.

As though he had called to her, she opened sleepy eyes —sleepy eyes that as she looked at him grew sweetly languorous.

"My own dear lord!" whispered Sharane.

She sat up, motioned the girls to go. And when they had gone she held out white arms to him. His own arms were around her. Like a homing bird she nestled in them; raised red lips to his.

"Dear lord of me!" whispered Sharane.

He heard no more the roaring wind—heard nothing but the whisperings, the sighings of Sharane; forgot all worlds save that which lay within Sharane's tender arms.

Long they flew on the tempest's wings. Twice Kenton took Gigi's place at the rudder oars, twice the Viking relieved him before the great wind died and they sailed once more on dimpling, sparkling turquoise sea.

Then for those upon the ship a hunted life began—and a haunted one.

Far, far behind them must lie Emakhtila by now, and yet on all the four rested clear certainty of pursuit. No fear, no terror—but knowledge that the ship was a hunted thing; knowledge that they could outwit, outsail the fleet they knew must be combing these strange seas until they found a safe and secret harbor, there could be but one end for them. Nor did one of them believe, deep in his heart, that there was such sanctuary.

Yet they were happy. Full tide of life beat round Kenton and Sharane. They took their fill of love. And Sigurd sang old Sagas, and a new one he had made of Zubran the Persian, while he and Gigi beat out huge shields and arrows for the bows. The shields they set around the bulwarks at the ship's bow and pierced them with slits through which arrows could be winged. Two they fastened on each side of the stern to guard helmsman.

And Sigurd would chant of battle to come, and shield maidens who would hover over the ship ready to bear the soul of Sigurd, Trygg's son, to his seat in Valhalla where Zubran awaited him. He sang of place for Kenton there, and Gigi too—but not when Sharane was in earshot, since in Valhalla was no place for women.

Hunted and—haunted!

Within the black cabin the shadows thickened and faded, grew stronger, passed and returned. Something of the dark Lord of the Dead was there, had retaken seizin of his deck. Nor Gigi nor the Viking cared to sleep in the black cabin now; they sought the open deck or the cabin of the warrior maids.

And the slaves murmured of shadows that flitted over the black deck and clustered at the rail and stared down upon them!

Once, while Sigurd drowsed over the tiller bar, he awakened to find that unaware to all the course of the ship had changed, that the greater needle of the compass pointed straight over the bow to—Emakhtila; that the ship was moving under the oars back to Sorcerers' Isle!

Thereafter they steered two by two—Kenton and Sharane, Gigi and the Viking.

Nor was there power within Sharane to banish the shadows.

One isle they made and replenished food and water. There was good harbor there, a hidden cover and, beyond, a great forest beckoned them. Here they stopped for a time; talked of drawing the ship up shore, concealing her; then finding place within the woods to build fort; meet there whatever attack might come.

The Ship of Ishtar drew them back to her.

Restless were they all, uneasy on the land, each afraid in secret heart that the other three would make up minds to stay; and gay as children they were when the ship drove out again and dipped her bow to the crested waves while the clean sea wind shouted to them and the isle dropped behind.

"A prison," laughed Kenton.

"No life, that!" growled Sigurd. "Hiding in a burrow till the dogs come to dig us out! Now we can see what comes."

They met a long ship, a *unireme* like their own, but of twenty oars. It was a merchant carrier and heavily laden, and it would have fled from them. But the Viking cried that she must not escape to carry tidings to Emakhtila. So they pursued and rammed and sunk her with the chained slaves wailing at the oars—Kenton and Gigi and Sigurd ruthlessly, Sharane white faced and weeping.

They met another—a light vessel no larger than the ship, but this time a war boat, a hunter. They feigned to flee and it gave chase. And when it was close to them the Viking swerved and fell astern; then drove the Ship of Ishtar swiftly against the other's side, shearing the oars. Those on that vessel fought bravely; yet, hampered by the black priest's command to take but not slay, they were no match for Gigi's great mace, the Viking's blade and Kenton's sword of blue lightnings. They fell before them and the arrow storm from Sharane and her maids. But they took toll before they were ended. One of the warrior maids died with an arrow through her heart and both Gigi and Sigurd had their wounds.

In this craft they found store of metal for the Viking's forge. Better still, balls of tow and oils to soak them in and flint to light them, strong shafts to carry the balls when blazing and oddly shaped crossbows to hurl the shafts with their heads of fire. All these and the metal

184

they took. Then they sank that vessel with its living and its dead.

On sailed the ship and on; while Sigurd hammered out his long shields and Gigi and Kenton set the crossbows in place by rosy cabin and dark, with tow and oils and flint ready for the firing.

And time passed; nor did the tides of life that flowed strong through Kenton of the ship wane ever; waned not —grew stronger and more strong for him and for Sharane.

Lying beside his sleeping love Kenton awoke—or thought that he awakened—and opening his eyes saw not the cabin but two faces gazing down upon him from some unknown space; vast faces, vague and nebulous. Their shadowy eyes dwelt upon him.

One spoke—and lo, it was the voice that had guided him through the temple's secret shrines! The voice of Nabu!

"Again Nergal centers his wrath upon the ship, O Ishtar!" it said. "The strife between him and your Sister-Self once more will trouble gods and men, deepening the shadows in myriad worlds. Great Mother—only you may end it!"

"My word went forth"—the other voice was like the wind rippling over thousands of harp strings—"my word went forth; and that Sister-Self of mine whom of old men have called the Wrathful Ishtar—has she not her rights? She has not conquered Nergal. Nor has Nergal conquered her. There has been no settlement such as I decreed. How, then, can my Sister-Self rest when the word I spoke in anger has not yet been resolved? And as long as she contends, so long must Nergal also who, too, is bound by that word."

"Yet the flames you kindled within the souls of Zarpanit and Alusar, the flames that were the life of those souls —they did not perish," the still voice whispered. "Did they not escape both your Wrathful Sister and Dark Nergal? And why, Ishtar? Was it not because you willed it so? Did you not hide them? What of that word of yours then?"

"Wise are you, Nabu!" came the voice of Ishtar. "Now let this man whose eyes we have opened see what that my priestess and her lover wreaked of ill when they brought into each other's arms the Mother of Life and

185

the Lord of Death! Let the man judge whether my anger were just or not!"

"Let the man judge!" echoed the voice of Nabu.

The vast faces faded. Kenton looked out upon depth upon depth, infinity upon infinity of space. Myriads of suns were hived therein and around them spun myriads upon myriads of worlds. Throughout that limitless space two powers moved; mingled yet ever separate. One was a radiance that fructified, that gave birth and life and joy of life; the other was a darkness that destroyed, that drew ever from the radiance that which it had created; stilling them, hiding them in its blackness. Within the radiance was a shape of ineffable light and Kenton knew that this was the soul of it. In the darkness brooded a deep shadow, and he knew that this was its darker soul.

Before him arose the shapes of a man and a woman; and something whispered to him that the woman's name was Zarpanit and the man's Alusar, the priestess of Ishtar and the priest of Nergal. He saw in each of their hearts a wondrous, clear white flame. He saw the two flames waver, bend toward each other. And as they did so, shining threads of light streamed out from the radiance, linking the priestess with its spirit; while from the black core of the darkness threads of shadow ran out and cooled about the priest.

As the bending flames touched suddenly the shining threads and shadow threads were joined—for an instant were merged!

And in that instant all space shuddered, the suns rocked, the worlds reeled and all the rushing tides of life paused!

"Behold the sin!" rippled the voice of harp strings.

"Open his eyes wider!" came the still, cold voice.

And now Kenton beheld a radiant chamber in which sat dread powers, veiled in glories of light—all save one who hid in the darkness. Before them stood the priest and priestess and at the side of the priestess—Sharane!

Again he saw the white flames within the hearts of those two—untroubled, serene, indifferent to gods or angry goddess! Bending toward each other, unquenchable, immutable, indifferent to wrath of gods or their punishments!

That picture wavered, faded. Now upon the floor of that radiant chamber he saw priest and priestess, Sharane and Klaneth and around them the bodies of many women and men. There was a high altar half hidden by a cloud of sparkling azure mist. Within the mist, upon that altar, a wondrous ship was being built by unseen hands.

And ever as that ship grew Kenton saw, far beyond it as though it were its shadow cast into another dimension, another ship growing; a ship that seemed to build itself out of a turquoise sea in a world of silver clouds! Step by step that shadow ship followed the building of the puppet ship upon the altar.

He knew that the shadow was the real—the toy being shaped upon the altar was the symbol.

Knew, too, that symbol and reality were one; things linked by an ancient wisdom; things created by ancient powers, of which the fate and fortune of one must be the fate and fortune of the other.

Duoform! One a puppet and one real! And each the same!

Now the unseen hands within the mists of azure had finished the ship. They reached down and touched, one by one, the bodies of Ishtar's priestess and Nergal's priest, Sharane and Klaneth and all who lay around them. And as they touched, those still forms vanished. The unseen hands lifted and placed, one by one, little puppets on the puppet ship.

Upon the decks of the shadow ship on the turquoise sea in the world of silver clouds bodies lay—one by one they appeared there as the toys were set in place upon the toy ship on the altar!

At last there were no more still forms upon the floor of the council chamber of the gods.

The ship was made and manned!

A beam shot out from the radiance that veiled Ishtar and touched the ship's bow. A tendril of darkness uncoiled from the blackness in which brooded the Lord of the Dead and this darkness touched the ship's stern.

That picture wavered and fled.

There appeared another chamber; small, almost a crypt. In it stood a single altar. Over the altar hung a lamp nimbused by an aureole of azure; and the altar was of lapis lazuli and turquoise and studded with sapphires of clearest blue. And Kenton knew that this was some secret shrine of Nabu, Lord of Wisdom.

On the altar rested the ship. As Kenton looked upon

it, it was borne to him again that this jeweled toy, his gleaming symbol, was linked inseparably with that other ship sailing in another space, another dimension; sailing on strange seas in an unknown world——

The ship on which he sailed!

And that as the toy fared, so fared the Ship of Ishtar; and as the Ship of Ishtar fared, so fared the toy; each threatened when one was threatened; sharing each the other's fate.

That picture faded. He looked upon a walled city out of which towered a high temple, a terraced temple, a *ziggurat*. A host besieged city; its walls were covered with its defenders. He knew that the city was ancient Uruk and the high temple that in which the ships had been built. And as he looked, the besiegers broke through the walls; overwhelmed the defenders. He had a glimpse of red carnage—that picture fled.

Again he saw the crypt of Nabu. There were two priests there now. The ship rested upon the floor of a lattice of silvery metal. Over the altar hovered a little shining blue cloud. It came to him that the two priests were obeying a voice in that cloud; saving the ship and those who sailed on it from the invaders. They poured over it from huge basins a fine mortar that was like powder of ivory flecked with dust of pearls. It covered and hid the toy. Where the puppet ship had been was now a block of stone. The cloud vanished. Other priests entered; dragged the block out, through corridors and into the court of the temple. There they left it.

Into the court swarmed the victors, looting and slaying. But ever, unheeding, they passed the rough block by.

Now he looked upon another walled city, great and beautiful. He knew it for Babylon in the full moon of its power. Another *ziggurat* took its place. That melted and Kenton looked upon another secret shrine of Nabu. The block lay within it.

Flickered thereafter before him fleeting pictures of battles and of triumphs; pageant and disasters; quick, broken scenes of temple and city lost and won and lost once more; destroyed only to be built again in greater grandeur——

Then fallen—abandoned by the gods.

Then crumbling—abandoned by man; the desert creeping on it; at the last covering it.

Then—forgotten!

There came a whirlpool of images, grey and indistinct in the swiftness of their passing. They steadied. He saw men working in the sands that were Babylon's shroud. He recognized among them—Forsyth! He saw the block unearthed; borne away by tall Arabs; saw it crated into a primitive cart drawn by patient little rough coated ponies; watched it tossing in the hold of a ship that sailed a sea he knew; watched it carried into his own house——

He saw himself as he freed the ship!

He looked again into the shadowy eyes.

"Judge!" sighed the harp strings.

"Not yet!" whispered the still voice.

Kenton looked again into that immeasurable space wherein he had first seen radiant power and dark. But now he saw within it countless flames like those which had burned in the breasts of Ishtar's priestess and the Lord of Death's priest; saw infinity flecked and flaming with them. They burned deep down through the shadows, and by their light up from the darkness came groping multitude upon multitude of other flames that had been shrouded by the darkness. He saw that without those flames the radiance itself would be but a darkness!

He saw the ship as though it floated in that same space. As he gazed a deeper shadow flitted from the soul of the blackness and brooded over it. Instantly something of the soul of the radiance rayed out and met it. They strove, one against the other. The ship was a focus of hatred and of wrath from which, visibly, waves swung out in ever widening circles. As the waves circled outward from the ship the shadow lines that ran from the core of darkness grew darker, thicker, as though they sucked strength from those waves. But under their beat the radiance dulled and the countless flames flickered and swayed, and were troubled.

"Judge!" whispered the cold tones of Nabu.

Now Kenton in this dream of his—if dream it was—faced dilemma; hesitated. No trivial matter was it to indict this power—Ishtar, goddess or whatever that power might be in this alien world where, certainly, it was powerful indeed. Besides, had he not prayed to Ishtar and had she not answered his prayer? Yes, but he had prayed to Nabu, too, and Nabu was Lord of Truth——

His thoughts shaped themselves into words of his own tongue, his familiar idioms.

"If I were a god," he said, simply enough, "and had made things with life, things with lives to live, men and women or whatever they might be, I would not make them imperfect, so that they must, perforce through their imperfections, break my laws. Not if I were all powerful and all wise, as I have gathered gods—and goddesses —are supposed to be. Unless, of course, I had made them only for toys, to play with. And if I found that I had made them imperfect and that therefore they did wrong, I would think that it was I who was responsible for their sinning—since being all powerful and all wise I could have made them perfect but did not. And if I had made them for my toys I surely would not heap upon them heart-break and misery, pain and sorrow—no punishments, O Ishtar—not if they were toys that could feel these things. For what would they be but puppets dancing through their day as I had fashioned them to do?

"Of course," said Kenton naively, and with no ironic intention, "I am no god—and most certainly could not be a goddess—nor until I came into this world have I had any conscious experience with either. Yet, speaking as a man, even if I had punished any one who had broken my laws I would not let my anger run on and hurt any number of people who had nothing whatever to do with the original cause of my anger. Yet that, if what I have just beheld was true, is what this strife for the ship seems to bring about.

"No," said Kenton, very earnestly, and quite forgetting the vague faces hovering about him. "I can't see any justice in the torment of that priest and priestess, and if the struggle for the ship does the damage it appears to, I certainly would stop it if I could. For one thing I would be afraid that the shadow might get too thick some time and put all the little flames out. And for another—if I had spoken a word in anger that made all that misery I wouldn't let that word be stronger than myself. I wouldn't as a man. And if I were a god or goddess—very certainly, indeed, I would not!"

There was a silence; then——

"The man has judged!" whispered the still voice.

"He has judged!" the vast ripple of the harp strings was

190

almost as cold as that other. "I will recall my word! Let the strife end!"

The two faces vanished. Kenton raised his head and saw around him the familiar walls of the rosy cabin. Had it been all a dream? Not all—those scenes he had beheld had been too clear cut, too consecutive, too convincing.

Beside him Sharane stirred, turned his face to hers.

"What are you dreaming, Jonkenton?" she asked. "You were murmuring and muttering—strange words that I could not understand.

He bent and kissed her.

"I greatly fear, heart of mine, that I have offended that goddess of yours," he said.

"Oh—Jonkenton—but no! How!" Sharane's eyes were terrified.

"By telling her the truth," answered Kenton; then unveiled to Sharane all of his vision.

"I forgot she is—a woman!" he ended.

"Oh—but beloved, she is all women!" cried Sharane.

"Well—that makes it all the worse then!" said Kenton, ruefully.

He leaped up; threw his cloak about him and went out to talk to Gigi.

But Sharane sat thinking, long after he had gone, with troubled eyes; at last walked to the empty shrine; threw herself before it, prostrate; praying.

29

How The Strife Was Ended

"WHAT BEGAN on the ship must end on the ship!" said Gigi, nodding bald head wisely when Kenton had told him also of that vision of the two faces. "Nor do I think we shall have long to wait before we see that end."

"And after?" asked Kenton.

"Who knows?" Gigi shrugged broad shoulders. "No rest for us, Wolf, while Klaneth lives. Nay—I think I know what this darkening of shadows on black deck means.

By those shadows Klaneth watches us. They are the thread by which he follows us. Also my skin is sensitive, and it tells me the black priest is not so far away. When he comes —well, we conquer him or he conquers us, that is all. Also, I do not think that you can count on any help from Ishtar. Remember that in your vision she promised only that the strife of the Wrathful One and the Dark One should end. She made no promises, I gather, as to Sharane or you—or the rest of us."

"That will be well," said Kenton cheerfully. "As long as I am given chance to stand fairly, face to face with that swine bred from hell swill Klaneth, I am content."

"But I think you gathered that she was not mightily pleased with what you had to say to her," grinned Gigi slyly.

"That is no reason for her punishing Sharane," answered Kenton, harking back to his old thought.

"How else could she punish you?" asked Gigi, maliciously—then suddenly grew serious, all impishness gone. "Nay, Wolf," he said and laid paw on Kenton's shoulder; "there is little chance for us. And yet—if all your vision were true, and the little flames you saw were real—what matters it. . . .

"Only," said Gigi, wistfully, "when those flames that were you and Sharane journey forth into space and another flame comes to you that once was Gigi of Nineveh —will you let it journey with you?"

"Gigi!" there were tears in Kenton's eyes. "Where ever we go in this place or any other, no matter what may happen—you go with us as long as you will."

"Good!" muttered Gigi.

Sigurd shouted at the rudder; he pointed over the ship's bow. To Sharane's door they sped and with her through the cabin of the maids and out beneath the sickled prow. Across the horizon ran a far flung line of towers and minarets, turrets and spires and steeples, skyscrapers and mosques; a huge chevaux-de-frise. From where they stood, the outlines of this bristling barrier seemed too regular, too smoothly shaped, to be other than the work of man.

Was it another city—the refuge they had sought? A place where they might stay, safe from Klaneth and his pack until they could sally forth to meet that pack and its master on more equal terms?

Yet if a city—what giants were they who had reared it?

The oars dipped faster; the ship sped; closer came the barrier——

It was no city!

Up from the depths of the turquoise sea thrust thousands of rocks. Rocks blue and yellow, rocks striped crimson and vivid malachite; rocks all glowing ochre and rocks steeped in the scarlet of autumn sunsets; a polychrome Venice of a lost people of stone, sculptured by stone Titans. Here a slender minaret arose two hundred feet in air yet hardly more than ten in thickness; here a pyramid as great as Cheops', its four sides as accurately faced—by thousands, far as eye could reach, the rocks arose in fantasies of multi-colored cone and peak, aiguille and minaret and obelisk, campanile and tower.

Straight up from the depths they lifted, and between them the sea flowed in a maze of channels both narrow and broad; in some of the channels smoothly, in others with swift eddies and whirlpools and racing torrents; and in others the sea lay like placid lakes.

There came another shout from the Viking, urgent, summoning—and with it the clangor of his sword beating upon the shield.

Down upon the ship and little more than a mile away rushed a long line of other ships, a score or more of them both single and double banked—boats of war racing on oars that dipped and rose with swiftness of sword blade stroke. Between them and the Ship of Ishtar drove a lean and black *bireme* leaping the waves like a wolf.

The pack of Klaneth with the black priest in the lead!

The pack, breaking out of the mists unseen by Sigurd, eyes like the others fast upon that colossal fantasy of stone that seemed to be the end of this strange world!

"In among the rocks!" cried Kenton—"Quick!"

"A trap!" said Sigurd.

"A trap for them as well as us then," answered Kenton. "At the least, they cannot ring us there with their boats."

"The only chance!" grunted Gigi.

The slaves bent their backs; through a wide channel between two painted monolithic minarets they flew. Behind them they heard a shouting, a baying as of hungry hounds in sight of a deer.

Now they were within the maze and the rowers must go slowly and the Viking's rudder-craft was needed indeed, for the currents swung them, gripping at bow and stern and the sheer rocks menaced. Twisting, turning, on and on they went until the painted decks closed from them sight of the open sea. Yet now, too, Klaneth and his fleet were in the maize. They heard the creak of the oars, the commands of the helmsmen, searching, ferreting them out.

Abruptly as though snapped out, light vanished and darkness fell! Darkness blotted out the channel they were following, blotted out the towering rocks. From the pursuing boats came horn blasts, orders shrill with fear, outcries.

A purplish glow sprang up within the blackness.

"Nergal!" whispered Sharane. "Nergal comes!"

The whole of the black deck was blotted out as though an inky cloud had dropped upon it and out of that cloud leaped Sigurd and ran to where the others stood.

And now from every quarter of the horizon whirled pillars of darkness. Their feet were in the sullen sea, their heads lost in the pall that spread above. Ahead of them drove a charnel odor, the breath of death.

"Nergal in all his might!" shuddered Sharane.

"But Ishtar—Ishtar promised the strife should end!" groaned Kenton.

"But she did not say how it would end!" wailed Sharane. "And, O Beloved—Ishtar comes no more to me—and all my power is gone!"

"Ishtar! Ishtar!" she cried—and caught Kenton in her arms. "Mother—my life for this man's! My soul for his! Mother Ishtar——!"

The van of the whirling pillars was close; the circle between them and the ship swiftly narrowing. On the echo of Sharane's cry a blinding light, pearl white and pearl rose flashed down upon them—on Sharane, the three men and the warrior maids crouched white faced at Sharane's feet.

High over their heads, thrice the height of the mast, a great globe of moon fire hung poised, effulgent, serene, and brighter, far brighter than a score of moons at full. From its periphery poured rays, enclosing the whole fore part of the ship as in a tent of light; a radiance that ringed them and in whose center they stood as though prisoned in a hollow cone whose top was the moon globe.

Around that radiant tent the pillared darknesses, churned, pressing for entrance; finding none.

Faint at first and far away began a keen edged shrieking;

louder it grew as though from racing hordes fresh loosed from Abaddon. The purple darkness lightened, turned to a lurid violet. It was pricked by countless points of crimson fire.

And now the myriads of fiery points were at the ship; striking like little snakes of fire at globe and sides of radiant tent, shooting at them like arrow heads of fire, thrusting like little lance tips of fire.

There was the whir and rustle of thousands of wings. Around calm globe and cone of light whirled doves of Ishtar in thousands. And as the points of fire struck and stabbed the doves darted to meet them. Like little living shields of shining silver they caught the thrusts of the fiery javelins upon their breasts.

Where were the doves coming from? Cloud upon cloud of them poured from above the moon orb yet, for each whose ashes were whirled away a score rushed in to meet the striking fires, and all the air was palpitant with the tumult of their wings.

The shrieking raised itself a full octave. The inky cloud that had leaped upon the black deck shot up, towering, gigantic, into the heavens. The countless points of fire rushed together, coalesced. They became a crimson scimitar of fire that struck down upon shining orb and ship!

Before the first stroke could fall the phalanxes of the doves had wheeled; had formed themselves into a shield mighty enough to have been held and wielded by Ishtar's own arm!

And ever as the scimitar of fire slashed and thrust at the radiant globe and ship, the shield of the doves met it. Fiery point and fiery edge struck and blackened the living argent—but could not pierce. And ever the seared wounds of that shield shimmered moon white, as soft, untouched silver breasts darted in and healed them.

In mid-sweep it met another sword of brilliant light—a sword forged all of those white flames he had seen in his vision and that were the life of that radiance that fructified the swarms of worlds!

The scimitar was dimming! No longer was its fire so crimson bright!

The moon orb pulsed; its radiance flamed wide, dazzling, blindingly, hurling back the darknesses.

Swiftly as it had come, it vanished!

With it went the doves!

Kenton saw the gigantic scimitar pause, quiver uncertainly—as though the dread hand that held it had been stilled with sudden doubt—then down it swept once more.

The red scimitar fell shattered!

He heard a voice—the voice of Ishtar——

"I have beaten you, Nergal!"

And Nergal, snarling——

"A trick, Ishtar! Not with you, but with your Sister-Self was my warfare to be!"

And again Ishtar——

"No trick, Nergal! I never said that I would not fight you. Yet this I will grant—though you have lost the ship —I will not take it! The ship is free!"

Then Nergal, grudgingly, snarling still——

"The strife is ended! The ship is free!"

For one beat in time Kenton seemed to see a vast vague face gazing down upon the ship, a face in which were all the tendernesses of all mothers, all loving women beneath the sun—the shadowy eyes dwelt softly on Sharane, softly but enigmatically upon him——

The face was gone!

As when a shutter is dropped before a closed lamp, so the darkness had fallen; and abruptly as when the shutter is lifted so the darkness fled; light took its place.

The ship lay in a wide channel; around it the phantasmagoria of the sea floored city of stone. At port a thicket of obelisks all dull greens and glaring vermilions raised tops on high. Three arrow flights on starboard a pointed moonlith arose, pyramidal, its pointed tip hundreds of feet in air.

Around an edge of it crept the black *bireme* of Klaneth!

30

The Last Battle

SIGHT of that lean boat that like a lank hound leaped at them was like wine to Kenton; like strong wine to all.

Heavy upon them had hung the conflict just passed—

196

they but midges, dancing helplessly now in the fierce radiance of life's spirit, now stilling as helplessly in the blackness of life's negation. The charnel odor was still in Kenton's nostrils; the chill of the grave on his heart; the touch of the worm upon his eyes.

But there—there on the black priest's ship—were things he knew!

Sword edges and arrow point; death—it might be; death with pulse beating like war drums; hot death striking in as the red tides of life rushed out; things understandable; reality.

He heard the golden clarion of Sharane's defiance, the roar of Gigi, the shouting of Sigurd. And he was shouting too—challenging the black priest, taunting him, menacing him.

Silently the lean ship drove down on them.

"Sigurd, to the helm!" Sanity returned to Kenton. "Make for a narrow channel. One we can row but one that will force them to draw in their upper bank of oars. Thus shall we equal their speed—at the least!"

The Norseman ran back to the tiller. The whistle of the overseer shrilled in the pit; the ship leaped forward.

It swept round the obelisks, the *bireme* now only two arrow flights behind, and into a wide lake of blue water bordered by a hundred domes, magenta set on huge cubes of damask; the turquoise tides ran between the mathematically spaced sides of the cubes in a hundred canals, each barely wide enough for the oars of the ship to dip without touching the stone.

"In there! Take any channel!" shouted Kenton.

The ship heeled, darted to the closest opening. A flight of arrows from the *bireme* whistled into their wake—five ship lengths short!

The huge blocks with their mosqued tops bordered the narrow canal into which they had passed; for a full mile the open way stretched, straight ahead of them. A third through and they heard the *bireme's* sweeps clanking, saw it come swinging on a single bank of oars into the entrance. Quicker, at Kenton's command, dipped the ship's blades; heavier than the ship, the *bireme* fell behind.

And as they flew through the blue water Kenton and Sharane took swift counsel with Gigi and Sigurd back at the stern.

"Ravens gather!" chanted Sigurd, eyes brightening with

197

fey fires. "Shield maidens ride from Valhalla! I hear the feet of their horses!"

"They may return empty handed!" exclaimed Kenton. "Nay, Sigurd—now we have our only chance. None but Klaneth has smelled us out. Let us pick our place and give battle to him."

"We are but seven, and there are many times seven on that *bireme*, Wolf," said Gigi, doubtful it seemed—although his little eyes sparkled.

"I run no longer from the black swine!" cried Kenton hotly. "I am weary of dodging and skulking. I say let us play the game out now! What does your thought tell you, Sharane?" he asked.

"My thought is as yours," she told him, tranquilly. "As you will it, so is my will, beloved!"

"What do you say, Norseman?" asked Gigi. "Quick now —decide!"

"I am with the Wolf," replied Sigurd. "No time better than now. In the old days when I was a dragon master there was a trick we played when we were chased. Have you seen the dog when the cat turns on him—ho!ho!" laughed Sigurd. "Swift flies the cat until it has reached a corner. And there it lurks until dog yelps past. Then out springs cat, digging deep its claws, striking at eyes, raking dog's sides. Ho! Ho!" roared Sigurd. "Swift we would fly like the cat until we had found a place to turn and skulk. Then as other dragon sped by, out we would spring upon it; like the dog, loud would it howl while we clung and tore! Ho—let us find such a corner where we may lurk till this hell dog leaps past. Then we shall spring. Give me two of the maids to guard me here as I steer. You three with the other maid, stand by the crossbows, and when I shear their oars, loose the fire shafts upon them."

"In the meantime," asked Gigi, face wrinkling, "what about their own arrows?"

"We must take our luck as it comes," said Kenton. "Gigi, I am one with Sigurd—unless you have a better plan to offer."

"No," answered Gigi—"No—I have none, Wolf"—he lifted his great body, shook long arms on high.

"By the Hollow Hells and Ischak their Keeper," roared Gigi, "I, too, am weary of running away! I ran away from my princess because of my bald head—and what luck did it bring me. By Nazzur the Eater of Hearts—by Zubran"

—his voice softened—"who gave his life for us—I run no more! Pick your place, Wolf—you and Sigurd—and let us fight!"

He waddled away; then turned.

"The end of the channel draws close," he said. "Sharane, between the hearts of you and your maids and their arrow points are only soft breasts and a fold of cloth. Don coats of mail like ours and caps and buskins and greaves for your knees. I go to put on another linked shirt and get me my mace."

He dropped down the steps; Kenton nodded, and after Gigi trooped Sharane and her three women to doff their robes and kirtles, don battle garb.

"And after you have shorn their oars—if you do?" asked Kenton of the Viking, lingering.

"Then we return and ram," said Sigurd. "So we did in the old days. The ship is lighter than the black priest's galley and far more quickly can she turn. When we ram, be all of you at the bow ready to beat off any who try to drop abroad. After Klaneth's galley is both shorn and rammed we can tear at it as we will—like the cat."

The end of the canal was near; half a mile behind, the *bireme* clung to the ship's wake.

Out of her cabin came Sharane and her three maids, four slender warriors in coats of mail, hair hidden under brown linked caps, leathern buskins on legs and greaves at knees. They piled arrows on stern and bow; with Gigi seeing to it that crossbows were in order, tow and oil and flints ready.

The ship swept out of the canal, hung on reverse oars while Kenton and the Viking took survey. At left and right, in two great arcs, ran high walls of unbroken crimson rock. Smooth and precipitous, continuing they would make a circle a mile or more in diameter—but whether they did so continue Kenton could not see.

Out of the waters they walled, in its center if they encircled it, a huge pinnacle lifted, its needle point thrice the height of the walls, shutting off the further view. Its pedestal was one colossal block, octahedral, shaped like a star. But from it rayed the star points, long and narrow like titanic wedges, their ends fifty feet high and edged like a knife.

"We go to the left," said Sigurd. "Let the black dog know which way we turn."

Kenton leaped to the cabin's top; waved derisive arms; heard shouting.

"Good!" rumbled Sigurd. "Now let them come. For here, Wolf, we make our stand! Look"—he pointed as the ship drove past the first star point—"between the tip of stone and wall there is a little more than room for ship and galley to pass each other. Also the stone is high and hides us when we have passed. Yes, it is the place! Yet not here beyond the first star shall we lurk— Klaneth may expect that and come by it slowly and alert; nor beyond the second—for again he may come slowly though surely not so slowly as before. But not finding us there he will believe that we have but one thought—and that to run. So he will pass the third tip at speed to close in on us. And it is there that we shall leap out upon him!"

"Good!" Kenton, and dropped down to the deck; stood beside Sharane and Gigi.

And Gigi grunted approval and walked away to test once more the crossbows. But Sharane locked mailed arms around Kenton's neck and drew his face close to hers and drank him with wistful eyes that seemed as though they could not drink enough of him.

"Is it the end, beloved?" she whispered.

"There shall be no end—for us, O heart of mine," he answered.

They stood so, silent, while the second star point wheeled by. And now the third leveled its tip at them and Sigurd cried out to raise oars; and when the ship had swam a hundred yards or so, brought her sharply around. He called to him the overseer.

"We strike at the *bireme's* left bank of oars," he said. "No wish have I to run risk of splitting the ship on that edge of rock. When I shout, draw in your left sweeps. When we have sheared and passed, whip the slaves again into full speed. When we have rammed, reverse oars and pull free. Is it clear?"

The black's eyes glistened; he bared white teeth; ran back to the pit.

Now from beyond the great stone wedge came faint rasp of sweeps, splashings of oars. Two of the warrior women sped back to Sigurd, crouched beside him, arrows ready at slits of the high shields. A tenseness gripped the ship.

"One kiss," whispered Sharane, eyes now misty. Their lips clung.

Nearer came the oar sounds, closer, closer—faster—speeding——

A low whistle from the Viking, and the rowers bent back under sting of whip. A dozen strong strokes and the ship leaped like a dolphin straight for the star tip.

Past tip it shot; heeled as the Viking threw the rudder sharp to port.

Ten ship lengths ahead of them was the *bireme*, racing on its four fold multiple feet of oars like an enormous water spider. And as the ship flashed out and at it a roar arose from its crowded decks, a shouting confused and clamorous, medley of wild commands—and filling all that clamor, bewilderment.

The oars of the *bireme* faltered; stopped at midstroke; held rigid, just touching sea.

"Faster!" howled Sigurd and as the pit's whip cracked, he drove with a twist of the rudder the ship down parallel to the course of the galley.

"In oars!" he howled again——

The prow of the Ship of Ishtar struck the *bireme's* port oars. It swept through them like a blade through brittle stubble. Broken, splintered, the long shafts fell, holding back the rush of the Ship of Ishtar as little as though they had been straws. But in the *bireme* those who gripped the great handles fell back with ribs crushed, backs snapped, as the heavy stocks were flung against them.

Up from the ship's side as it passed, up into the ranks staring down on it, ranks turned wooden with surprise of that unexpected attack, hissed the fireballs from the crossbows. Hissing like serpents of fire, expanding as the air fanned them, the fire-balls struck—hurling back the soldiers, searing them, flaming up as they fell on deck and into open hold and touching with fingers of inextinguishable flame all that would burn.

Again the galley roared—and now with terror in its voice.

The Ship of Ishtar was clear; down thrust the withdrawn oars of it; straight ahead she flew into the wider space beyond the star tip of stone and circling wall. Swift once more the Viking turned her. Back raced the ship upon the *bireme*.

And the *bireme* swung helplessly, sidled grotesquely like a huge spider from one of whose sides all legs have been cut, slithered like that same spider toward the knife edged tip of the stone star ray. From hold and deck little columns of smoke swirled.

Now Sigurd realized all that galley's peril; saw that it was close to piercing stone ray; saw that he might drive it upon that ray; send stone blade biting into it; destroy it.

"Guard bow!" shouted Sigurd.

He threw back the rudder, made wider turn, hurtled upon the galley not at stern as he had planned but far toward midship. The ram of Ishtar's ship struck and bit deep; prow too. Under the shock Kenton and the others toppled over and before they could set foot on bow fell prone on faces, clutching at deck.

Beneath the blow the *bireme* reeled, heeled until the seas sucked over its farther side. Down dipped its starboard oars seeking to thrust back from the menacing stone. The sweeps churned, but under the weight of the ship clinging to its flank, its bow turned sharply in.

It struck the knife edge of the rock.

There was a crackling as rock bit through hull.

"Ho!" roared the Viking. "Drown, you rats!"

Down upon the ship whistled an arrow cloud. The shafts shrilled over Kenton, staggering to his feet. They pierced deck and pit. Before the rowers could back sweeps, pull free, they dropped, hung limp over oars, bristling with quivering bolts.

On the ship's bow fell a dozen grapples, holding it fast to the wrecked galley. Ropes whirled and sliding down them came the swordsmen.

"Back! Back to me!" shouted Sigurd.

The *bireme* shuddered, its gashed bow slid down the rock edge for a dozen feet or more, the water pouring over its fore deck. Up from the sea bobbed heads of soldiers, washed away and swimming for the ship. On the deck of the *bireme* a milling began as those on it fought to drop upon the ship.

"Back!" cried Kenton.

He caught Sharane's arm; they ran with heads bent low as from the steerman's place the arrows of Sigurd and his flanking maids winged into the mass of men swarming over the rosy cabin.

The *bireme* slipped again along the cleaving edge of

stone; checked fall with bow half under water, yet held by the ship's ram. But that last slipping had wrenched sharply down the ship's own prisoned bow. As the deck tilted Kenton fell, dragging Sharane with him. He caught swift glimpse of men dropping from the *bireme's* side, throwing themselves into the sea, striking for the ship.

He scrambled to his feet as the soldiers at the bow rushed. And now Gigi sprang past him, twirling his great mace. Kenton leaped to his side, Sharane at his heels.

"Back! Back to Sigurd!" grunted the Ninevite, club sweeping the soldiers before it like a flail among wheat.

"Too late!" cried Sharane.

Too late!

Men were swarming up the stern chains, clambering up from the sea, tearing away the shields.

From the *bireme* came a howling, frenzied and beast-like. At its sound even the soldiers halted, Gigi's mace hung in air.

Then upon the ship of Ishtar leaped—the black priest!

Pale eyes pools of hell fire, mouth an open square from which black hate flew screaming, he hurled himself through the swordsmen, dived under Gigi's falling mace and flung himself on Kenton.

But Kenton was ready.

Out flashed the blue blade and met the thrust of the black priest's sword. Quicker than he, that sword swept back, bit into that old wound in his side!

Kenton staggered, hilt half dropping from his hand.

Howling triumph Klaneth swept down the death blow.

Before it could fall Sharane had thrown herself between Kenton and priest, had parried the stroke with her own sword.

The left hand of the black priest shot out, dagger in its grip. He buried that dagger in Sharane's breast!

Now all the world was but one red flame before Kenton—one red flame in which was nothing but Klaneth's face. Ere the black priest could move, swifter than the lightning stroke, Kenton had struck.

His sword bit down, shearing away half the black priest's face, leaving in place of cheek and jowl, only a red smear—swept on half through his shoulder.

The black priest's sword clanged upon the deck.

The sword of Kenton bit again—straight through his neck.

The head of Klaneth leaped from his shoulders, struck

the rail and whirled into the sea. For another instant the gross bulk of the body stood, the neck spouting. The body crashed.

No further heed paid Kenton to him nor to the *bireme's* men. He bent over Sharane, raised her.

"Beloved!" he called, and kissed the pale lips, the closed eyes. "Come back to me!"

Her eyes opened, her slim hands made effort to caress him.

"Beloved!" whispered Sharane. "I . . . Can not . . . I will . . . Wait . . ." Her head dropped upon his breast.

Kenton, standing there with his dead love in his arms, looked about the ship. Circling him were those who were left of the black galley's crew, staring at him, silent, making no move.

"Sigurd!" he cried, paying no heed to them. On the helmsman's deck where the Viking had fought was only a heap of slain.

"Gigi!" he whispered.

There was no Gigi! Where Gigi had wielded his giant flail the dead were thick.

"Sharane! Gigi! Sigurd!" Kenton sobbed. "Gone! All gone!"

The ship lurched; shuddered. He took a step forward, Sharane clasped to his breast.

A bow twanged; an arrow caught him in his side.

He did not care . . . let them kill him . . . Sharane was gone . . . and Gigi. . . .

Why was it that he could no longer feel Sharane's body in his arms?

Where had the staring soldiers gone?

Where was—the ship!

There was nothing around him but darkness—darkness and a roaring tempest sweeping toward him out of farthest space.

Through that darkness, seeking as he fled for sight of Sharane, reaching faltering hands for touch of her, whirled Kenton. . . .

Swaying, weeping with heartbreak and weakness, he opened his eyes. . . .

To look again upon his old room!

31

KENTON stood there, half in stupor seeing less the room than swift fleeting pictures on that last battle. A bell struck three times.

Three o'clock! Of course . . . this was a world of time . . . not like the world of the ship. . .

The ship!

He staggered over to the shining mystery that had given him everything he had desired of life—and at the end had taken everything away.

Sharane!

There she lay . . . on the ivory deck . . . close to the rowers' pit . . . a gleaming toy, a jeweled puppet with hilt of tiny dagger in breast . . .

Sharane who had held for him all joy, all sweetnesses, all desirable delicious things.

The headless manikin so close to her—

Klaneth!

He looked upon the black deck—why, where were all the dead? There on the rubber platform lay only three puppets, one with yellow hair and battered armor. . . . Sigurd and the two warrior maids who had fought beside him! But where were the soldiers they had slain?

And there beyond the headless body of the black priest . . . was Gigi! Gigi with his great arms a-sprawl and his

205

dwarf legs doubled under him! His dead—they too were gone!

Gigi! Kenton's hand left Sharane, caressed him.

An agony bit deep into his side. It brought him to his knees. He thrust down his hand and clutched a feathered shaft. The arrow! Suddenly he knew that life was ebbing fast.

Beneath the other hand he felt the ship tremble. He stared at it, bewildered. In that brief moment of agony its bow had vanished, melted away—and with it the rosy cabin!

The ship lurched. As cabin had gone, so went the ivory deck almost up to the rowers' pit and with it—Gigi!

"Sharane!" he sobbed and gripped the puppet tight. "Beloved!"

The ship crumbled to within an inch of where the toy lay.

"Sharane!" wailed Kenton—and above him the servants wakened to that heartbroken cry and came hurrying to his door.

He threw the last of his strength into his fingers, wrenched at the toy . . . it was loose . . . in his hand . . . he raised it to his lips. . . .

And now where the ship had been was nothing but the oblong base of pearl crested, lapis luzuli waves!

He knew what that meant. Down into the depths of the strange sea of that other world had gone the *bireme*, dragging with it as it went the Ship of Ishtar. As fared the symbol, so must fare the Ship—and as the Ship fared, so must fare the symbol. And had so fared!

There was a hammering at the door, and cries. He gave them no heed.

"Sharane!" they heard him cry, but now with voice that sang with joy.

Kenton fell forward, the toy woman at his lips, gripped tight in stiffening hand.

The base of little waves dissolved. Where ship and it had been something stirred and took form—a shadowy great bird with silver wings and breast and feet and bill of scarlet. It arose. It hovered over Kenton.

A dove of Ishtar.

It hovered—and was gone.

In crashed the door; the servants clustered at the threshold, peering into the darkened room.

206

"Mr. John!" quavered old Jevins. There was no answer.

"There's something there—on the floor! Turn on the light!" whispered one.

The electrics gleamed upon a body stretched face down upon a bloodstained rug; a body in cut and t̶ dyed crimson; in its side the shaft of a black one strong arm a wide bracelet of gold. Back body they shrank, looking at each other wondering eyes.

One bolder than the others advanced, t̶ form over.

Kenton's dead face smiled up at them, and a great happiness.

"Mr. John!" wept old Jevins, and kneel in his arms.

"What's he got in his hand?" whisp hand was at Kenton's lips, clenched. stubborn fingers.

But Kenton's hand was— Empty!

THE END